Promise Me

CARLIE JEAN

Printed in the United States of America
First Printing, 2023
ASIN: B0CBHLRKPT
Kindle Direct Publishing

Editor: Salma R.
Proofreader: Isabella B.
Cover Designer: Cat Imb at TRC Designs
Formatting: Qamber Designs
PR: Greys promotions

*To all the girls that have been through some shit and want that
soft kind of love, the one that feels like a cozy blanket
on a fall night, this is for you.*

Content Warning

Explicit sexual content

Mentions of death of parent, grief, anxiety, alcoholism, domestic abuse, and sexual assault.

Contents

Playlist

Thought you Should Know - Morgan Wallen

Girl in Mine - Parmalee

Trophies - Young Money ft. Drake

Sparks Fly (Taylor's Version) - Taylor Swift

Bed - J. Holiday

In the Morning - J. Cole & Drake

Under My Skin - Nate Smith

Come and Get Your Love - Redbone

Roll Up - Wiz Khalifa

Ain't no Mountain High Enough - Marvin Gaye, Tammi Terrel

Promise - Ciara

XO - Beyonce

Better Together - Luke Combs

Star of the Show - Thomas Rhett

Motivation - Kelly Rowland & Nelly

Celebration - Tank ft. Drake

She - Jake Scott

Chapter One

Aurora

"Ah, fuck," Brad groans into my neck as he finds his release, cumming into the rubber wrapped around his cock.

I wish I could say I came too.

I didn't even really want to answer his text because practice today was brutal. Coach Tilly made us do fifty tuck jumps every time a serve hit the net. I think we did about five hundred in total, and my thighs are jelly now.

But after being high off of a win as the quarterback of the football team at Rockland University in Colorado, Brad had a different kind of energy.

He's not my boyfriend, just a fuck buddy.

I don't do boyfriends since I don't have the time between school and volleyball practice, and Brad gets that.

He's the star of the football team, and I'm the star of the volleyball team.

Call me vain, but it's true. I'm damn good at what I do. It's my goal to make it to the Olympic team once I graduate this year, so I have no room for distractions.

Rolling off of me, Brad sighs as he comes down from his high while I remain still, wishing I had just stayed home when he texted me after his game.

What a lame lay.

For an athletic guy, he sure is lazy in bed. He's always been more into receiving than giving. Honestly, I'm not even sure why I am still fucking him. It's time to end it and go celibate until the end of the school year.

It's only September, but I can do it, and if not, my vibrator will do the job just fine.

Better than Brad could ever.

"Brad, I think we should stop whatever this is," I say into the dark.

"Sweet cheeks, relax. I'll get you off later. I'm just tired," he sighs, sounding annoyed.

"No, thanks. I'm going to go. We're cool, but we're not hooking up anymore," I tell him as I sit up and pull my panties back on because Brad was in such a hurry they never came off.

Even my dress is still on.

At least it makes this less awkward. I couldn't imagine having this talk naked.

"The hell we're not. Get back in bed," Brad grumbles, sitting up as he watches me gather my things.

"Brad, you're the quarterback of one of the best football teams in the country. You won't miss me, trust me." I pull my backpack over my shoulders and wait for his response, my body eager to flee this frat house for good.

A scowl forms on his lips, his words biting. "Good fucking luck making Team USA. You're not even that good, because all you're good for is a place to stick a dick in. So you know what, you're right. I won't miss you, just like I'm sure the many before me don't."

It seems like Brad is a little boy who's not used to not getting what he wants—a typical trust fund kid.

I square my shoulders, not letting him see how his words affect me because even though I'm furious, a part of me is also hurt. Who wouldn't be? The man just called out my worst fear and called me a whore in under two seconds.

"If your football career is anything like your cock, it'll be small and unsatisfying," I snap and turn on my heel, hightailing it out of this house for the last time.

Thank God.

The walk back to my house is only about fifteen minutes off campus, but it feels a lot longer since it's the middle of the night. The wind rustles against my 5'9 frame, the early fall chill wrapping around me, but mixed with Brad's harsh words, I feel colder than usual.

I wrap my arms tightly around my body, trying to bring me some much-needed warmth and love because right now, his words are hitting my worst insecurity—not being good enough to reach my goals.

A tear pokes at my eyelid because I'm frustrated that I'm letting his stupid words get to me.

"Aurora." I hear my name yelled from behind me. I turn around and see my friend Theo, a player on the football team, chasing after me.

"Wait up, what's wrong?" he huffs as he stops beside me, his blue eyes searching my hazel ones.

"Nothing, just wanted to go home, that's a-all," I stutter, my teeth chattering.

"You cold?" He goes to hand me his jacket, but I shake my head, noticing the mini fidget cube in his hand.

"Thanks, Theo, but I'll be good."

I'm not sure if I believe it yet, but I know it's true.

He ignores me and throws his coat over my shoulders, exposing his muscular arms to the cold.

"Let me walk you home, Aurora. It's too late to be out here alone."

Theo is one of my closest friends. Super nice and a total goofball. We met when our training schedules coincided last year. Thanks to a renovation in our facility, the football team and the women's volleyball team had to share the weight room during junior year.

Yes, we have our own facility. Rockland University is known for its varsity teams being the best in the country, which means each team has its own separate facility.

Theo and I became good friends from the day we met. I was loading a plate on the squat rack when he walked in and literally ran up to me, joy all over his face. He told me his sister was a huge fan and how impressed he was by my signature spike that's given out a few concussions when not appropriately received by the opposing team.

I instantly liked him. Not because he was a fan, but because he was genuine. You can tell some things about a person right away, and I could tell he was a good one.

"Okay, thanks." I smile, tucking a stray lock of dark blonde hair out of my face.

The rest of the walk home is more comfortable with Theo by my side, taking my mind off the words that were wrapping around my brain.

You're not good enough. You won't make it.

He walks me to my house and waits until I've unlocked the door to leave, waving at me with a smile as I close the door behind me.

I slump against the door, lock it, and blow out a deep breath, willing it to center myself. I won't let Brad get to me, and I'm done with men.

Volleyball and school are the only two things I'm putting my energy into anymore. That and my part-time bartending job on the weekends. My dad may be the dean, but I'd like to earn something for myself, not wanting to rely on his handouts.

I got into RLU on my own merit through an athletic scholarship, and I plan to continue to work hard for myself.

"Ro! What's wrong?" my roommate and best friend, Jasmine, asks, scaring the crap out of me.

"Jesus, Jasmine! What are you still doing up?" I deflect her question, slipping out of my sandals.

She groans from her spot on the couch, running a hand through her midnight curls. "I have a paper due tomorrow morning, and I may or may not have just started it two hours ago."

"Ouch, that sucks." I cringe, not envious of the all-nighter she's about to pull.

I plop onto the cushion beside her. My stomach growls, and my mind wanders to the pumpkin-spiced muffins I know are on the counter because Jasmine spent all day making them.

"If you're hungry, try a muffin. They're delicious, but they keep reminding me of how stupid I am for baking them instead of writing this damn paper."

I fidget on my lap, flattening out my dress. "I will later," I say, trying my best to sound excited.

Jasmine peers up at me from her laptop, a scowl on her lips. "What happened at Brad's?"

"You know I never spend the night with a hookup. It's simply a pleasurable transaction, and then I leave," I answer, hoping that avoids further questioning.

Jasmine supports my lack of interest in a relationship because, as my fellow teammate, she understands how demanding it is to be a student-athlete.

She shrugs her shoulders. "That's true. I guess I expected it to last longer. What would I know, being a virgin and all."

I sit back down and cover my hand with hers, resting them on her thigh. "There's nothing wrong with being a virgin, Jasmine."

She nods at my statement. "I know, just like exploring your body and options isn't either. But I'm not going there until I find someone who can stimulate me mentally first, then we can see about physical intimacy."

Typical Jasmine, always leading with her head first.

Her mom is a doctor, and she reinforced the importance of education throughout Jasmine's childhood, which is why she's so damn smart and focused. She prefers reading over TV, has never kissed anyone because she's deemed them unworthy, and is good at everything she does. Jasmine's a great volleyball player, an excellent baker, and on her way to earning her degree in business.

"I don't blame you, Minnie. In fact, I'm going celibate for the rest of the year. Forget men." I hold my hand up high for a high five, feeling triumphant in my pledge.

Jasmine smacks her palm into mine before wrapping it around and squeezing it tightly. "Good. Now, tell me what the hell Brad did to you tonight before I walk my ass down there and ask him myself, which will only wind up with my fist in his face and my paper unwritten. So talk, now."

"Easy there." I chuckle. One of the reasons why I love Jasmine is her ability to understand me and really listen. She's a people reader, and even though she's a year younger than me, she's always filled the mom role between us.

"He came within two minutes, and I didn't even have an orgasm. So, I told him I was done… and he," I pause, my body caving in on itself as the words play back in my mind. "He said all I was good for was sex, that I slept around a lot, and that I'm not good enough to go pro," I tell her, tallying each insult with each of my fingers.

Jasmine's mouth gapes and fury fills her lean, petite body. "Please tell me you don't believe that?"

I grimace, shrugging my shoulders and dipping my chin to look at the fluffy white rug. "No…I mean, I know I'm good at what I do. There's a reason I'm on every poster around campus, but it still gets to me when I hear stuff like that. You know how important it is for me to make it big. And the whore stuff…well, he's probably not wrong."

She turns to face me now, her hands cupping my face as she looks at me intently. "Aurora Vallacourt, you listen to me, and you listen well. You are the most talented player I have seen on the court. Your skills speak for themselves. As an athlete himself, Brad knew what words would hurt you the most because he has the same fears. As for the whore part, are you kidding me? Guys at school screw different girls every day, and they are celebrated for it, but when you decide to do so, that's a problem? To hell with that and anyone who looks at you differently for it. There's nothing wrong with my choice to be a virgin, just like there's nothing wrong with your choice to casually hook up with people."

Tears sting my eyes, like the softie that I am, and I throw my arms around her body, hugging her. "I love you so much, thank you."

"I love you more, Ro," she says into my hair, then pulls back with a sly smile, "Any chance you want to help me with my paper?"

I stand and yawn dramatically, taking small steps back toward the kitchen, where I snag a muffin. "Would you look at that? Bedtime. Night, Minnie!" I smile, then run up the stairs to my room, Jasmine's chuckle filtering in from below.

Chapter Two

Aurora

Two months later

I shift uncomfortably in my chair, my eyes darting to the last autumn leaves hanging on to the trees in the November chill.

I wish the trees stayed colorful all year round.

I also wish I wasn't sitting across from my Dad, aka the dean, with his stern, hard eyes on me.

"Ms. Vallacourt, did you hear me?" he asks, tapping a pen on his desk to fill the silence. When I got the email last week, I knew exactly what this would be about. How could I not when I know I haven't been doing so well lately.

My dad is the picture of professionalism, so much so that we had to talk about my current situation in his office rather than him sitting me down at his home. I love the guy, he's truly a great dad. But sometimes, he takes his different roles too seriously, always trying to find the fine line between the two with me.

I twirl a piece of my dark blonde locks around my finger, not looking at him because I'm embarrassed at how I got here. "Yes, I certainly did."

"Good, so you understand that you will now be required to meet with a tutor twice a week—Coach Tilly's demands, not mine. Your average is slipping, and in order to stay on the team, you need to get it back up as soon as possible. This tutor is the last available one, so don't mess this up."

My head tilts up quickly, my eyes meeting his blue ones for the first time since I've entered his office. "Twice? How am I supposed to fit that into my schedule?"

He picks up a paper off his desk, pushing his glasses further up his nose as he reads, "According to your class and varsity schedule, I see you have an opening Monday and Thursday from 5-7 pm."

"That's usually my downtime to relax between classes, studying, workouts, and practices." I groan, feeling defeated that I have to add more to my plate in the year that matters most.

I was supposed to be doing nothing other than work toward my goal, but in doing so, my tunnel vision caused me to forget the other aspect of being an athlete.

The student part.

I've been running myself empty, fitting in longer workouts, and staying later after practice ends, which means my grades have started to slip because I don't have the energy to keep up with my readings or studying.

I'm majoring in kinesiology, but the elective I chose— Introduction to Coding— is what I'm struggling with. It was the only elective that fit with my busy schedule. While I'm hovering around the 70s in my other courses, I'm nearly failing this one, bringing my overall average down.

My dad takes his glasses off, signaling he'll act as my dad now instead of my dean. "Cupcake, if anyone can do this, it's you. You're a Vallacourt, and Vallacourts don't give up. I wanted to be a dean, and I did that. Your brother wanted to own a business, so he did. Mom wanted to be a gymnast, and hell, did she ever do that. She was the best the sport had ever seen," he chokes up. He clears his throat, coughing up the emotions swelling in his throat.

The same emotions are now swirling in my stomach, a familiar yet unwelcome feeling of grief overwhelming me.

My mom was a renowned gymnast and was on her way to making the Olympic team. But then, she got pregnant with my brother, Nate, and decided to step back from her dreams to pursue another.

While she still loved gymnastics, she loved being a mom even more. My mother loved it so much that she had me two years later. Dad made her promise him she'd chase her dream again despite her age, knowing she had more talent than anyone else in her field, but life had other plans.

My mom died in a car accident the year she qualified for Team USA. The roads were icy that day and the other driver lost control of their car.

Losing someone so unfairly is fucking awful. Unexpected losses always hurt differently, and I was ten when I lost my best friend.

My dad clears his throat again, continuing. "And you, Cupcake, will get exactly what you want. If you work hard, that is, because the best things—"

"Don't come easy," I finish for him, the Vallacourt family motto.

"Exactly, so tell me, what are you going to do?" he prompts, his forearms resting on his oak desk.

I sigh, running a palm up and down my thigh. "I'll go to this tutoring thing and get my grades up. Then, I'll smash my first game of the year in two weeks."

"That's my hardworking girl. Speaking of hard work, have you stopped working for your damn brother yet?"

"Dad, we've had this argument before. I won't stop bartending. It's a good way for me to make my own money. I know you and Nate can easily support me, but I want to be able to support myself."

My older brother owns a sports bar near campus, Beers n Cheers, and I've been working there as their bartender since it opened two years ago. It's fun, and I honestly enjoy it. I meet a lot of people and get great tips.

He chuckles. "That's what makes you a Vallacourt— headstrong and respectable. Now, get out of here. Your tutor will be meeting you at the library in fifteen minutes." He puts his glasses back on, switching back into dean mode.

I stifle a giggle at him for wearing fake glasses. He says it makes him look wiser.

I salute him like a soldier. "Yes, sir. I'll see you tomorrow for my pre-birthday dinner."

My dad smiles and rolls his eyes, knowing how much I love my birthday. It's not for another three weeks, but I like to celebrate all month long.

Starting with a pre-birthday dinner with my family tomorrow, then next weekend will be a spa session with Jasmine after our first game, and the following weekend will be the main event.

A day spent hiking by myself. Well, with Pickles, my chocolate lab.

His name is a long story.

I usually go by myself because it was something I liked to do with my mom. The two of us went hiking together all the time, so I like to think of this as a way to feel connected to her.

He ushers me out of his office and I hustle my way into the library fifteen minutes later, peeling my scarf off as warmth starts to replace the coolness on my cheeks.

I pull out my phone and see that my dad texted me my tutor's information on my way over.

Dad

Cameron Fields
Meeting you at the table next to the window overlooking the mountains.

I've never heard of him before, and I don't plan to know much more than what my dad texted me.

I scale the stairs two at a time, eager to meet him and get the hell out of here. I pause at the top, feeling a little lightheaded. In the midst of my busy schedule, I forgot to eat today and I have a team workout right after this.

Damn it.

I pass the white shelves stacked high with books and head toward the back. Rockland's library rivals the inside of a church with its high ceilings covered in art, and the tall windows that encase the entire space in natural light all around. I don't spend a lot of time here, but it's my second favorite spot on campus, the first obviously being the volleyball court.

I wind around a corner and find the table by the window overlooking the mountains. Along with a man sitting with his head buried in front of his laptop.

"Hi," I huff out, feeling out of breath from how I bolted up the stairs. I tug my headphones out of my ears. "I'm Aurora Vallacourt."

The man's head snaps up, and cinnamon-tinted eyes take me in from behind his glasses. His dark brown eyebrows furrow as he stands and removes his glasses.

Holy hell.

My mouth dries out while another place gets a different memo. He's tall, at least 6'4, and let's just say he looks like he's well-acquainted with the weights at the gym. His ball cap sits atop brown hair that curls slightly at the ends. I get the sudden urge to run my hands through it.

No, dammit.

I need him to help me get my grades up, not satisfy my needs.

Forget men, crush the volleyball over the net. That's my motto for the year.

"I know who you are," he grumbles. He crosses his arms in front of his chest, making his olive Henley shirt stretch against his frame. My eyes skim over his features as quickly as I can without being obvious, and something weird happens.

I've found guys attractive, but there's something about him that's different, something more than the fact that I want to climb him like a tree.

I feel a warmth spread throughout my body, fuzzy and sweet. Realizing I've been staring for far too long now, I quickly shake my head, burying the dirty thoughts away.

"Do tell, what's your review?" I tease as I inch forward, wanting to know why the hell he's so grumpy and claiming to know who I am.

"Ask yourself why you care?" His words hit me in the chest, making it ache for some unknown reason.

What did I do to this guy? I'm pretty sure I've never met him before because I would definitely remember someone as beautiful as him.

"I-I, I'm just trying to be friendly that's all," I stutter.

Jesus, when the hell have I ever tumbled on my words in front of *anyone?*

"Don't. We're not friends, this is a job," he says, sitting back down in front of his screen, and putting his glasses back on.

This guy is a real charmer.

"Ooookay," I drag out, because this is awkward. "Uh, I'll just give you my number then, so we can figure out—"

His head whips up again, his eyes burning into mine for a brief second, but he breaks his gaze away before I can decipher it. "Don't need it. We'll meet here Mondays and Thursdays at 5 p.m."

I pop my hip out, resting a hand on it. "And what if I can't make it one time, or you can't? What then, *Fields?*"

He doesn't look up from his screen this time, but I hear his sigh. "Fine, leave your number. But I'm only using it for that reason."

My chest aches again. Is he… does he think I sleep with every guy I meet? That I'm going to sext him or something? Un-fucking-believable. The double standards in this world suck. Why did he have to be the *last* tutor available?

Usually, I'd have no problem telling this guy to screw himself, but I can't find it in me to do so. He kind of intimidates me because I equally want to ride him, while also flipping him the bird.

I scribble my name and number down on a sticky note that I found in my purse, because I always carry some with me, and stick it to the back of his computer screen.

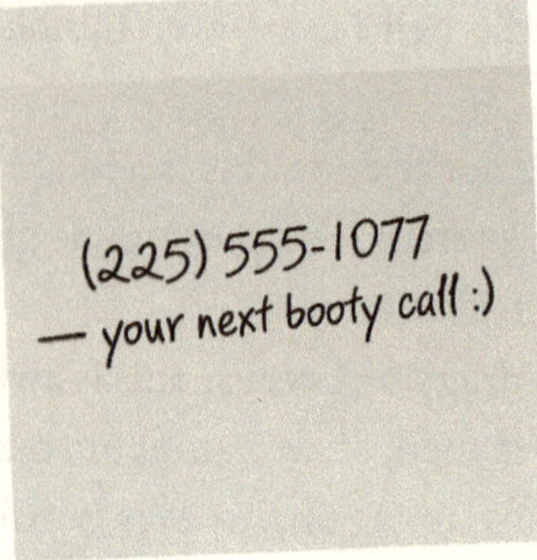

If he wants to be a dick, then so can I.

For a moment, I thought it would be a struggle to work so closely with this insanely attractive and quiet man, with my celibate pact and all. But now? Call me Aurora, the one with no goddamn worries because absolutely nothing will happen between us.

Chapter Three

Cameron

Fuck. Fucking fuck.

It might seem a little overboard, but that's exactly how I feel right now.

I run a hand down my face, rubbing my eyes. Being a computer science major means spending a lot of time in front of a screen, resulting in itchy, irritated eyes, which is why I wear glasses when working.

But that's not why I'm frustrated.

Oh no, that would be because of the somewhat tall blonde, with bright hazel eyes that could peer into my fucking soul if I let her close enough.

Aurora Vallacourt—Rockland University's star athlete, the dean's daughter, and the current 'it' girl, if you use that kind of lingo.

She's loved by everyone and wanted by all. Except for me because I refuse to let myself want anyone that way.

Sure, she's good-looking, anyone would think so.

But there's nothing there for me beyond that. I know her type, spent my teenage years loving one, all to have that go to shit when she cheated on me. I've been through some things, but that was just the cherry on top.

So now, I keep to myself. I'm here to get my degree, get the job I want, and provide for my little sister and my mom.

I haven't had any interaction above anything platonic with a girl since Layla, my high school girlfriend. That was a whopping seven years ago. I took three years off after high school to help my mom get back on her feet after Dad went to jail, hence why I'm twenty-five and still in school.

My father was an abusive alcoholic. It started when I was nine, the year after Lexa was born with spina bifida.

I think caring for a disabled child was too much for him, and he sought a bottle instead of support.

Fucking prick.

His behavior deteriorated shortly after that. It started with shoving my mom when he got drunk, and eventually, moved to punching.

I often sat there helpless. I wanted to help but knew I wasn't strong enough. Besides, Lexa wouldn't let me leave her side, not that I wanted to either. If he had ever come after her, I would've called the cops a lot sooner than I did.

That's my biggest regret, not calling them fucking sooner.

Mom begged me not to, too afraid of how we would cover Lexa's medical bills. But the important thing is that I eventually did.

Our family is doing better now that he's gone. My mom is now a waitress, makes great tips, and enjoys meeting new people every day. While Lexa is still in high school, the class president and she loves every second of being the boss.

Sometimes, I worry I'll turn out like him, but then I remember I'm in control of my actions, and would never lay a hand on someone. It's one of my two most important rules.

Number one—never fight or drink.

Number two—stay focused on school and graduate with no distractions.

I keep to myself, go to class, work out, study, tutor, and develop websites for clients in between. All to send money back home to help cover Lexa's medical bills.

Any spare time I have is spent outside.

Colorado is known for its beautiful mountains, and I like to take advantage of that by hiking. Growing up in Detroit, where there are no mountains, I quickly fell in love with this city when I moved here for school. I didn't want to leave my family, but Rockland offered me a full ride, and I couldn't say no. Plus, their computer science program is one of the best in the country, and I want to be the best at what I do.

But you know what has the potential to ruin rule number two?

Aurora fucking Vallacourt.

I've tutored girls who've ogled me before, and I usually let it go respectfully, but for some reason, I couldn't do that with Aurora. I was a dick to her, the curt words tumbling out of my mouth before I could even stop them.

I think it was a defense mechanism to keep her out, because I knew I was in trouble the moment my eyes met her pretty hazel ones. She unnerves me, and I don't fucking know why. But what I do know is that I need to apologize. I'm not a rude person. I've worked my whole life actively avoiding that.

Or at least, on the inside, I'm not.

I don't show that side of myself to anyone but my mom, Lexa, and Finn, my best friend and cousin who lives here, another reason why I came out here for school.

Leaning forward, I grab the sticky note Aurora stuck on my laptop and read the scribble she wrote. I don't plan on nee—*wait,* what the fuck?

She left her name as 'your next booty call'? When the hell did I say that?

I think back to our brief interaction, but there's nothing I can think of that points to me insinuating anything about that. I honestly don't know much about her since I mostly keep to myself.

The only reason I know she's our university's star athlete is because I see her face in ads all around campus, and I assume that a girl like her is exactly like the one I used to know.

Should I not judge and assume? Probably. But I don't care enough to find out, my rules and all that.

"Fuck," I mutter to myself, trying to come up with a way to fix this. We're going to be spending a lot of time together, and I don't want her to feel uncomfortable, despite the fact that her being so close to me is going to make *me* uncomfortable.

I already know it.

Hours later, I'm lying in bed, working on the coding for a gaming job I'm applying for. It's a cartoon mash-up racing game from popular shows. I was one of three chosen from the applicant pool, which is huge.

We all have to code and design the game, essentially doing the work for them, and whoever they like the best will get the position.

Knowing how much of my life hinges on this job has been a huge stress. Sure, I could apply elsewhere, but this is an aspect of coding that I particularly enjoy, which makes me want it all the more. The salary alone would allow me to take care of my mom and sister for life.

So, I *need* this job.

"Cammmm," a voice sings from the living room.

"What?" I shout back, not averting my eyes from the string of numbers I'm working on.

"Get your ass out here for a minute!"

I stifle a grumble, bookmark where I left off with annotations, and set my laptop on my desk. Coming out to the living room, I see Finn has the hockey game on, his feet up on the coffee table. "What do you need?"

He turns his head to meet my dumbfounded look because as my one and only friend, he knows how annoyed I get when I'm interrupted during work. I think that's why he does stupid shit like this. He gets a kick out of it.

"I was missing your beautiful face," his eyes droop like a puppy, and I can't contain my eye roll.

"What do you want?" I chuckle, trying to sound annoyed but failing. Finn has always been able to make me laugh. The guy is such a goofball.

"Since my woman is busy, I wanted to have a guys' night."

"Oh, so I'm your backup plan?" I quirk a brow at him.

"You were my first choice if that helps." He smiles while patting the seat next to him. That's when I notice how late it is, the clock on the wall showing it's 8 p.m., Jesus, I've been working for six hours straight.

The smell of pepperoni pizza hits me, and I'm a goner. I plop my ass down on the seat next to him and go right for the pizza because I'm starving.

"Ashlyn is right. The way to a man's heart *is* food," he remarks, winking at me as he bites into a slice.

Something I love about Finn is that he never pressures me to drink or party. He knows everything there is to know about me and respects it. While we may differ in certain ways, our friendship couldn't be better. He's two years younger than me, but due to my delay in coming to school, we're both graduating this year.

Throughout the game, I can sense Finn's eyes on me periodically. "What is it?" I finally ask.

Finn smiles like a kid who knows something they shouldn't. "I haven't seen you like this in a while."

My face scrunches. "Like what?"

Keeping his gaze trained on the game, he casually states, "Like you've met a girl."

I nearly spit out my water. "Excuse me?"

He turns to look at me now, a knowing grin on his lips. "Exactly my point. You've been acting off ever since you got home. I've known you long enough to know it's not usually routine, so it has to be something new. Who is she?"

"You don't know shit, Finn." I shove his shoulder, and his grin just gets wider.

Asshole.

"Wait," his eyes nearly pop out of his head, fist to his chest as he tries to quickly swallow, "You had your first meeting today with your new tutee right?"

I'm beginning to regret telling him everything. "Yes," I grumble, crossing my arms over my chest.

"Oh, this is rich. Who is it?" He beams, sitting up a bit taller.

I know if I tell him, he'll know who she is because *everyone* does. But what's even worse is that Finn probably knows her more than some. They have the same major, kinesiology, and I'm willing to bet they have a few classes together.

With a sigh, I relent. "Aurora Vallacourt."

Finn's face tells me he's confused. "Wait, what? Aurora is at the top of our class. I've never seen her struggle in our three years in classes together."

Part of me wants to dig deeper into that and figure out exactly why her grades are suddenly dropping. But the other part of me knows better. The less personal I can make our sessions, the better. I don't have time for a girlfriend or want one.

"Hm, weird," is all I comment back, trying but failing to keep my brain focused on the puck shooting back and forth across the screen. I hope Finn drops the topic, but knowing him, he won't.

"So, you're into her eh? Pull a number and join the waiting room," he chuckles to himself. "Don't get me wrong, she's a great girl. Whenever I've talked to her, she's been really nice and funny. But everyone wants her for that reason, she's a great person and smoking hot."

"What would Ash say if she heard you say that?" I deflect.

"Pssh, Ash thinks she's hot as hell. Told me if we ever break up, she'll try and get with her, convince her to take a ride on the other side."

Ashlyn is Finn's girlfriend, and he's obsessed. My guy is a softie when it comes to her.

"I'm not into her. Sure, she's good-looking, but something about her unnerves me. I can't put my finger on it." I sigh, running a hand through my hair.

Finn claps his hands together. "Oh, I am here for this. It's love at first sight, huh?"

I shoot him a sharp glance. "Do you ever stop being annoying? Is it curable?"

He smiles. "You didn't deny it, though."

"I'm not in love. You know my stance on that. It's just pent-up sexual frustration, that's all," I reasoned, trying to convince myself more than Finn.

That emits a howl of laughter from Finn. "Yeah, I'd have a fuck ton of sexual frustration if I was twenty-five, still a virgin, with no intimate contact whatsoever in seven years."

"Fuck off." I kick his leg off the coffee table as he continues to laugh. Even though my ex and I dated for a while in high school, we never made it that far. We did everything but go all the way.

Finn mock winces, pretending like I snapped his leg in half. "I'm joking, you know I support your choices. But don't you think you owe it to yourself to have some fun? You've nearly got the degree, and you're going to get that job. Even if you don't, there's a huge demand for computer nerds, you'll easily get something. So, it looks like you got all your shit together. There's no excuses."

I hate how he strung those words together and how they rang with truth. "Aurora's not the kind of girl for me. I know her type all too well."

Finn pauses his bite, pulling his mouth away from the cheese nearly falling off his slice. "What in the hell is that judgemental shit?"

I huff in frustration, knowing he's right again. "Fuck, I know, I'm sorry. I was kind of a dick to her today too, and it's been messing with me. I feel like shit over it."

"Well, look on the bright side. You get to spend two hours with her twice a week. Plenty of time to fix it."

I nod, seeing the truth in his words again, but another part of me wants to keep her at an arm's length. Not by being a dick, but by not letting things between us be more than a tutor/tutee relationship.

I got this.

Chapter Four

Aurora

Spago's is my absolute favorite place to eat.

It's a hole-in-the-wall Italian restaurant on the outskirts of town. It's quaint and authentic, the pasta noodles made from scratch every meal. I've eaten bruschetta, salad, pasta, and a dessert to boot. This place is too good not to go home feeling ten pounds heavier.

My dad, Nate, and I are here, all of our schedules aligning for once.

We are done with dinner, our dessert plates nearly empty, when our Dad says something I never expected him to.

"I'm seeing someone," he states, his tone neutral, not giving anything away. He's waiting to see how we react to the news first.

My brother's fork clatters to his plate. "That's amazing. Who is the lucky lady, or not so lucky because you can be corny as shit."

I can't seem to form words because they're all stuck behind the lump in my throat at the idea of someone trying to replace my mom.

Dad looks hesitantly between us—one is filled with excitement, while the other is not. "Her name is Jodi. We met at the ski lodge last winter. She's a veterinarian and owns her practice in the city. Lovely lady whom I think both of you would like very much."

My throat finally clears, and I try not to sound offended. "You've been sneaking around for a year? Why hide it?"

Dad gives me a sad smile. "Cupcake, I only did it because I wanted to make sure she would be permanent before I introduced her to my life, to the two of you."

"That's really great dad, I'm happy for you. When do we get to meet her?" Nate asks, his smile genuine as he kicks my leg under the table.

I sit up straighter, willing myself to sound as genuine as my brother. "Yeah, right. When? This is so exciting." *Miserable fail.* I overshot my confidence to hide my emotions. I've always worn them on my sleeve.

"Aurora, you don't have to pretend to be happy for me. It's okay to feel sad or angry, I felt that way with myself at first. But it's been eleven years, and it's time I allow myself to love again. No one will replace your mom as the love of my life, but I'm a firm believer that we can have different kinds of love in life. Your mom would want all of us to be happy." His tone is gentle and kind, the way it always is when we talk about Mom.

"Thanks, Dad, I know I'll come around. I just need to wrap my head around the idea of someone replacing her, that's all," I nearly whisper as I wipe a stray tear from my cheek.

My dad's hand covers mine on the table, his eyes going glassy as he speaks. "No one will ever be able to do that, no one. There's nothing to replace. She was and still is your mom. Jodi will just be another person for us to open our hearts to, with no other role involved than caring for one another. Just as we Vallacourts do."

My heart breaks and mends at his words, knowing he understands and respects how hard this might be for me. I will do my best to open my heart to Jodi. I know it's what my mom would want me to do.

I smile, feeling lighter than moments before. "Love you, Dad."

"Love you more, Cupcake."

"What am I? Chopped liver?" Nate teases, his eyebrows quirked up.

My dad grins. "Oh, Muffin, are you jealous?"

Our table erupts into laughter at that, and we continue with our conversation until it's time for Nate and I to head to work.

I stand and bundle myself up in my knee-length puffer jacket because winter in Colorado is something else. I top my look with a beanie, scarf, and wool mittens just for the walk to my car.

"You know, you could just come home and snuggle with Pickles. He misses you," my dad goads, always trying to get me to quit my job.

"Dad," I groan. "Don't blackmail me with Pickles. You know he's my weakness, but I need to work."

It's one of the reasons why Pickles lives with my dad and not with me. Besides, between training, games, work, and classes, I'm never home.

Nate runs a hand through his light brown hair before pulling his beanie over it. "I need her. Having the star of the school boosts the traffic at the bar. I ran the data once."

Our dad chuckles, a teasing glint in his tone as he says, "Are you two ever going to let me just spoil you? Most kids would jump at the opportunity."

"We're not like most kids, Dad. Remember? We're Vallacourts," I hum back to him, smiling up brightly at the man I look up to.

"Damn right, you are. Raised too well, apparently." He pulls us both into a hug, and we all say our goodbyes as Nate and I drive back to his bar on campus.

My dad and brother mean the world to me, and I'm grateful for the small pockets of time we share together as we work around our crazy schedules.

If there's one thing I've learned since my mom passed, it's to make time for those who matter as much as possible.

Because you never know when you won't be able to.

Chapter Five

Aurora

Holy hell, the bar is busy tonight.

Since I stepped foot into this place at 8:30 p.m., I've been going non-stop, and it's edging on midnight now. Midterms finished two weeks ago, so students are flocking here to catch a game on TV, catch up with a friend, or let loose.

Admittedly, we're always busy on weekends, but tonight's been more than usual. The entire hockey team is here, on a high from their first win of the season, and their opposing team apparently decided to join them. If I have to make one more vodka cranberry for all the puck bunnies in this joint, I may lose it.

"Dude, that goal today was insane!" Isaiah Thomas, a power forward, cheers from the bar top, sloshing his beer on the surface with his enthusiasm. I roll my eyes and quickly wipe it up because I don't trust him to wipe it properly.

"Thanks, Zee," his teammate Dan remarks, his eyes sliding over my body for what feels like the hundredth time since they took residence at the bar fifteen minutes ago.

As a bartender, I'm used to dealing with drunken men and their lingering gazes or potty mouths. It sucks to say that, but it's what I've come to learn as part of the job at this point. It used to really bug me at first, but I quickly learned how to use my voice to shut them the hell up.

"You know what's insane?" He shifts in his seat, facing me as I clean glasses with the reprieve I've been given from making drinks. I look past him at the TV on the wall, watching the hockey game. He doesn't seem to notice or care. "How sexy Miss Bartender over here is."

I don't miss a beat. "You know what else is? Your ratio of slap shots taken and goals actually scored."

His friend covers his mouth to hide his laughter, knowing I'm right. The man before me scowls, no longer finding me oh so sexy—tough shit.

"Fu—"

My brother appears out of nowhere, fuming at my side. "Think about those words before you spit them out, 'cause they'll be the last ones you ever say here."

Dan zips his lips, throwing two twenties down for his tab and leaves with his friend.

"I had it under control, you know," I say to Nate, who's helping me wipe down glasses.

"Don't care much. No one is talking to you like that here, or anywhere else for that matter."

The vein in his neck that pulses when he's angry might pop if only he knew what the quarterback said to me a few months ago. Before I can comment back, a new customer takes a seat at the bar,

A customer I know.

"Hey, Finn. What can I get for you?" I smile at him. I like Finn. We've had some classes together since we're both majoring in kinesiology, and he's always been nice. We usually goof off whenever we have to work together on a project, his silly personality meshing well with mine.

"Aurora, it's nice to see you. I'll take a lager, please."

I nod, grab a glass, and put it under the tap for the beer he wants. When I return, I grab a coaster and put his beer on top, sliding it across to him.

"Did you finish the persuasive paper on the best cardiovascular exercise yet?" I ask as I fiddle with things behind the bar, cleaning up and whatnot.

"Yup, I did it the night it was assigned. I'm a good boy like that." His eyes tell me he's full of bullshit, and it makes me shake my head as I grin at him.

"Asshole," I mutter.

"I heard you met an even bigger asshole yesterday," he prods, but I have no idea what at.

Another puck bunny demands a vodka cran, so I hold up my finger to him, letting him know I'll answer in a minute. Once I finish, I return to his spot at the bar. "Sorry, who?"

He chuckles to himself like there's an inside joke I'm not aware of. "Cameron."

Oh, right, *that* asshole. I roll my eyes. "Yeah, I don't think Fields is too fond of me, which is a first."

Finn's smile grows at my comment. "I wouldn't count him out, just give him some time to warm up to you."

I put my hands on the bar, feeling the need to ground myself. "Look, I don't know if you're friends or whatever. But it's fine if he doesn't like me. He's my tutor. We don't need to be friends."

Liar.

If I'm being honest, I don't like when people don't like me. I'm very much a people pleaser.

"Aurora, I can tell it bugs you just by how you're fidgeting right now."

I look down and see my fingers pulling at the sleeves of my black long sleeve top.

Whoops. There's that whole wearing my emotions thing I was saying.

"Okay, don't tell him I told you this, but he said—"

My eyes widen. Cameron told Finn about me? How close are they?

"Wait, why did he tell *you* about me? What did he say?" I ask, leaning my elbows on the bar top, all too nosey to care how it sounds to him. I trust him, not sure why, but I do.

Finn has a knowing look on his face, one that I don't think I like. "We're cousins and best friends."

My mouth gapes at the confession, and I quickly close it at the realization.

"He feels bad about how cold he was with you. Like I said, just give him time to warm up. He's a cinnamon roll, okay?"

My face scrunches up. "What the hell does that mean? A cinnamon roll?"

He takes a long pull of his beer before answering. "It means he's the best guy I've ever known. A total softie."

My mouth gapes again. "Cameron Fields? A softie? Does he have a twin or something? Because I'm finding that very hard to believe."

Finn brushes the comment off. "The one and only." He finishes his beer and stands, fishing a bill out of his wallet. "That stays between us, okay?"

I take his money to the register and salute him. "Of course."

"Oh man, Cameron is in trouble. I can't wait to watch him fall," he muses as he shoves his arms into his jacket.

"Fall?" I ask, my eyebrows furrowed in confusion as Finn's body retreats.

Turning around, his head twists over his shoulder, and he says, "In love with you."

He strolls right out of the bar like he didn't just send my mind into a tailspin. My jaw is hitting the floor because did he really say that? I don't for a second believe that will happen, but even if, a *heavy* if, I can't give it back.

I also don't miss how it seems he came here tonight specifically to talk to me, as he only ordered one drink and left. He usually comes with Ashlyn, his girlfriend, but tonight, it seemed like he was on a mission.

I've gone my whole life without falling in love, and right now, with my senior year ahead of me, and that Team USA spot looming, it's impossible for me.

No matter how much space Cameron's been occupying in my mind since we met.

Chapter Six

Cameron

Mondays are my favorite day of the week.

I only had one class at noon, algorithm designs, but I woke up early, regardless, needing to stick to my routine. I started my day at the gym for an hour, went home to shower and eat, worked for an hour on the coding game, did some actual coding work for local businesses, and then went to class.

I'm back home, working at my desk since I have three hours until I need to meet with Aurora for our first official tutoring session. This reminds me of the question that's been playing in my mind all weekend. Why does she need help? It doesn't make sense to me if she's as smart as Finn says.

She's slowly starting to become a code I want to crack. A series of numbers out of order that I want to put back in their proper place to function again.

My phone ringing pulls me out of my head, and I smile when I look to see who is trying to video call me.

"Aren't you supposed to be in class?" I tease, trying to make my face look stern.

My sister's baby blue eyes beam at me, knowing I can never give her shit. "I have a free period, so I thought I'd call you."

"How are things? How did the appointment with Dr. Marsh go?" The pit in my stomach starts to fill with anxiety. I worry every time she has a checkup on her ventricular shunt.

Lexa's face gives nothing away. She's not afraid of her condition, and she embraces life with a smile no matter what. "Dr. Marsh said everything looks good, as always. I'm perfect, remember?"

I chuckle at that, loving how confident she is.

"I'm great. Senior year is off to a good start. I'm planning the Christmas spirit week, and I could not be more excited."

The anxiety pool starts to drain, a sense of relief washing over me that she's okay. "That's great. I'm glad to hear it. How's Mom?"

Lexa groans, "Cam, she's great, and you talk to her every day. You know this." A soft smile forms on her lips, her tone gentle. "Do you ever turn it off?"

I narrow my brows at that. "What do you mean?"

She rolls her eyes at me while she sighs softly. "Being a caregiver. You worry all the time, and you're always thinking of us. Tell me something about you, marvelnerd11?"

Lexa will randomly bring up my old email handle in conversation, and every time, it makes me smile, although I try to fight it like I am now. "Not likely, and to answer your other question, nope. Same old, marvelnerd11 here." I chose to leave out my new tutoring gig because the last thing I need is both Lexa and Finn on my ass about it.

"Boring. Live a little, will you? For me?" she pleads, her big blue eyes intent on mine.

"Nearly everything I've done is for you, Lexaroo, you know that." It's true, she's been my motivation for years to work hard.

Lexa's face goes from soft to stern within seconds, and I already know I'm about to get a load off from her. "I know, Cam, and while I am so grateful for that, I also sometimes feel like a burden. Go out and have fun every once in a while, okay? I can't stand the thought of you working your life away for me."

I sit up straighter, looking her in the eyes with finality. "Lexa, you listen to me. You never have been and never will be a burden. I enjoy taking care of you, okay?" She nods, and I continue. "And I do have fun. I work out, hike, camp, read comics by the lake, play video games, watch Marvel movies, or hang out with Finn when I'm not outside. That's all stuff I enjoy, which means I am having fun."

With a sigh, she gives it up – for now, knowing her. "Fine, but can you promise me something?"

"Anything," I say easily, knowing I'd give her the world if she'd ask for it.

"If you ever meet someone worthy of sharing your big ass heart with, give them a chance. I'm willing to share," she says, and before I cut her off, she adds, "I want to be an aunt already, help me out, would ya?"

I pretend to look at the watch on my wrist, knowing Lexa can see there's nothing there. "Wow, look at the time, I have to get going. Bye, love you, Lexaroo!"

I hear her mumble something just as I hang up on her. I love my sister, but she'd go on forever if I'd let her.

And while I said I'd promise her anything, letting someone in is the one thing I can't do.

Chapter Seven

Cameron

I'm ten minutes early for our first tutoring session, as I always am.

I set up my laptop, notebook, cue cards, and pencil case, getting out everything we may need.

I looked up the class that I'm tutoring her for—Introduction to Coding—and read the book front to back over the weekend to make sure I knew what to go over. I blame my actions on the rainy weather and a sudden interest in refreshing my mind about coding. That's all.

I rap my knuckles on the desk, feeling unease course through my body.

It's 4:55 p.m.

Aurora will be here in five minutes, and I feel like an ass for how I acted last week. But I also don't know if I want to turn it off. I'm afraid of what will happen if I do, and I'm not sure why the fuck she has this effect on me.

I hear the padding of feet getting closer. Aurora rounds the corner of the bookshelf and finally comes into view. Her dark blonde locks are in a messy bun, and she's wearing our school's forest green hoodie with gray sweatpants.

My brain screams one word so clearly and dominantly that I can't ignore it.

Beautiful.

She's fucking beautiful, and I can't deny it, as much as I want to.

She sits across from me, silently setting her backpack on the table. She starts unpacking it, pulling out her notes and textbooks while I fail to pull my gaze away from her.

"Uh, hi," she says, sounding unsure.

Realizing I've been staring for far too long, I cough and look at my laptop screen. "Can I apologize?" I blurt before analyzing what the hell I'm even saying.

Hazel eyes snap up, looking cautious as they stare into mine. "For what? I definitely wasn't offended in the slightest when you thought I just wanted to be your late-night texting buddy." The bite in her tone makes my chest ache. I hate that I upset her, a stranger or a client, I hate it.

I hold her stare, letting her know that her words don't put me off. "I'm apologizing for making you feel like that, because that wasn't my intention, and that's not what I think of you. I don't even know you. I'm sorry for being a dick overall. I just—" I pause, not wanting to reveal the walls I've built around myself. "I had a bad day, and you didn't deserve that."

Her shoulders drop slightly at my words, but her eyes remain guarded. "I thought you knew all about me, mister 'I know who you are.'"

I pull on the brim of my cap, feeling frustrated with myself for being such an asshole that day. "I know you're the star of this school, captain of the volleyball team, and the dean's daughter. That's it."

Aurora crosses her arms under her chest, making her breasts more pronounced. I use every ounce of self-control to not check her out. "Let me guess, you think I'm entitled, selfish, arrogant, pretentious, and an attention-seeking partier? Does that sound about right?"

My face remains passive while my stomach flips because that's exactly what I thought. I automatically compared Aurora to my ex, Layla, who was everything she had just described. The only difference was that she was a soccer player and not our principal's daughter.

Does Aurora deserve to be judged? No. Does anyone? Also, no.

Layla did a fucking number on me when she cheated on me during the worst time of my life. It made me distrust those around me and judge them based on what happened to me. It's taken me a while, but I've started to learn that my experiences aren't the only ones out there, and I can't go through life letting that affect how I react to people who may remind me of her.

I know I'm in the wrong. No one's perfect, and that's why I don't deny it.

I opt for blunt honesty, wanting to give us a clean slate. "I did at first, but I'm learning I shouldn't judge others."

Aurora rolls her eyes at my admission. "Typical," she mutters, blowing a blonde strand out of her face, "I accept your apology as long as you agree not to be a judgy asshole. Sound easy enough?"

I nearly smirk at that, but I control it before it starts. "I agree. Now tell me, what are you struggling with exactly?"

She pulls out a hefty textbook, placing it in the spot between us. The title reads *Introduction to Coding*.

"It's the only class I have below a 70, and to keep my spot on the team, I need to get it there. I didn't even want to take this stupid elective, but it's the only one that worked with my schedule," she mumbles, sounding embarrassed.

It bothers me that she does. Everyone struggles with courses at times, but it's nothing to be ashamed of.

"Then let's get you there," I said, wanting to ease her apparent stress.

Aurora just nods, not seeming to want to talk about it further, which is fine with me. The less details I know about her, the better. I can't control my body's attraction to her, but I can prevent getting close to her.

While we're starting over with our tutor/tutee relationship, I don't necessarily plan to become friends either. *Or anything else, for that matter.*

"What chapter are you on right now?" I ask, trying to figure out what material to start with.

Aurora flips open the book to a pink tabbed page titled 'Programming Languages.'

"This is currently the bane of my existence," she scoffs as if the subject offends her.

"Nothing I can't help you with."

Aurora's eyebrow raises slightly. "And you thought I was the arrogant one?" she teases, her tone playful.

It takes all my control to stifle a smile, but I do. "I'm a tutor for a reason, Aurora. I'm good at what I do." I grab her book and pull it to me to look through the chapter's content.

She pulls out a worn-out pink notebook while I flip through the pages, along with a pencil, and begins writing or drawing on a page. I can't tell which because I'm trying not to stare.

I quickly avert my gaze, focusing back on the material in front of me, although my mind is curious about what she's doing. I notice that she pauses for moments at a time, putting her pencil to her lips in thought before resuming her scribbling something.

It's distracting, her every move catching my attention and pulling me away from the textbook I need to focus on.

I take a few moments to jot down how I want to present the information to her, chunking it into sections we will tackle each session.

I look up at her, noticing a small smile on her lips as she stares at whatever she did on her paper. Her knees are pulled to her chest, the notebook resting against her thighs. My hand itches to reach across the table and yank it from her to see what it is, but then I remember my rules and the itch disappears.

I clear my throat to get her attention. Her soft eyes land on mine as she peers at me over her knees. "I'm ready to get started if you are."

Her head falls to one shoulder, a breath leaving her pouty lips in defeat. "If we must." She really does not like this class, she's making that evidently clear.

We spend the next hour reading the contents of the first four pages. I explain the bolded terms to her, and we decode each paragraph to understand what their point is.

Sometimes textbooks explain shit with too much fluff. I've learned that there's usually something valuable in each section, you just have to look around the extra words to figure out the main point.

And I think that's Aurora's problem—looking beyond the mess of technological terms and academic writing to understand it in a more simple way. This type of information is heavy. Coding is no joke, but math is easy for me. It's not like sociology-based classes where you have to prove or debate things, there's only one correct answer.

I check the time on my phone, seeing that we only have two minutes left of our time together. "That's it for today. Did that help?"

Aurora closes her textbook with a giant smile on her lips. "Yup. Your arrogance is well-deserved, Fields. What a smart cookie you are."

My damn lips twitch, nearly letting her see how she has the ability to make me smile when no other girl has. I also find it interesting that she calls me Fields instead of Cameron or Cam. What's even more interesting is the fact that I like it. I don't say anything, though. I just pack up my shit while she does the same.

"Which way are you heading?" she asks over her shoulder as she shoves her things into her backpack.

I pause because I'm not sure where she's going with this. Does she want to hang out? I don't want to hurt her feelings, but we can't do that.

"Home. I have work." It's not a lie, I do need to get some coding done tonight.

Slinging her backpack over her shoulder, she sighs. "Are you ever going to say more than five words to me at a time?"

I grind down on my jaw, trying once again to stifle a smile. She calls me out on my shit and is not afraid to do it. I'm not used to that.

"Maybe. Where are you going?" I ask, exactly five words. Four of them should've been kept to myself because what the fuck am I doing asking her personal questions?

Aurora laughs for the first time, her eyes squeezed shut as her head tilts back, being one of those people who laugh with their entire body.

You know when you hear an old favorite song and it fills you with a warm, happy feeling at the familiar tune? Yeah, that's what listening to her laugh did to me, and despite it being new, it feels like my heart knows its tune already.

I'm in trouble.

"Exactly five words. Nice one," she lets out between pants. "I'm heading home too. I have early morning conditioning tomorrow."

Even though her body is hard to see accurately in her loungewear, I know she's in better shape than I am. Sure, I work out a lot and have the body to show for it, but training for a Division I sport is another thing entirely.

Our eyes meet, her specks of green and blue vivid against the brown. They're intriguing, just like her. I feel myself slipping, staring longer than I probably should, but I can't seem to stop myself.

"Night, Fields," she says all too quickly, turning on her heel as she walks away, shoving her headphones into her ears.

I groan, rubbing a hand over my face in frustration. I can't stop making this girl uncomfortable it seems. I need to get it the fuck together. I'd like to think my communication skills are good, but apparently not with her.

Or maybe Finn is right. Maybe I need to get laid for once. My pent-up sexual frustration must be causing me to act like a fucking idiot because I'm attracted to her. But I know I won't do that—have a meaningless hookup.

At this point, I want to wait for someone meaningful. Despite my determination to avoid women to focus on my goals, realistically, I know I can't keep that shit up forever. I want a family, a big house full of laughter and love. I just don't want to lose sight of my goals and fail to provide for my family.

Maybe I could work on both?

I'm good at focusing and pushing myself to be the best at everything I do, and hell, maybe I'd be good at that, too. But the idea of opening myself up to that again is also scary.

What I need is some confidence, knowing that I can handle anything that comes my way. My mind is clearly swirling, and it's fucking tiring.

I throw my backpack over my shoulder, the few minutes it takes to walk to my house off campus not doing much for my thoughts that seem to be on a never-ending loop. As I get ready to set up my workstation for the night, I see a text on my phone from Lexa.

It's a meme of three people sitting in a booth. Two are making out while the other is sitting there stuffing his face with pizza.

Lexa Roo

This is your present and future, Cam.
Third-wheeling Jordan and I,
just saying.

Jordan has been with my sister for two years now, and they're fucking adorable. Although I was stressed when I first found out because I'm overly protective of her, he's turned out to be the best thing for her.

Her message is a reminder that I need to open myself up to dating if I want the life I always dreamed of as a kid—the one I've put on hold for my family.

Maybe I can have it all while providing for them, too.

While Layla gave me slight trust issues with her cheating, I've seen enough healthy relationships to know they exist and not let a few bad ones taint my perception completely. Lexa might be my baby sister, but sometimes, it feels like she's the wiser one.

Lexa's incessant demands from our earlier video chat play in my mind before I attempt to sleep a few hours later. Her words, along with the melody of Aurora's laugh, cause me to toss and turn for what feels like forever.

I'm not sure if Aurora's worth lowering my walls for yet, but I know I spend every restless minute before sleep thinking of her.

Chapter Eight

Aurora

The chirps of birds float through the air, the early morning chill wrapping itself around my body.

I pull my blanket tighter around me, sipping on my vanilla matcha latte and feeling the sweetness warm me from the inside out. It may be November, but I love sitting outside. The orange hue of the sun starts to peek over the mountain peak, casting a glow on me as I sit on the back porch of my house.

I always start my home game day mornings like this, enjoying the calm feeling that the early morning brings as I watch the sunrise.

It gives me time to set myself up for the day, and to think about what I need and want to accomplish. I'll bring my notebook with me, in case inspiration strikes. Whether it does or doesn't, I always keep it on me, needing the comfort it provides me to know I can jot down whatever I feel.

Something no one knows about me is that I love to draw. It may seem silly or odd with my athletic persona, but it's my thing. Growing up, I've always loved drawing, and when I went to therapy after my mom's passing, my therapist encouraged it even more to sort out my feelings. So now, I still do it, drawing whenever I want to remember a moment or need a release.

I opened my worn pink notebook to one of the last things I drew during my tutoring session on Monday. I didn't know why I had the urge to draw him, but I did.

I drew his eyes, the different hues of brown that make up the primarily cinnamon hue, capturing the honesty I saw in them the moment I knew he wasn't bullshitting me.

He's the first guy I've ever drawn.

Every time I look at it, butterflies take flight in my stomach. It makes me nauseous. I have no idea why I'm so confident that my conversation with Cameron was honest, but I felt it regardless.

There's something about him.

His first words were an apology, which surprised the hell out of me, along with his brutal honesty when I called him out. I've never had a guy speak to me that way. With his whole body. The way his eyes flicked over my face, trying to read my emotions, while his hands wrapped tightly around his forearms to suppress his nerves, which I noticed through the bounce of his knee under the table.

On one hand, it was relieving that we'll be able to get through these tutoring sessions without being at each other's throats, but, on the other, it's also unnerving. It was easier to ignore my attraction to Cameron when I thought he was an asshole, but getting previews of his softness here and there? It's making me want to be around him for more than a few hours a week, and not as his tutee.

Hell, Cameron could have a girlfriend, for all I know, and I'm celibate, so it shouldn't matter.

It's a relief that our sessions won't be as unbearable as I thought they would be. Our last session on Thursday went well. He was nice once again, but we didn't talk outside of coding.

In fact, he didn't say more than five words unless it was course-related.

I've made it my goal to not only improve my grade but to a) get Cameron to smile, and b) get him to speak to me with more than a few words at a time. We may not hook up, but we could be friends.

I hear the patio door slide open and slam my book shut. Jasmine's seen it before, but she doesn't know what I draw in there.

"Morning," she yawns, blowing a smooth black curl out of her face.

Ever since we became friends in high school, our families became close as well. Especially once her dad got hired as the hockey coach here. Ned Park has been the head of the coaching staff for the last eight years while her mom, Madelaine, is a doctor specializing in cardiology. "I'm thinking about going for breakfast at Cora's before our first game today. You want to come? Breakfast is on me for your birthday."

Cora's is our campus's famous pancake diner, serving only pancakes all day long. They even have vegan options, which is perfect for Jasmine since she's allergic to eggs. She's not vegan by any means, but she'll often opt for that option for baked goods and breakfast to be on the safe side.

I stand from my seat, keeping my blanket wrapped tightly around my body. "I'd love to. Let me change and grab my gym bag."

If there's anything people need to know about me, it's that I love food—specifically sweets.

Jasmine's face beams at my answer. "Perfect, I'll warm up my car."

After devouring a stack of chocolate chip pancakes with a peanut butter drizzle, my absolute favorite, we arrive at the volleyball facility around 10:30 a.m. Our first game of the season starts at noon, which is an irregular start time. We usually play on Fridays and Saturdays at 6 p.m., but our home opener warrants a special time.

After today's game, Jasmine and I are going to the local spa for some much-needed relaxation. I've been saving up for this, and I can't wait.

We head to the locker room, where most of our teammates are getting ready for the game. I changed into our home uniform, a white long-sleeve top with my name and number 25 on the back. The school's mascot, a coyote, is on the sleeve in forest green.

Before pulling on my socks, my finger strokes over the ink on my inner ankle. A 'V' with a hyacinth wrapped around one side of the V because those were my mom's favorite. I do it before every game, reminding myself that I want to make her proud.

I have to.

After pulling my hair into a tight ponytail, I pop my Airpods in place, tuning out the room to focus on the game. Some people like to chat or read, but I just like to listen to music, usually something upbeat, nothing that will put me to sleep.

Before I know it, my team is on the court, finishing our warm-up and drills. We're playing the University of Florida, the home of the Sharks, a decent team, but not enough to beat us.

I feel good today, confident in my team and my skills. It's not something I usually doubt, but it always feels good when I have that extra confidence boost.

I get called up for the captain's meeting with the referee, where they spiel the same story as always about rules, lines, and behavior.

Then we're on the court, the crowd's roar fueling up the adrenaline in my veins as we get into formation. Volleyball is huge at RLU, and our gatherings match that of our equally famous football team.

I look out into the crowd and easily spot my dad sitting next to my brother because they both have foam fingers and a sign that says "Vallacourt owns the court." I flash them a wide smile, feeling eternally grateful for having them as my biggest cheerleaders on and off the court, despite how embarrassing they can be at times.

I keep scanning the crowd and see a few faces I know, but my eyes zone in on a particular couple I never would've looked at twice until now—Finn and his girlfriend, Ashlyn. My gut sinks for a moment when I realize Cameron isn't with Finn.

Why the hell do I care if he watches my games or not? He just started to be nice this week, and while I may think about riding him a few times a day, there's no reason I should feel the way I do about him not being here.

I push the thoughts and feelings aside as the ref blows the whistle, indicating it's game time.

I'm our lead server, so I bounce the ball four times like I always do, then toss it up with my right arm and smash it over the net. The ball skims the net perfectly, seeming like it's going to hit it, but coasting just above and heading downward quickly.

The Shark's center dives just in time, hitting it up to her setter, who volleys it. Their spiker hits it, but Jasmine is better, blocking the hit before it has the potential to come on our side.

Despite her lack of height, she's able to jump higher than anyone on the team.

We easily won all three sets, and Coach Tilly pulled me out in the third set to let our second-string players get some court time. I didn't mind because it's the beginning of the season and there were no scouts here today.

My dad says that my mom always knew the importance of rest and that the best players are the ones who know how to balance training with rest. I like to think I do that well, but with it being the year I have the best chance to make the Olympics, I'm doing more training than resting. I have to make it, there's no other choice for me.

I've never had a plan B, C, or D. I've only ever had a plan A, and that's to make it into Team USA and go to the Olympics in two summers and every four years after that until I physically can't anymore.

I could do something with my degree in kinesiology, but nothing sparks a fire in my soul like competing does.

After our post-game shower and meeting with Coach Tilly, Jasmine and I head to our spa retreat. It'll be the perfect remedy for my sore limbs from endless practices, training, the game, and for my mind.

Which seems to keep circling back to a particular guy when it shouldn't.

Chapter Nine

Aurora

"Can we make it a pact to do this once a month?" Jasmine sighs peacefully, resting her head on her shoulder as steam from the hot spring mists her face.

I hum happily, the bubbles blasting from the jet into my back working wonders on my body and mind. "If I pick up some extra shifts at the bar, then yes."

Refresh in the Rockies is the best retreat in the area. They have an outdoor oasis with three different hot springs with differing temperatures and features, along with three different saunas, some more intense than others.

We spent the first hour getting a massage, and now we're resting the day away outside, rotating from the hot springs to the saunas and back.

"Ro?" Jasmine's voice is a whisper over the sound of the jets.

"What, Minnie?"

"My dad texted me last night. He wanted me to remind you about celebrating the Korean New Year with us."

I smile, my hands swaying back and forth as I gather foam in them.

Jasmine's family has always been like my own. "Tell him I will, without a doubt, be there."

Her lips twitch, and I sit up, my back going straight. "What is it?" My hand finds hers under the bubbles, and I give it a squeeze.

Jasmine's deep mocha eyes flick to mine, sadness in her features. "This year it falls on the day….you know, *the* day."

She doesn't need to say what it is because it hits me then.

The day my mother passed away—January 22nd.

It never gets easier. Every year on that day, I feel as if I'm transported to that exact moment ten years ago when I'd first heard the news, a rush of pain wracking my entire body.

"Oh," is all I can muster to say, the familiar tug of grief inching its way around my throat, threatening to pull me under. In some ways, it gets easier, but sometimes, it hurts just like a fresh wound.

Jasmine's hand falls to mine on her knee, squeezing it. "Ro, don't even worry about it. I know how hard that day is for you. I just want you to know the option to celebrate with us is still there. We love you either way."

"Thank you, Minnie," I choke, suddenly feeling a bit overwhelmed. From our conversation to my hectic schedule, the pressure about scouts in the new year, and my new tutor who seems to mess with my brain while helping it.

Jasmine speaks up before my mind can go off on a whole tangent with all things Cameron-related.

"I love you, Aurora," she says softly, resting her neck on the headrest of the hot spring.

"How much?" I quip, raising a brow at her.

Jasmine's eyes flit to mine, a small smirk on her lips. "So much that I watched every goddamn Marvel movie with you when you had the flu that one time. And you know how I feel about TV."

My smile grows with hers as I recall the memory. Even though I felt like crap, it's one of my most cherished memories of us. Jasmine took care of me the entire four days I was out. She fed me, bathed me, and did whatever she could to get me to smile, including watching my favorite movies of all time—anything Marvel.

"And I love you for that. Want to do it again sometime?"

Jasmine scoffs, sinking further into the water. "Hell no. Please don't ever catch the flu again. My brain can't handle watching Peter Parker say he doesn't want to go."

"Aha! So you do have a heart," I tease, shimmying my shoulder against hers.

"I'm not a psycho, that shit was sad," she chuckles, then stares at me more seriously. "You know, I always thought you were a conundrum before we became close."

"What do you mean?"

"You just have so many different sides to you, you know? You dress super girly, but you're also an athlete who loves to wear sweats. You nerd out over superheroes, but you also love to be outside and away from technology. You love to draw and be soft, but pretend you aren't."

My bottom lip falls, my breath hitching in my throat. "Wait, how do you know I draw?"

"Don't hate me, but one day our freshman year, it fell out of your gym bag and opened up to a page. I couldn't help myself, but I only looked at one, then stopped." She confesses, her words rapid as if I'll forgive her as quickly as she tells me.

I groan, rubbing a hand down my face from embarrassment. "I don't hate you, Minnie. But don't tell anyone, please?"

"I swear it," she says, her pinky up in a scout's honor, "It was really good, by the way. I don't remember the picture exactly, I just remember it made me feel something when I looked at it."

I smile at that, liking that my drawing had an effect on her. Even though I don't draw for anyone else to see, it's still nice to hear.

"Good, because if you tell anyone, I'll be sure to tell them all about your extensive sex toy collection for a virgin."

Jasmine gapes at me, splashing water on my chest. "I have needs, okay!"

We both break out into a fit of laughter, which is how we spend the rest of our time at the retreat. Laughing and relaxing in the hot springs until it's time to head home.

My birthday celebrations have been amazing thus far, from the dinner with my dad and brother (despite the bombshell my dad laid on us) to my spa day with my best friend.

All that's left is my big birthday finale. A hike by myself next Saturday, spending it in the place I love the most and with the person I miss the most.

My mom.

Chapter Ten

Cameron

After tightening the laces on my boots, I stand tall, peering at the mountain ahead.

Bear Trail is a popular trail in Colorado known for its infamous Emerald Lake, drawing in tourists all summer.

But since it's edging towards winter, it's nearly empty despite the snow having held off so far this season. I didn't intend on spending my Saturday here, but plans changed. I knew the trail well and needed something I didn't have to focus on while I sort out my mind.

Aurora has been living in my head rent-free all week. Our two sessions this week had gone well academically, with nothing vastly changing from the week before, except it's becoming harder and harder not to smile around her.

I often find myself lowering my head to my laptop screen to avoid letting her see that she's putting a dent in my walls.

I don't think she's even trying, and that scares me.

What if she actually put some effort into getting to know me and vice versa? I'd be fucked.

As if the universe wants to mock me, guess who I see sitting on a log right in front of Emerald Lake about an hour into my trek?

None other than Aurora Vallacourt.

She's wrapped up in a long, white puffer jacket. Her beanie, mittens, and scarf are all the same shade of pale green. That worn-out pink notebook she carries everywhere is open to a page on her lap. I can't see the details from here, but it confirms my theory that she draws rather than writes in it.

A brown dog is sitting at her feet, ears flickering at the sound of my approach, but she doesn't seem to notice.

What I find the most interesting, though, is her face. She's beautiful, I already knew this, but the look of peace she's projecting is mesmerizing. Her hazel eyes are beaming at the view in front of her. Even from a distance, I can tell how relaxed her body is, the lack of tension in it.

I could turn around, pretending I never saw her here, but as soon as I think about it, my stomach recoils at the idea of leaving her. There's a magnetic pull I feel toward her. It's something intangible, yet it feels like I could reach out and grab it. That's how strong it is.

I step out of the path, and her dog immediately barks at my presence.

Aurora's head whips over to me, her eyes widening when she takes me in. She sighs, a mixture of shock and relief. "Fields? What the hell are you doing here? I thought it was a bear, for fuck's sake." She puts her hand over her chest, and I notice how rapid her breaths are coming in and out.

Crap, I didn't mean to scare her.

"I like being outside." It's probably the most I've ever told her about myself, and I'm not sure why I did it or what I say next. "I could ask you the same thing."

"It's my 21st birthday, and this is where I like to spend it. I enjoy being outdoors too, whenever I get the time," she adds, tucking her notebook into her backpack resting on the log beside her.

I'm not surprised by her easy admission, the way she opened up with no struggles. In the short time I've spent with Aurora, I've learned that she wears her emotions easily.

"Happy birthday," I tell her with a small smirk, but not quite a full smile.

She returns it with a wide one of her own. "Thanks, Fields. This is Pickles." She gestures to the brown dog panting happily at my feet.

I sink to my knees, giving Pickles the attention he desperately wants. "Pickles? Interesting name."

Aurora turns away from me, her gaze locked on to the crystal blue lake before her. She's quiet for a moment, and I think she'll ignore my intrigue in her dog's name until she blows out a breath. "My dad has pet names for all of us: my mom, brother, and I. They are all dessert-based, so I wanted to give my dog the opposite. Something snack-related."

I don't know if it's the cold getting to my head or the invisible pull I feel towards her that propels me to keep asking questions. "What dessert are you?" I ask while running my hands over Pickle's belly, who's happily sprawled on his back.

"I'm Cupcake, my brother is Muffin, and my mom was Pudding," she tells me, her voice turning quiet at the end.

I don't miss that she referred to her mom in the past tense.

"Did your parents divorce?" I ask softly, my gaze trained on her as I take a seat next to her. Not close enough that we're touching, but enough that I catch a whiff of her scent.

Lime and coconut—refreshing yet comforting.

I don't know why I sat down, but standing over her for this conversation feels wrong. Her eyes flick back to mine, and those hazel irises swim back and forth with indecision. I don't blame her, I haven't told her anything about myself, yet here I am questioning her like it's a goddamn interview.

Aurora's head tips to the side. We've never been this close before. There's always a table between us, and we never leave our session together, aside from our first one. I intentionally stay back and fiddle on my laptop to avoid that now.

"When I was ten, there was a bad snowstorm," Aurora pauses, pain etched onto the surface of her face.

The sudden tightness in my chest at her palpable pain surprises me.

What is going on?

"The other driver lost control and stole my best friend from me."

Jesus Christ. I can't even imagine losing my mom. The thought alone makes my body ache with sadness.

"I come here on my birthday because we used to hike together all the time. It makes me feel closer to her," she finishes, a sad but somewhat there smile on her lips.

I don't even know how to reply, but it's changing how I look at her. It makes me want to know more, to keep learning about the things that make her who she is.

"I am so sorry, Aurora, that must have been tough," I say, my tone gentle and my hand itches to hold hers.

Well, that's new.

Her arms wrap around her middle. "It was, but so am I. She's my motivation. I plan to make it to the Olympics for her, to finish the dream she never got to."

I have a newfound admiration for her strength because I don't think I could do it. Living out her mom's dream must bring a certain weight to her life, even if she enjoys it at the same time. It also explains why it's so important for her to get her grades back up, keep her spot on the volleyball roster, and be recruited for Team USA.

The pieces are starting to fit, but a few are still missing. Pieces I find myself wanting more and more to uncover.

"You will. If anyone is going to make it, it's you." I'm not sure why I said that, but it's out there now. No taking it back.

Aurora tilts her face to look at me, a smile on her lips. "Thank you."

Our eyes stay locked on one another, and something weird happens. The scenery starts to fade, the green of the trees not as vibrant, the rustle of the pond silenced. I can feel my heart beating my chest more than I ever have before. My lips feel dry, my throat tight.

What the hell is happening?

Pickles interrupts our trance with his barking, demanding some attention. Aurora breaks away first, leaning forward to give her dog some love. "You don't have to stay. You can finish your hike," she offers.

I don't like the sound of that, so I tell her the truth. "I was coming here to clear my mind, actually, but I can leave if you want to be alone."

She ponders it for a moment, her lips twisting. "You can stay under two conditions."

"Proceed," I motion, waving my hand in front of me for her to continue.

Her body shifts on the log to angle herself toward me. "One, you have to tell me something about yourself-"

"I like the color green?" I smile for the first time, not a full one, but it's a start.

Aurora freezes, her bottom lip parting from the top. Her eyes widen in awe like she's just seen fireworks for the first time. "Is that a smile, Fields? You just fulfilled condition two."

I smile again at her request because I should've known she's smart and would eventually catch on to the fact that I never smile around her. It's a tough feat, one I'm growing tired of doing.

"Hey, I fulfilled condition number one, too," I reminded her.

Her nose scrunches at my words. "Something real, Fields. It doesn't have to be diary-level deep."

Why I'm even going along with this is beyond me, but I'm learning to stop questioning my heart and following it for once in my life.

I take a deep breath, steadying my emotions for what I'm about to reveal. Wanting to be as open as she was with me, I tell her what only Finn knows. "I'm 25 and still in school because I delayed coming to university to support my mom after we sent my dad to jail."

Aurora's breath hitches. "Cam… you didn't have to—"

I notice it's the first time she's called me Cam, and while I like her calling me Fields, this feels different. Warmer.

"I want to," is all I say, then continue because, for some reason, the words don't want to stop tumbling out of my mouth. "My dad was abusive and an alcoholic, which is why I'm sober."

Aurora's gloved hand rests on top of mine, and although there are layers between us, I feel the weight of its significance throughout my body. "Did he… did he ever hurt you?" she asks, her voice quiet.

I shake my head. "No, but I wish he would've instead of taking it out on my mom. I'll never forgive myself for not calling for help sooner, but we needed his money to take care of my sister, Lexa. She has a condition that requires a lot of monitoring.

I never stood up to him because I was afraid my sister wouldn't get the proper care she deserved, and Lexa was too afraid for me to leave her alone when he had his episodes."

"It wasn't your fault. You have to forgive yourself." Her hand squeezes mine. "Forgiveness is hard, but you know what else is?"

"What?" I ask, my voice rawer than I'd like.

"Believing that we have control over everything in our lives."

Her words hit me square in the chest, nestling themselves in my heart. I look away from her eyes to the pond because the emotions swelling inside me threaten to burst, and I'm not sure what that will look like.

I might sigh with the relief her words bring or kiss the hell out of her. The latter scares me more than anything has since my dad went to jail.

"Tell me about Lexa, if you want, that is," she pipes up. She lifts her hand from resting on mine, seeming to know that I need a change of conversation.

I smile as Lexa's big blue eyes and brown curly hair shape into my mind. She'd like Aurora; their bright personalities are a match made for one another.

"She's in senior year, student body president, has tons of friends, goes out like a typical teenager, and has a boyfriend. Her hobbies include giving me shit, baking, and event planning."

Aurora winks, a playful grin on her face. "Sounds like my kind of girl."

I shake my head. Even though my sister's condition doesn't define her, I find myself wanting to share more with Aurora.

"She's amazing. Lexa has spina bifida which is a neural condition that affected her spine at birth. She only needs a walker now, which is huge in itself for her condition. She lives life to the fullest every day and doesn't let anything hold her back."

"Ah, the superior Fields sibling, I see," she teases, and I erupt into a full-blown laugh.

Aurora's face lights up at the sight, her eyes locked on me.

"You're not wrong," I muse, looking up at the slowly darkening sky, wisps of pink and orange hanging lowly against an ocean blue.

We should probably head out soon, but I find myself wanting to extend my time with her. The two of us feel different here, surrounded by nature and away from the noise of our lives.

I like it, and I like this version of Aurora that I'm getting to know better.

We sit in silence for a while, the only sounds being the ripple of the pond, the whispering of pine trees in the wind, and the occasional bark from Pickles. It's the first time I've felt truly at peace in a long time, the worries about my mom and sister absent. All while being next to Aurora Vallacourt, of all people.

I know it's not merely the scenery because I've spent countless hours here. It's her. And I want—no, *crave* more of it. Of the feeling that being around her brings me.

Which is why I find myself asking her something I wouldn't have two weeks ago. "What are you doing after this, birthday girl?"

Aurora tilts her head, studying me like I've got two heads. "Are we becoming friends, Fields?"

I level her with a no-bullshit expression. "Yeah, I think we did. So, what about those plans?"

"Who knew you were so pushy?" she teases, her voice light and happy. "Honestly, nothing. Probably watch a Christmas movie and snuggle with Pickles."

"Christmas? It's your birthday?" I pin her with a quizzical look.

"Yeah, but my birthday is literally the month mark to Christmas. And I love the holiday, so I start celebrating on my birthday."

Half of my lips tug up into a crooked grin. "I like it. Have you had cake yet?"

It's her turn to look at me in confusion, her dark brown eyebrows inching up her forehead. "Nope, why do you ask?"

"Lexa always says that you can't age until you have a slice of cake."

Most families eat cake during birthdays, but Lexa's spin on it made it even more important to ensure we always had a cake.

"Oh, is that true? Well, I never want to age, so maybe I should avoid it." A smirk forms on her plump lips and I wonder what they would taste like.

I push the thought away and stand, waiting for her to follow suit. "Not a chance, let's go."

"Where?" she asks from her spot on the log.

"To get you some cake," I state, bending to pick up her pink and gray backpack and slinging it over my shoulders.

Aurora stands at that, clutching Pickles's leash in one hand. "Why are you carrying my backpack?" She steps beside me, and we begin descending as I think of what to say.

"You have the dog, and it's dark. I don't need your heavy bag slowing you down," I somewhat lie because although it's partly true, I also want to do something for her. I want to take care of Aurora Vallacourt, and once I start, there's no stopping.

Chapter Eleven

Aurora

"This is amazing." I nearly moan as my lips lick my spoon clean, trying to savor the swirl of chocolate and peanut butter.

Dad told me that my mom's pregnancy craving was chocolate and peanut butter, and I think that desire was transferred to me. It's my weakness, my one true love.

"I told you this place is the best." Cameron's lips tug, forking another slice of his cookies and cream cake into his mouth.

After we made it down the mountain, I drove Pickles home to my dad's house, then went back to my house on campus while Cameron followed me in his car. He refused to let me drive separately, and that's how he ended up driving us to a little cafe outside of town. It's quaint, with a few regulars sitting in booths with either headphones tucked in, reading a book, or furiously typing on their laptops.

It's cozy, the little shop making me feel like a hot chocolate on a snowy day—comforting, sweet, and warm.

Cameron told me on the ride over that this place has the best cake he's ever tasted. He didn't lie. This cake is freaking phenomenal.

Do you know what else is unreal? This weird friendship forming between him and me. If someone told me two weeks ago that I would be willingly spending my birthday with Cameron Fields, I would've laughed in their face.

But now? I would smile.

I don't know whether it was the emotions of the day for me or the peaceful setting at the lake, but things between us shifted. It was so easy to open up to him, something that's hard for me to do despite wearing my emotions on my sleeve.

It felt good, cathartic even.

And I think he felt the same way, letting me have a glimpse behind his secure walls. I may not have been given full access, but I'm grateful for what he allowed me to see.

There's more to Cameron than I ever thought, and I find myself wanting to uncover more.

Don't even get me started on his smile. I felt the breath leave my lungs in a whoosh and those dimples. I so badly wanted to pull my notebook out and draw them.

Mixed in with his sandalwood and fresh linen scent, it was a deadly combination.

Cameron is already beyond attractive to me, with his slightly curled hair, the cute glasses he wears when he works on his laptop, and his large, muscular frame. But that smile of his? Easily his best feature.

It makes me wonder if he's single, not for me, but because I find it hard to believe he is, and I find myself unable to stop from asking.

"Can I ask you something?" I ask him while dragging my finger along the peanut butter frosting on my plate.

His eyes zero in on my finger for a moment before lifting to my own. "The deal was I had to tell you one thing. Don't get carried away now," he smirks.

I bring my frosting-covered finger to my lips, letting my tongue get a small taste before sucking my finger into my mouth. I didn't think anything of it, but looking at Cameron, I know it came across as sexual.

His eyes narrow, his jaw ticking as I release my finger with a pop. *Interesting.* Not that it matters because of my whole no dating/celibate rule, but it's nice to know he may be attracted to me.

"I thought we were friends, Fields?" I pout, my bottom lip jutting out.

His demeanor relaxes, his jaw less rigid as he swallows another bite. "Valid point. What do you want to know?"

"Are you single?" I blurt out.

Cameron's eyes widen, then a chuckle leaves his full lips as he runs a hand under his beanie. "That's uh, random…"

I shrug my shoulders. "I've never been shy to speak my mind before, and it crossed my mind, so here we are."

He studies me for a moment, then with a nod, he tells me, "Yeah. I haven't dated anyone since high school. And to answer your next question, I haven't been with anyone since."

Wait, what? How does a guy like him not have girls all over him? What happened to him with his ex to make him that way? Does he still love her?

"I respect your choice, but I am curious, why? If you're comfortable telling me, that is."

Cameron holds his gaze steady with mine, never wavering or backing down. It's a bit intimidating, but I like it.

"My ex, Layla, cheated on me. Mix that in with my dad and having to step up to take care of my family, I didn't have time for that stuff anymore."

My heart breaks for him because, amid his shitty home life, his piece of shit ex cheated on him. How someone could do that, I have no clue. Cameron deserves so much more. It makes sense, along with his past, why he's so closed off and mistrusting toward others. I can't imagine the pressure he feels to be his family's caregiver.

Actually, I do. It's a bit different for me, but I get it. Maybe Cameron and I have more in common than I thought. While the thought soothes me, it also troubles me.

I reach across the small bistro table and rest my hand on his, just like I did on the log. "Cam, I'm so sorry that happened to you. You deserve so much more than that, I hope you know it. If I ever see your ex, I will avenge you."

Cameron removes his hand from under mine, but before I can feel his rejection, he rests his hand over mine. My body zones in on the contact, it's warm and protective, and I feel it spread from my hand to the rest of my body, wrapping me up completely.

When the heck have I ever felt this way when a man touched me? *Never.*

"Don't be sorry, it was shitty, but it pushed me in the direction I needed to go—no distractions—and I've had absolutely none until…" he trails off slowly, removing his hand from mine. He glances back up to me, a playful smile on his lips. "No avenging needed, but thank you."

I look at him quizzically. "You mean…nothing? No sex, no kissing, no touching since then?"

Cameron crosses his arms against his chest and shrugs. "Nope, nothing. I'm—"

My phone rings in my pocket and cuts him off. Dammit, I want to know what he was about to say. I look to see who's calling, a picture of Nate and Pickles filling the screen. "I'm sorry, mind if I take this?"

"Not at all," Cameron says sincerely before bringing the last bite of cake to his lips.

I slide my finger across the screen, my ear suddenly filled with loud shouts and music. "Hey, Nate, what's up?"

"Hey, sis, I'm sorry to bother you on your birthday. But do you mind coming to the bar? I'm slammed right now. You know I wouldn't ask if I wasn't."

There goes my Christmas movie marathon and snuggle session. Even if my brother weren't my boss, I'd still go. If someone needs me, I'm always there.

"Yeah, I'm just outside of campus. Give me half an hour, and I'll be there," I say as I stand, putting on my jacket.

"Get here safely. It started snowing, so don't rush. Love you, see you soon," Nate tells me, hanging up before I can respond.

Cameron stands, putting his jacket on, too. "What's going on?"

"My brother just called. He needs me at the bar," I explain as I pull cash from my wallet. "I'll get an Uber, thanks for today-"

His hand halts my movements. "Aurora, put your money away," his voice warns me, taking a tone I have yet to hear from him, and I kind of like it, the assertiveness yet caring undertone. "And you're not getting an Uber. I'll drive you."

I give him a quick, appreciative glance as I tug my mittens on. "That's okay, you've already done enough for me today." I pull out my phone and attempt to pull up the app when my phone is snatched from my hands.

"I'm not putting your life in the hands of a stranger, no thank you. Just get in my car, please?" he pleads, his tone full of concern. His words etch themselves into my skin, leaving goosebumps in their wake.

We may have just become friends, but it's evident how much he cares about me, and that makes my goosebumps triple.

My body is feeling out of tune, so I just nod, earning my phone back. Then, I follow him out of the cafe to his car. He opens the door for me, like he did at my house, then runs around to his side. We wait for it to warm, both of us just whispering 'fuck' over and over again as if that'll make it less cold somehow. The car warms up within a few minutes, and we're off to the bar.

Our conversation from earlier jumps back at me, and I don't know if being around a bar would make him feel uneasy because of his past. So instead of wondering, I ask, "Are you okay with bringing me to the bar? From what you told me today, I don't want you to be uncomfortable."

Cameron's gaze is locked on the road, two hands on the wheel and driving under the speed limit. "I can make my own choices, and being around alcohol doesn't tempt me. Seeing what it did to my family, it's never had an appeal. I'll be fine, Aurora, don't worry."

"Okay, I wanted to make sure, that's all." I sink back into my seat, feeling the emotions of the day weighing on me.

"Can I ask you something?" Cameron asks, slightly shifting in his seat.

"Anything, we're friends, remember?" I tell him.

He quickly looks at me, then back at the road. "Right. Are *you* single?"

Not at all what I thought he would say, but I should've seen it coming. I asked him, so it's only fair that he asks me the same thing.

"Yup. I don't date, never have. I've always been too busy training, working out, or competing since I was eleven."

It was right after my mom passed that I started to take volleyball more seriously.

He nods to himself, his voice carrying a stoic tone. "I understand that, trust me. That's why I haven't bothered either. Between working, tutoring, and studying, there's no time, really."

"Where do you work?"

Cameron beams, full of pride. "I do side jobs, coding for different local developers and whatnot. I'm currently applying to Disney, and they're having me work on a racing game for them."

I turn toward him in my seat, excitement brimming to the surface. "Cam, that's really cool. I know you'll get it. They'd be idiots not to pick you."

"Thanks, I hope so. I want to finally be able to securely provide for my mom and Lexa."

"So you may have time for a girlfriend, then. Since everything in your life is almost put together?" I ask out of curiosity, of course.

His eyes dart to mine at the question, then back to the road. "If I find someone worth it, maybe."

I wonder if I would be worth it to him, and then I remember Brad's words about being a whore. Not that I believe them, or at least I try not to. But I do wonder what Cam would think if he knew I've been hooking up with guys over the years.

We remain quiet the rest of the drive, the sound of whatever pop hit is trending on the radio filling the space. We're parked outside the bar a few minutes later, and I can see how busy it is already.

"I hope you had a good birthday. Thanks for letting me spend it with you," Cameron says, breaking the silence first.

I smile at him, grateful for having spent the day together. "I did. Thank you for the camaraderie and for that cake. I'm going to need to go back there ASAP."

"Maybe I'll use that to motivate you during our next study sessions."

I roll my eyes, my hand on the door handle. "Not even that cake can save me from coding."

"No, but I can," he teases, all too confident. His eyes fall behind me to the bar, a frown tugging at his lips. "Are you going to be okay in there? It looks rowdy."

I glance over my shoulder at the chaos inside and shrug. "I'm used to it, and my brother's there. He steps in when he can tell I've had enough."

Cameron's frown deepens. "What do you mean?"

"Some customers are dicks, that's all, but it comes with the job. Which I need to go to. Thanks for driving me."

"Aurora, that's not okay—"

I start to climb out of his car, needing to help Nate sooner rather than later.

"Wait!"

I stop with my hand on the top of the door, looking at his panic-ridden face.

"Do you need a ride home?" he asks, his tone concerned yet gentle.

I smile at him, feeling that damn warm buzz flowing through my veins. "Nate can give me a ride, thank you though. Have a good night, Fields."

I don't wait to hear his response. I shut his door and book it inside, needing to get away from my tutor/friend, who I feel could very well be more, which is my worst fear. Because I *can't* have him.

No matter how much I may want to.

Chapter Twelve

Cameron

It's 3 a.m., and I can't sleep, so I'm lying on the couch, watching *Iron Man*.

I had the best day with Aurora. Our friendship is unexpected but one I didn't realize I needed. We have a lot more in common than I thought, and she makes me smile so fucking much. A feat I thought nearly impossible.

I stare at the texts between us shortly after I dropped her off since sleep is avoiding me.

Me

> Hey, it's Cameron. Let me know when you get home, please.

Aurora

> Will do, Fields.

Leaving her at the bar made my gut heavy with anxiety, especially after her off-hand comment about some of her customers. Are they rude to her? Do they tip like shit? Do they try to touch her? I can't even imagine it without my blood pressure rising through the fucking roof.

Part of me wanted to stay there and make sure she was okay, but I didn't want to seem overbearing. Aurora doesn't know my protective side like Finn and Lexa do.

And even though we're friends, I can't fight the way my body kept wanting to be near her tonight. Holding her, touching her, hell, *kissing her.* But I know we can't.

I'm her tutor and her dad is the goddamn dean. If shit goes wrong, who's to say he won't kick me out before I graduate. Even if I was willing to try, my rules be damned, she's not interested in dating. So, I need to keep my shit together and be her friend.

Should be fun.

The door opens, and Finn bustles through, brushing the snow off his jacket. "Holy fuck, it's cold out there," he mumbles to himself, not having seen me yet.

"That's what happens when it snows, you know," I reply, and he jumps.

"Jesus fuck, Cam. What are you doing up this late?" he asks while kicking off his boots, then comes to plop down on the loveseat next to me.

"Couldn't sleep, clearly," I grumble.

Finn eyes me, his dark eyes penetrating my soul. "You were waiting for me."

My brows narrow at his statement. "What makes you think that?"

"Hmmm, maybe because you texted me asking if I was at Beers n Cheers right after a certain blonde arrived amidst the chaos."

He's not wrong. I did text him, knowing that he and Ash usually spend their Saturdays there. I wanted to make sure she was okay, and that seemed like my only option. I knew he would immediately understand what I was asking without me actually asking. I wanted him to look out for her, plain and simple.

So, instead of trying to bullshit him, I give in. "How was it? Anyone give her trouble?"

Finn runs a hand through his auburn hair, patting it down after removing his hat at the door. "She was busy. I sat at the bartop after you texted me, and nothing happened. She can handle herself, don't worry."

I nod, the pit of anxiety in my stomach shrinking at his words. "Thanks, Finn."

He reaches for the remote, pausing the movie. "When are you going to let yourself acknowledge that you like her?"

I sit up, feeling the need to escape into my bedroom suddenly. "When that *actually* is true. We're friends. I was worried, that's all," I say with as much conviction as I can muster for Finn and maybe myself too. I stand and start to retreat to my room when Finn's next words halt my steps.

"I haven't seen her smile that brightly in a while."

He's spent more time with Aurora than anyone I know, so his words pack a certain punch. In a good way. I'm glad our time together made her smile a bit brighter.

As I lie in bed before falling asleep, I can't help but think of all the ways I want to continue to make her smile brighten more and more. So much that it blinds me enough from my rules and excuses to make her mine.

My phone pings on my side table, and I roll over so quickly that I nearly fall out of bed. Christ.

Aurora

I'm home and cozy in bed.
Thanks again for today.

Me

Stop thanking me, please.

Aurora

Never. Now I know it bugs you,
so I won't stop. & why are you up??

Her text makes my lips twitch, a near smile forming on my lips. My face seems to do that often when she teases me. I like it, that fiery mouth of hers.

Me

I couldn't sleep until I knew you were home safely. Goodnight.

Aurora

Night, Fields.

Chapter Thirteen

Aurora

I open and reopen my latest drawing that I started on my birthday.

After my shift at the bar that felt never-ending, I finally got in bed at 3 a.m. and had the itch to draw. I couldn't sleep until I let some emotions out first. I drew a rough sketch of my green mitten over his black one, the crystal blue lake shining in the background.

I don't know why I picked that specific moment, but I wasn't ready to analyze it, so I looked out the window. It's days later, and the snow has finally come to stay, covering the campus in a white sheet. It's not an overwhelming amount, just enough to be pretty.

I admire it from the comfort of the couch in my house that doubles as a pull-out, meaning it's one big bed of cushions.

This morning, I had an early workout, two classes, and a practice, which I got through with ease. I came home after practice, wanting to squeeze in a nap before my tutoring session with Cameron. Whenever I'm on my period, I'm more tired than usual and get the worst cramps. Sometimes, they take me out, leaving me glued to the couch or my bed. They're that awful.

And today is one of those days.

I felt it coming just as I was getting ready to head to the library. I groan as pain radiates across my lower stomach, an ache that pierces with a stinging force every so often. Canceling on Cameron this late makes me feel like crap, but I don't think I can get off this couch.

I fumble to find my phone under the blanket, then finally find it under the pillow. With my body in a ball on the couch-bed, my knees crunched into my body, I text him.

Me

I'm so sorry to cancel last minute, but I physically cannot make it to our session. I'll have my dad make sure they still pay you.

I set my phone beside me just as my stomach rumbles, but I don't think I can muster the strength to get up and grab something. Jasmine left to work on a group project tonight and said she didn't know when she would be back because 'everyone in my group is an idiot,' as she put it. I know I could text her, and she'd come home right away to take care of me, but I would never do that to her.

My phone vibrates, so I pick it up and see it's a text from Cameron.

Fields

Are you okay? What's wrong?

Butterflies threaten to take flight at his concern, but I'm beginning to learn that this is his personality. He'd do this for just about anyone. There's nothing special about me.

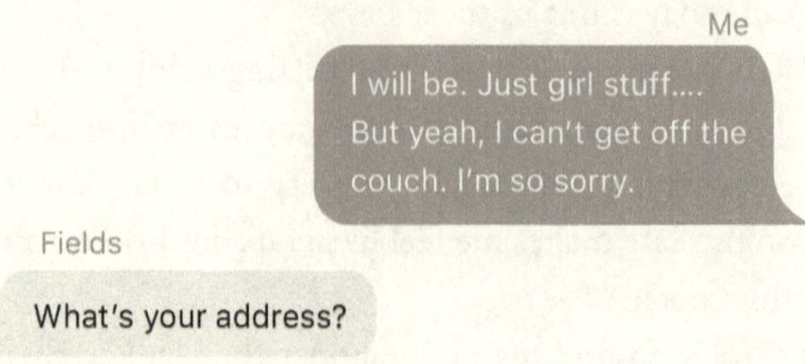

That has me sitting up straight, then groaning at the ache below my belly. What is he doing?

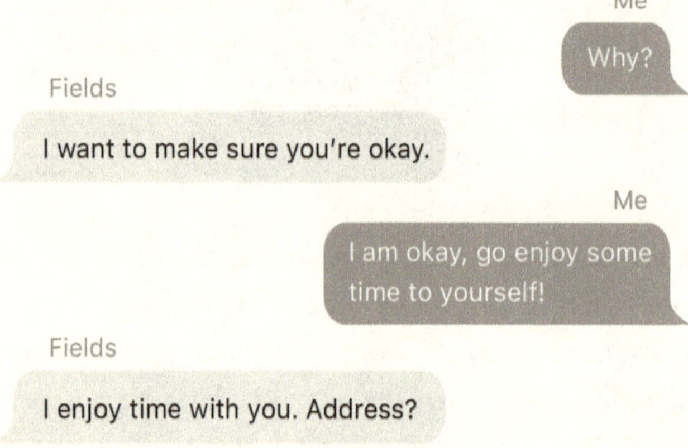

My heart pitter-patters in my chest, and I try my best to ignore it as I text him back my address, knowing he will persist until I tell him. Remembering that I can't get up to unlock the door, I also send him the code for the number lock pad.

About twenty minutes later, I hear a car pull into the driveway, but I don't bother sitting up to check that it's him because my cramps are at an all-time high at the moment. I pause the Christmas movie I was watching about a man who realizes he's not actually an elf when I hear the beeping of the keypad lock.

I hear the lock of the door turn, and then the removal of his boots on the foyer mat fills the silence. "Aurora?" he calls out.

"Right here," I wince, the ache intense and debilitating.

Cameron comes into view, his tall, broad frame and warm eyes taking the breath right out of my lungs. He instantly frowns when he notices me. My knees are curled into my chest, a blanket wrapped around me, my hair in a messy bun, and my face grimacing from the pain.

He mutters a string of curses to himself, taking a deep breath. Then, he crosses the room and sits on the edge of the couch.

It's then that I notice the backpack in his hands. "Fields, I don't think I can study. Look, I'll pay you whatever they normally pay you, but I can't do it today. I'm sorry."

His jaw clenches as he stares at me, his eyebrows dipping inward. "I don't care about studying. I care about you."

Oh. My lips threaten to break into a wide smile, but I control it. We're friends, and he cares for me like he would his sister. Nothing more.

"Then what's in the bag?" I ask, my voice barely there as I stifle a whimper.

Cameron unzips his bag, pulling out a bunch of items. "I stopped at the campus store and grabbed a few things I thought might help." He then begins to sort through the different items. "I figured you liked chocolate and peanut butter from the cake you loved, so I got you a pint of chocolate peanut butter ice cream. I also got you some ibuprofen and this," he says, pulling out a plushie cupcake. "It's a weighted heating pad. My sister has one and swears by it."

No, no, no. This is not good. He can't do this to my poor, secretly hopeless romantic heart. This man. This sweet, kind, caring man. He remembered my favorite food combination and got me a heated stuffed cupcake, which I told him is what my dad calls me.

What a goddamn sweetheart.

I've always had a sweet tooth, and he's on his way to becoming my newest craving.

"Cameron, this is…wow. I don't even have the proper words. Thank you," I say, my voice sincere and full of gratitude. I would say it's the hormones that make tears a possibility, but I think any other day would warrant the same reaction. No one's ever done anything like this for me.

"You're welcome. Take one of these," he says, uncapping the medicine and placing one in my palm. Then, he passes me my water jug from the side table, and I swallow it down with the water. Once I'm done, he takes it from me and places it beside the couch.

"Okay, pizza will be here in ten minutes. Do you want to eat your ice cream now or later?" he asks, standing from the couch and heading towards the kitchen with the ice cream in tow.

I want to argue with him and tell him that he didn't need to order me food, but I know it's pointless. Cameron doesn't know how to be anything less than protective and caring, but I also do know my manners. "How much was it? I can pay for it or split it at least. And ice cream now, please."

Cameron fiddles around with the drawers in the kitchen until he finds the utensils, coming back with one spoon in his hand and the ice cream in the other. "Don't ask me stupid questions," he sighs, sitting on the edge of the couch once more, passing me both the spoon and ice cream.

I attempt to sit up, wincing with each movement.

"Aurora, stop," Cameron's panicked voice causes me to look at him, the worry clear as ever in his eyes.

"I'll be okay, I have to move eventually," I groan, moving myself to a sitting position, my back against the cushions, my legs stretched in front of me.

He shuffles around, grabbing the cupcake stuffy and turning it on, pausing when he turns back to face me. "Can I sit beside you?"

His question throws me off, especially with how intimate it feels. I've never had a guy ask me that. They've always just come into my space freely. Not that I didn't want most of their advances, but I never realized how nice being asked is.

"Of course," I tell him.

He shuffles his body backward until his back rests against the cushion, his sweatpant covering long, muscular legs stretching in front of him.

Noticing my hands are full, he eyes me, asking silent permission to place the heated pad on me. I nod and wait with bated breath as he places it on my stomach. His fingers brush against the sliver of skin exposed between my long-sleeved crop top and sweats. My body lights up at this touch, sparks erupting where his skin touches mine.

Cameron pulls his hand away quickly, and I wonder if he felt it too.

"What movie are we watching?" he asks, crossing his arms over his defined chest that's hidden but noticeable through his black, Dri-Fit quarter zip.

I pull off the lid on the ice cream, "*Elf*, it's one of my favorites."

"I'm more of a *Home Alone* guy, but since Lexa is obsessed with *Elf*, I grew to like it." His mouth pulls up, a crooked grin on his lips. He's so freaking cute I want to squeeze his cheeks and dive my tongue between his lips, finding out what he tastes like. I decided to blame my hyper-awareness of him on my hormones.

I press play on the movie, ignoring the fantasies in my head, and dig my spoon into the ice cream when it dawns on me. "Why didn't you get a spoon for yourself?"

Cameron shoots me a sideways glance. "I got it for you, not me."

"I know, but you can have some," I tell him, taking a mouthful. The chocolate peanut butter creaminess melts onto my tongue, and I briefly close my eyes as I enjoy every bit of it.

"Nah, I'll taste it another time. I don't like to have dessert before dinner," he says, causing my eyes to fly back open, all too aware of how dirty that sounded.

There's a knock on the door before I can comment back or go down a rabbit hole of imagining him making *me* his dessert.

I go to remove the cupcake and get the door when a hand lands on the stuffy, pushing me back gently. "Don't move," Cameron urges, his tone demanding yet caring.

So, I do as he says because, in all honesty, I don't think I could.

He shuffles off the couch, and within a minute, he's back, scooting closer than before. His shoulder brushes mine this time, and his proximity threatens to overwhelm me…in a good way.

His signature scent comforts me, while his nearness excites both my heart and my clit.

These goddamn hormones.

"I didn't know what you liked, so I got a large with different flavors split into quarters. One quarter is cheese, the other pepperoni and cheese, one is full of veggies, and the other is Hawaiian if you're into pineapple," he tells me, opening the lid, the heavenly scent of cheese and dough wafting towards me.

"I'm a vegetarian, so cheese and vegetables are good with me," I smile, taking in how considerate he was to get so many options.

"Shit, I'm sorry, Aurora, I didn't know. I can get rid of the mea—"

"Cam, stop, it's fine. I have no problem cooking meat for friends or watching them eat it. I just personally don't like it."

Those cinnamon eyes bore into mine, searching for any hint of dishonesty. "You're sure?"

"Positively, eat whatever you like. And thanks for this. I'll pay next time?" I offer, wanting this friendship to be fair.

Cameron rolls his eyes, and we both laugh at that. He'll never let me pay for anything, so I'll have to be sneaky about it. We fall into a comfortable silence, eating pizza and watching as Buddy tries to bond with his dad.

My eyelids fight to stay open, and I find my head slowly lowering to the right, resting on Cam's shoulder. The contact startles me awake. "Sorry," I murmur.

"Hold on a sec," he tells me, setting the pizza box on the side table next to him, then getting up to put my ice cream in the freezer. I watch him in confusion until he slides back down next to me.

"What are you doing?" I ask him, my lips twisted to the side.

"Cleaning up so that if you fall asleep, there's nothing to worry about when you wake up," he admits, his shoulder again bumping mine, sending a chill down my arm.

What in the hell is up with that anyway? My body has never reacted to a man like this before.

"Okay," I say, my voice cutting off at the end as a cramp rocks my entire body.

Cameron's face tightens, "Can I try something that used to help Lexa? I saw my mom do it all the time."

"Anything, please," I wince, feeling weak and needy.

"Put your head on my lap and lay on your side. I'm going to rub your back and massage your scalp. My mom says massaging the lower back helps with the cramps, and the head massage just feels nice and gets your mind off the ache in your stomach."

If I were in my right mind, I'd realize how bad of an idea this is. Getting so close to him, letting him touch me, but right now, I'll do anything to relieve the pain.

I lower to my side, resting my head on his leg, praying his cock is tucked into the other thigh. I don't think I could relax if I felt it beneath my head.

A large, rough hand meets my bare back. My body reacts, as it always does to his touch apparently.

His hand starts to kneed my lower back, digging into the muscles there. It feels so good that I want to moan in relief, but I stop myself. Just as his hand gets comfortable on my back, he brings his free hand to my hair, running it through my strands lightly at first, then returning to massage my scalp. The double sensations are enough to make me zone out, into a state of complete bliss.

"That feels so good," I softly moan, unable to control it this time.

Cameron's breath hitches in his throat, his hands stilling for a beat, but then he swallows and continues.

"Is it helping?" he asks, his tone lower than before.

"Yeah, it is." Eu-fucking-phoria. That's the best way to describe how his hands make me feel. The ache in my stomach is still there, but it's duller now, not a throbbing, piercing pain like it was before. I feel relaxed now, my breaths slowing, my eyelids closing.

But before I drift off into my inevitable sleep, I whisper, "Thanks for being the best friend, Cam. I appreciate you."

"Shh," he coos, "Get some rest."

I'm not sure how much later it is when I stir awake from the sound of two people talking, but when I realize who they belong to, I know it's late because Jasmine's home.

I keep my eyes closed, not wanting them to know I'm listening.

"Is she okay?" Jasmine asks.

"She seemed better before she fell asleep," Cameron says with hope in his voice.

"Thanks for coming by to take care of her. She's stubborn and would've just sat there in pain, starving all night until I got here," Jasmine tells him, and she's not wrong. That's exactly what I was going to do because there was no way I was getting off this couch.

"It's no problem. Have a good night, Jasmine."

"Cameron?" she whisper-shouts, and that makes me nervous. What is she about to say?

"Yeah?"

"I know she has some walls up…in certain aspects of her life if you catch my drift. But if you see her, truly see her. Try, okay?"

Part of me wants to do my best to jump off this couch and slam her lips shut, while the other part is on the edge of my seat, waiting to hear his response. There's a short pause until his smooth, deep voice penetrates the silence.

"I do see her."

Then, the sound of the door closing fills the room while my heart thuds louder than it ever has.

Chapter Fourteen

Cameron

I rub my eyes beneath my computer glasses, feeling a tension headache forming between my eyebrows.

I've been sitting in my room at my workstation since 6 a.m., and it's nearly ten. I have my first class of the day at eleven, so I really need to get going despite the pounding my forehead is taking.

My ability to put numbers in a sequence is harder than usual today because my mind keeps flicking back to last night. When I went over to Aurora's house to take care of her. All it took was just one look at her and seeing how much pain she was in, and I knew I was fucked.

As in I knew then how much I liked her, more than a friend probably should.

What really sealed the deal for me was having her head in my lap, her body under my touch. Feeling her bare skin for the first time was an experience I wasn't expecting, my entire body wanted to react to the feel of her. Especially my cock that threatened to harden, but I kept thinking of code algorithms to avoid it.

The slight moans she made didn't help the situation. Her voice is like music to my ears, but her sighs and moans? Those are a siren call right to my cock.

But more than anything, I enjoyed taking care of her.

Aurora comes off as this confident, assertive, and strong woman, which she is, but I've seen her vulnerability and the kindness she exudes. And it makes me like her that much more, learning more of the different pieces that make her who she is.

I want to know them all.

A phone call interrupts my thoughts, the name Lexa Roo popping on my screen. I swipe across to answer, a smile on my lips as I put it to my ear.

"Lexa Roo, what's up?"

"I just wanted to call my favorite brother in the whole wide world," she giggles, and from that tone, I know she wants something.

"I'm your only brother, so…" I remind her.

"Still, you're the best there ever is."

"What do you want?" I cut to the chase.

"Mom's here too, say hi!"

"Hey, Mom, how's it going?" I ask warily, suddenly feeling anxious. Why are they both on the phone?

"Hi, Sweetpea, everything is really great. We just miss you!" my mom says, her sweet, Southern accent booming through the phone. My mother grew up in Tennessee and only moved to Detroit when she was pregnant with me because my dad found a better job there.

"That's good to hear, Mom. Lexa, is everything okay with you?" The nervousness in my tone doesn't go undetected.

"Ugh, yes, I am fine, Cameron James. We have a question for you!" Lexa chimes, her voice upbeat despite the use of my middle name.

"What's that?" I ask, feeling my stomach sink with a million different scenarios.

"Can we come to you for Christmas this year? Lexa has never left Michigan, and I've been getting real good tips at work and saving plenty, too," my mom pleads.

"Of course you can, you know I'd never say no. Why did you feel like you needed to ask?"

Lexa comes back on the line, "Because we know how stubborn you are with us spending money and whatnot. We were worried you would say no. But, before you ask, I already talked to Dr. Marsh, and he said I'm good to go."

"That's great, Lexa Roo, but you're right. I'm not going to let you guys pay for your flight. I'll be done with exams by the 19th. When do you want to come?" I ask, feeling excited that they want to come here instead of me going there.

My mom and sister are my entire world, but I'd be lying if I said I didn't hate going back to my hometown. It just reminds me of *him*, and it just makes me fucking sick.

"Sweetpea, you aren't paying for them. I know damn well you won't let us pay for anything once we get there, so please let me do this one thing, okay?" my mom asks, sounding exasperated. And it's with that tone that I relent.

"Fine," I mutter.

"Yay! So we plan to fly out on the 22nd since that's when I'm done with school, and we'll leave on the 26th to go to Mom's side of the family's party back home. Is that okay with you? You have enough room at your house?" Lexa asks, her inner planner coming out to play. She'll probably have our entire five days together planned down to the minute.

"Yeah, Finn is going to Ash's family's house for the break, so I'll have lots of room."

"You gonna fly back with us, Sweetpea?" my mom asks.

Something gnaws at me, an uncomfortable sensation sitting in my gut. I love my family, but I can't ignore how I don't want to be away from Aurora.

Hell, I don't even know what her holiday plans are, she could be leaving. But all I know is that I don't like the idea of putting so many miles between us.

"No, I have to meet some work deadlines before the new year," I say. It's not a total lie, but not fully honest either. I do have some aspects of the game I want to finish over the holidays, but there's no deadline. The network understands I'm still in school and has given me the freedom to work at my own pace.

"Fine, we'll optimize our time together then, go to all the Christmas markets…." Lexa jumps in, filling me in on everything she has planned.

I love the holidays and can't wait for my mom and sister to get here. It'll be nice to show them around the place I've come to make my own. As much as I want Aurora to meet my family, part of me wants to keep her away from them because I know the minute my sister sees how I am around Aurora, she'll know how I feel about her.

And Lexa with that kind of information? She's going to become the biggest instigator I've ever seen.

After my 11 a.m. class, I make my way to the kinesiology building.

I've never been inside it before, but my body moves toward it without my brain even knowing why. But the closer I get, the clearer it becomes.

I want to see *her*.

Opening the large front door, I start to panic. What the hell am I doing? We're friends, and friends don't go out of their way to walk across campus to get a glimpse of each other during a bleak day.

I walk through the halls until I reach the one where I know her class is just finishing. Nerves swirl in my gut. I need to turn around and go home. I know I like her, but that doesn't mean she feels the same and wants to see me right now.

She's Aurora fucking Vallacourt, for Christ's sake. Who's sworn off dating and is so far out of my league that I can't even tell you which one it is.

She's far too beautiful, kind, loving, and bright to be with me in a more than friendly way.

I'm about to turn on my heel and book it out of here when I spot her standing off to the side of the hall with a guy I recognize from one of my first-year classes towering over her.

It only takes me a second to feel a wild and hot jealousy run rampant in my veins. Who is this guy? Why is he so close to her?

I want to be that close to her.

But then I see it. She's uncomfortable, evident from her posture and the way her eyes avert his.

My body propels me toward them without a second thought. He's making my girl uncomfortable for whatever reason, and to hell if I'm going to let it continue.

As I get closer, I hear the tail end of Brad's words, his tone harsh.

"Aurora, come on. Just think about it, for fuck's sake."

I instantly step between them, putting Aurora safely behind me. "I don't think she wants to. You should leave," I tell him, trying to keep myself calm and collected.

I know I said I'd never put my hands on someone, but I feel pretty close right now. Just seeing him near her, upsetting her, makes my body buzz with a need to protect her.

"What are you? Her new flavor of the week?" he scoffs.

"That's none of your business."

Brad chuckles to himself, seeming amused. "Whatever. Sweet cheeks, call me later when you come to your senses." He turns at that, heading in the opposite direction towards the exit doors.

Once he's gone, I turn around to face her, and my knees nearly give out at the look on her face. Her hazel eyes are soft yet strained with hurt. It makes me want to forget my rule and chase after him to make him apologize for whatever it is that he did to her.

"Cam, what are you doing here?" she asks in disbelief.

"I…uh, I came to see you after my class ended. You forgot your pen at our last session," I swing my backpack off my shoulder, rummage around until I find a pen, and hope she thinks it's hers. I've never been one to lie, but I couldn't just admit I missed her and wanted to see her.

"Are you okay? What happened with Brad?" I ask, holding onto a blue ballpoint pen. It's generic enough that she probably won't notice.

"I'm fine. He just wouldn't leave me alone, that's all. Thank you for stepping in, but you didn't need to," she says, eyeing the pen with scrutiny.

"I don't like how he talked to you or seeing you scared like that," I admit, my voice hushed.

Her head tilts to the side. "No, I-I wasn't scared."

"Aurora, your body looked like it wanted to curl in on itself. Your posture was rigid, and your eyes kept avoiding his."

This time, she averts her gaze from me, tilting her chin down. I bring two of my fingers under it and tilt her head back up until her pretty eyes meet mine.

"What does he want you to think about?"

Aurora eyes me for a beat, then lets out a breath. "To get back together…We weren't dating. He just wanted to hook up again. And I keep telling him no."

Anger roars in my chest, battling to set itself free and chase after Brad to explain what the fuck 'no' means.

A growl manages to escape, and it causes Aurora's eyes to widen.

"Cam, it's fine. He's entitled and isn't told no very often. He will get over it. Just let it go," she pleads, her hand coming up to caress my cheek.

The softness of her palm against my cheek has the anger subsiding, replacing it with a burst of warmth at the contact. It soothes me, pushing the anger into the back of my mind.

"If he corners you again like that, you call me, okay?" I breathe, staring at her intently.

"I can take care of my—"

I cut her off. "You. Call. Me. Got it?" I demand, my voice colder than I'd like it to be, fueled by the need to protect her. I soften my voice this time. "You know why Aurora."

It must be the reminder of my father that causes her will to break, her head nodding. "Okay, I will."

It's then that I feel it. My heart beating to the rhythm of her name.

Her hand is still on my cheek, making it hard to think straight, so I thrust the pen toward her. "Here, your pen," I cough, breaking up the emotion clogging my throat.

Aurora eyes the pen in her hand, a small smile on her lips. "This isn't my pen, Fields."

Oh, fuck me.

"Are you sure?"

"Yeah. Maybe you got me confused with another girl," she remarks, pulling away.

"Impossible," I mutter.

"What's that?" she asks, stuffing the pen in her backpack.

"Nothing. You're just going to steal my pen, then?"

She turns to me with a teasing smirk, a glint in her eyes. "Yup. I'll think of it and remember the time my best friend missed me so much, he pretended I forgot a pen just to come and see me."

I laugh. "You couldn't spare me?"

"Nope, I like teasing you. And if you want to see me, you can just ask. That's what friends do," she quips, tugging on my arm to get me to walk with her toward the front doors.

I fall into step with her, noting how she keeps bringing up the words *friends* with me. I hate it because I know I don't want to *just* be friends with her.

Sure, that's part of it. But I also want her heart, her lips on mine and mine all over her damn body.

I'll have to keep an eye out for a shooting star because I think I'll need all the luck I can get.

Chapter Fifteen

Aurora

"Ugh, Fields, my brain is fried. Can we stop?" I groan, blowing a loose strand of hair out of my face.

We've been working on different programming languages for the last hour, and I need a break. I don't plan on using this information come graduation, so the motivation to remember any of it is severely lacking.

Cameron looks up from my textbook, his cinnamon eyes on me. And just like every time they meet mine, I feel a shiver run down my spine. "We can take a small break."

"Small?" I pout, giving him my best puppy dog eyes.

"Yeah, small. I'm here to help you pass this test tomorrow," he says, sounding all too responsible. But he also knows how much getting a good grade means to me.

"Fine," I reply, unfolding my leg from the other, flattening my sweater dress so it's not giving him a show. Not that he can see anything, but, you know, class and all of that.

It's Wednesday, not our usual tutoring day or time, but I have a test tomorrow. I glance at my phone and see that it's already 8:30 p.m. We still have an hour left, making this late for me since I'm always up early, but it was the only time that worked for the both of us.

Cameron stretches in his chair and yawns. My eyes track the way his muscles flex underneath his plain white t-shirt. I don't know his workout regime, but I can only imagine it's intense.

He catches me staring, raising one brow at me, causing me to snap out of it as I dig in my bag for my notebook. I open and rest my notebook against my thighs, put my pen on the paper, and begin to draw, letting go of whatever needs to be released.

Keeping my chin tilted downward, I quickly glance up at Cameron to see that his computer glasses are on, but instead of looking at his screen, he's looking at me.

"Is there something on my face?" I mock as if I'm in shock.

Cameron rolls his lips together, "Yeah, right here," he says, lifting from his chair and leaning over the table, totally in my space now. He brings his finger to my face, pressing it lightly against the spot just above the corner of my lips. His finger being this close to my mouth is doing things to my brain they shouldn't.

"What is it?" I ask, actually worried now.

Cameron puts his finger to his lips, licking it before saying, "Looks like pasta sauce," and tries to wipe it off my cheek.

I dodge his finger, laughter bubbling from my lips. "Ew! Don't even think about it."

He laughs with me, the deep sound vibrating against my bones. "C'mon, it's just a smidge. Let me get it."

"That is such a dad move, Fields. I'm mortified, please stop," I wheeze, feeling out of breath. He backs up out of my space, so I take the opportunity to grab my phone and check my face.

When the camera flips to selfie mode, I quickly move it to the spot he touched and frown in disbelief. "Wait, I don't see anything? Is it the wrong side—" I stop myself, realizing Cameron is still laughing.

"You did that on purpose, didn't you?" I narrow my brows at him, trying to give him my best '*I'm mad. Do not mess with me*' look.

"Guilty." He shrugs, his eyes flitting to my notebook. "I want to ask what that is, but I know you would tell me if you wanted to."

"Isn't that still kind of asking?"

"Nope, I said I wanted to ask, but I didn't," he corrects me.

I shake my head at him. He can be so technical at times. "It's a notebook and I draw in it, but that's all I'm telling you."

His eyes bounce around my face, giving me a slight nod of his chin. "I'd love to look at it one day if you ever become okay with that."

Yeah, I don't think that day will ever come, but I also never thought I'd be this close to Cameron, so never say never.

Before I can say anything, an alarm goes off. "Time's up. Your break is over," Cameron says, hitting a button on his phone and grabbing a deck of flashcards.

"You seriously timed the break?" I ask, sounding perplexed.

"Yup, I told you that you're going to crush this test and I'm following through on my word," he replies smoothly.

"Fine," I grumble, putting my notebook away and giving him my full attention.

"If you get all of them right, I'll bring you a slice of cake tomorrow from the cafe that you like," Cameron says, convincing me to sit up a little straighter.

"Alright, you have my attention now, Fields. Proceed." I smile at him, folding my hands on the table, motivated to get my damn cake.

After an hour of flashcards, and much to my dismay, I got through them with three mistakes. Three fucking mistakes cost me a slice of my favourite cake tomorrow.

"Aurora, you okay?" Cameron asks, eyeing me as I set my things into my backpack.

"Yeah, just thinking about how smooth the peanut butter frosting is," I reply, fake sniffling and pouting my lips.

"I didn't take you for a big baby," he teases, his tone light.

"Yeah, well I am when I lose, okay? Especially when there is food involved," I inform him, putting my arms through my knee-length puffer jacket.

It covers my maroon sweater dress, making it look like I have nothing on but sheer tights. This isn't the ideal outfit for December, but I like to wear dresses. I spend most of my life in Spanx shorts or sweats, so when I can dress up, I take advantage of it.

"Noted," he says, doing up his jacket. His eyes roam down my jacket, then back up to my face, a scowl on his face. "You don't have sweats to put on?"

"Nope, I'll be fine. It's not a far walk, and I'm used to doing this to myself."

"How about no more dresses until the spring?" he asks.

I smirk at him, wanting to rile him up a bit. "You don't like my dress? Do I look bad?"

He growls. "Aurora, you know you look good. That's not it. It's the fact that it's nearly winter, and you're walking home with nothing to cover your legs from the cold."

"I wouldn't call these tights 'nothing'," I chuckle.

He glares at me, "I can see your legs through them. They're basically nothing."

I start walking backward, a smile on my face. "Stop worrying, Fields. Cold exposure is good for your health."

I don't hear his exact words, but it's something about me not being good for his health and him having a heart attack. I think he's being a bit dramatic, but I like to push his buttons.

Realistically, I know he's right, but now I just have to go down with my stance.

We reach the library doors, the cold air hitting my legs instantly. Motherfucker, it's chilly. I put my gloved hands into my pockets and nestle my nose into my scarf. I turn to wave Cameron goodbye as we usually do, parting to go different ways, but tonight, he's falling into step right beside me.

"What are you doing?" I ask him, a cloud of air leaving my lips.

"Walking you home. It's late," he says matter of factly.

"Hmm, but who will protect you when you leave my house?" I ask, not ready to quit bugging him.

He huffs, a cloud of air forming in front of his face. "I can protect myself, don't worry about me."

Those words have me turning serious for a moment. "I do, Cam. Worry about you, that is."

We both glance over at each other at the same time, an intensity charging the space between us, but just as quickly, we refocus our attention ahead of us.

"Call me on your walk from my house?" I ask him, not liking the idea of him walking alone either.

"I can do that," he agrees easily.

Wanting to change the subject to something less serious and more fun, I ask, "Tell me one of your most embarrassing stories."

"And why should I do that?"

"It'll make me smile?" I suggest, hoping that's enough.

"Okay."

That was easy.

"When I was in first grade, they were testing us on our reading skills to see what level we were at and if we needed to be placed in a learning support classroom. I knew how to read well already and loved it, but the table had a pack of Oreos. I assumed if I got it all wrong, they gave cookies to kids to make them feel better. So, I purposely answered them incorrectly to get the cookie."

I gasp. "What? Are you serious?"

He laughs at himself, "Yup. I got placed into the learning support class, but a week later, I was removed because they realized I was reading just fine. They asked me why I read them wrong… and let's just say that was embarrassing."

"Wait, did you get the Oreo the day you read incorrectly?"

"Nope," he says, popping the p. "All that and no goddamn Oreo. The cherry on top? I found out they were for the kids who did well."

His story does what I asked, a big smile filling my face as I start to laugh. I never would've expected him to say that, which makes me love it even more. I can't believe my smart boy once pretended not to be able to read for a cookie.

He juts his chin out in my direction. "Hit me. I want to hear one of yours,"

I take a minute to think, knowing there are too many things to choose from, but I think this one will make him laugh.

"My very first date ever was back in sophomore year, at the movies. I was so excited to go and finally experience what the dating world was like. But when we got to the movies, my dad and brother were there, ironically seeing the same movie."

"Oh no," Cameron chimes in.

"*Oh no*, is right. My dad sat beside me while Nate sat on the other side of my date since they knew each other from being in the same grade. At one point, I think my date forgot about them and tried to put his arm around my shoulder, you know, making *the* move."

"Your dad freak out?" he guesses.

"That he did. He not only removed his hand for him, which was super awkward, but he went on to give us the talk of the birds and the bees, right in the middle of the movie about some mean girls in high school."

"Please tell me you're joking," he balks.

"I wish I were, Fields, I wish. My date got up just as my dad started talking about teen pregnancies, and I never heard from him again."

Cameron's deep laughter rumbles through the air, making me laugh along with him. "That's brutal, tell me more," he chuckles.

"Sorry, looks like your time has run out." We've reached my driveway now, the end of our time together. There's this part deep within me that feels empty whenever we have to separate, but I try my best to ignore it.

Pulling out his phone, he taps something, and my phone rings. He winks just as I answer the phone. "Nope, you wanted to talk on the phone, remember?"

Then, he walks away.

We not only end up staying on the phone for his entire walk home, but for an hour after that, too. We share embarrassing things, stories from our childhood, anything that's easy and light.

The whole time I wore a huge smile on my face, and I could tell through his tone that he was happy too. Our friendship has become this pure, wholesome thing, reminding me how important it is to keep it that way.

No matter how much my heart screams at me to cross that line.

Chapter Sixteen
Aurora

The next day, I took a trip to my dad's house off campus, located near my favorite hiking trail, hidden among the trees.

My mom had chosen the location of course, and my dad never moved after she passed. It was bittersweet, having a house full of memories that kept mom close to us. Sometimes it soothed the ache that never went away from missing her, and sometimes it just added to it.

I missed Pickles and decided to take my class readings there to spend some time with him. We spent the afternoon playing in the snow in the backyard, throwing the ball around and making a snowman. Pickles loved to charge at them and knock them over. It was childish to do, but we enjoyed it.

Pickles nuzzled his nose into my lap, laying his body on the couch to nap after dinner. I stroked his brown fur while sipping hot chocolate by the fire with a Christmas movie on the screen. I was finally relaxing until Pickles started throwing up.

I wasn't too concerned at first, but when he started whining, I got scared. I quickly threw my jacket on, got his leash, and we were in my car within minutes.

I look in the rearview mirror to see him lying in my backseat, his light brown eyes sad, which breaks my heart.

Snow starts to come down as I pull out of the driveway, igniting my anxiety as I think of what happened to my mom that day. It always happens whenever I drive in the snow, making it an uncomfortable drive. Mix that with my worry for Pickles, and I start to feel overwhelmed.

Before I realize what I'm doing, I hit the Bluetooth system.

"Aurora?" Cam's raspy voice fills the car, his voice already soothing my anxious mind.

My voice trembles over the line. "Hey, were you sleeping? I'm sorry, I can let you go—"

"What's going on? Are you okay?" he asks, his tone full of concern and no longer drowsy.

"Pickles is throwing up, which is making me worried sick. I'm taking him to the vet, but now it's snowing." My lip quivers, tears threatening to fall, but I keep them at bay for fear of not being able to see the road ahead of me.

"Fuck," he mutters to himself, but it still comes through on my end. "Where are you? Pull over, and I'll come to get you both."

"Cam," I trail off, my grip tightening on the steering wheel because it all feels like too much. The snow, my dog, the way he cares for me. "Don't do that, I'll be okay. Just distract me, please?"

I hear the intake and release of a deep breath, briefly wondering why the hell he is taking one. He's not the one driving while it's snowing with a sick pup in his backseat, now is he?

"You want to know another embarrassing story?" he offers, knowing it'll probably make me laugh.

"Always," I reply, my voice not as shaky but still not great.

"Alright, so I was 16 when I had my first kiss. Which, where I'm from, is considered to be a late bloomer. My friends always hyped it up, joking about when I'd finally lay one on someone. It only made me more nervous and anxious to get it over with, so I asked my chemistry lab partner, Charlie, with whom I was good friends, to meet me in the gym at lunch. It was usually empty and unlocked. She agreed, so I took it that she knew what would happen and was okay with it. Once in the gym, we sat on the bleachers, where we talked for a bit, and then I asked if I could kiss her. She said yes, and then we did. Shortly after, the entire basketball team started cheering from the gym teacher's office, which had a window looking into the gym. They watched the whole thing and had a front row seat to my probably not-so-good first kiss."

A genuine laugh bubbled out of me, "Oh my goodness, Cam! That is awful, what assholes. It's kind of funny, but I also feel bad for you because one of your firsts was ruined."

"Don't feel bad. I learned to laugh about it and let it go," he says, and I knew he was shrugging his shoulders without seeing him. "What about you? Was your first kiss anything special?"

"Uhm, no," I chuckle, realizing that I felt calmer but not wanting to remember why I was anxious in the first place. I kept on with my story. "I was 14, and it was at a volleyball camp I attended in the summer. It was your classic spin-the-bottle story. There was a guy I was crushing on all summer but didn't have the confidence at the time to do anything about it. So, I was really excited when we played, hoping it would land on him the first go, and it did. But, sadly, he was a sloppy kisser. He instantly kissed me with an open mouth and left his drool on my chin. It lasted about ten seconds. It was quick, and I had no idea what even happened. I ended up leaving because I was so disappointed in the idea of kissing after that."

"I can't even laugh at the guy because I probably wasn't much better during mine," Cameron laughs at himself, the sound comforting me through the car's speakers.

We spent the next twenty minutes laughing and talking, filling my brain with easy topics to keep the worries at bay. It worked because, before I knew it, I was pulling into the city's vet hospital.

"I'm here. Thank you for talking to me and keeping me calm," I say, shocked at the emotion clogging up my throat. Why was I getting worked up over something so small?

"Anytime, Aurora. Seriously, if you ever need me, call me, okay? And let me know what they say about Pickles."

"Okay, and I will."

"You sure you don't want me to meet you there?" he asks, sounding so genuine it makes my heart pinch.

"Yeah, I'll be okay. If not, I'll text you."

He agrees, and we both say goodbye as the call ends. I turn the car off, rushing around to the back seat to let Pickles out, where he slowly and, with my help, gets out of the car. I walk him inside, and to my luck, the waiting room is empty.

The receptionist perks up instantly. "Hi there, what can I do for you?"

"My dog, Pickles, isn't doing so well. He started throwing up nonstop about an hour ago." Fear echoes in my voice because I am still worried about my pup.

"Oh no, poor puppers. The vet is here. I'll take you back there to see her," she says, sounding too cheery for someone who constantly sees sick animals. We follow her through the door, down a hall, and into a room, where I see a tall woman with short brown hair.

"Hi, I'm Dr. Lewis. What's wrong with your boy here?" she asks, her voice full of warmth as she examines Pickles, not even glancing at me.

My mouth gapes as I connect the dots. She's the woman my dad has been seeing for the last year. We were supposed to formally meet at a dinner this weekend, but I guess the universe had other plans.

"Uh, he started throwing up nonstop about an hour ago, and he seems lethargic," I reply, feeling slightly awkward.

She glances up at me, and a knowing look crosses her face. "Aurora! It's nice to meet you. A little informal and under poor circumstances, but it's still great to meet you."

I wasn't sure how I felt about her yet, so I was going to keep an open mind, but a closed heart. "Yeah, it's not ideal, that's for sure."

She smiles at me, then quickly returns to assessing Pickles. She feels around his belly, then takes her stethoscope to his heart. "His heart sounds good, and I didn't feel any obstructions in his stomach, but I'd like to do an X-ray just to be safe."

"What do you think it is?" I ask.

"Well, did you guys play roughly today? Did he eat anything he shouldn't have?"

"We did play a lot outside, but he didn't eat anything out of the ordinary."

"Hmm, okay. I think it could be from the exertion, and I can give you an antacid for that, but I'd still like to do the X-ray to be safe."

"And that's going to cost me how much?" I question, knowing how costly those damn things are for dogs. My budget was tight between paying rent with Jasmine, groceries, bills, and everything in between. This vet trip alone would derail the budget this month. I didn't get handouts from my dad. I wasn't brought up that way. I work hard for my money and everything I have.

"Free of charge. I can see how upset you are, and I personally want to make sure he is okay," she says, resting her hand on my shoulder for a beat before taking Pickles to the radiology room with her.

It hit me then that my mom would've liked her, just off of that alone. The kindness she's showing me by taking care of my dog, and waiving fees that usually cost owners a lot of money, would make my mother happy. And it's genuine. I can tell she's not doing it to get on my good side or anything like that. I have a feeling she does this quite often for certain patients.

I take the time to text my dad, Minnie, and Cam, giving them all an update on Pickles.

My brown furry boy returns to the room, looking a bit happier than when we came in. I scratch behind his ears and give him a kiss on the nose as Jodi comes in.

"I gave him the antacid and some treats while he sat patiently during the X-ray. I hope that's okay. I didn't find anything in his stomach that would be of concern and cause him to throw up. So, I'll say he was overly excited today and needs to take it easy with his age."

I sigh a breath of relief, *thank god*. I crouch down, squeezing Pickles's face with joy. "You're going to be okay, old man."

Jodi chuckles, and I stand to face her. "Thank you so much for taking care of him and doing that. It means a lot to me, and I'm glad my dad has someone so caring in his life."

"Aurora, I hope you don't think I did this to sway you—"

"No, I don't."

Her brown eyes crinkle, a shy smile on her lips. "Well, thank you for saying that. I know it must be hard for you, and if I am ever crossing a line or make you uncomfortable, let me know, please."

"I'll be honest, it's hard because I miss my mom so much. But I know we can't live in the past. And that means moving on, and living in the present. My dad deserves happiness, and I know he has it with you, so thank you."

She pulls me into a hug, and I willingly let her. I stay a little longer, talking to Jodi as we get to know one another a bit more until she gets a new patient.

On my way home, I take a few minutes to appreciate all that I have.

Grief tends to remind us of what we lost, but sometimes a little gratitude helps you to remember what you have and to be thankful for it right now. Because you never know when something you're grateful for could become something you grieve.

And right now, I'm grateful for my dad, who raised us with so much love despite losing the love of his life. I'm grateful for my dog, for giving me unconditional love, and for Cameron.

That man is etching his way into my heart, and I don't know if I want to even try to stop it.

Chapter Seventeen

Cameron

I've been more exhausted than usual this week with everything I'm trying to fit into my schedule.

Classes, tutoring sessions, side jobs, studying, working out, and designing the code for the company I'm applying to. It's been a lot, all while trying to check in on my mom and sister and avoiding the temptation I feel towards Aurora.

It's tiring as hell.

I decided to take a day off from working out and studying on my no-class day because this is more important. If I can secure this job, it'll mean a stable future for my mom and Lexa.

Which is all I've ever wanted.

It would mean I could take a deep breath and pause for a moment, maybe do something for myself.

My mind immediately drifts toward thinking about Aurora, so I grab my blue light glasses and get to work to avoid thinking of her.

I spend hours working with codes, only having completed an aspect of the race track. It's a massive project that'll take me some time to finish, but the deadline isn't until April 1st, meaning I have time.

I'm about to log off when I get an email from Kim Sepena, the competition manager for the job.

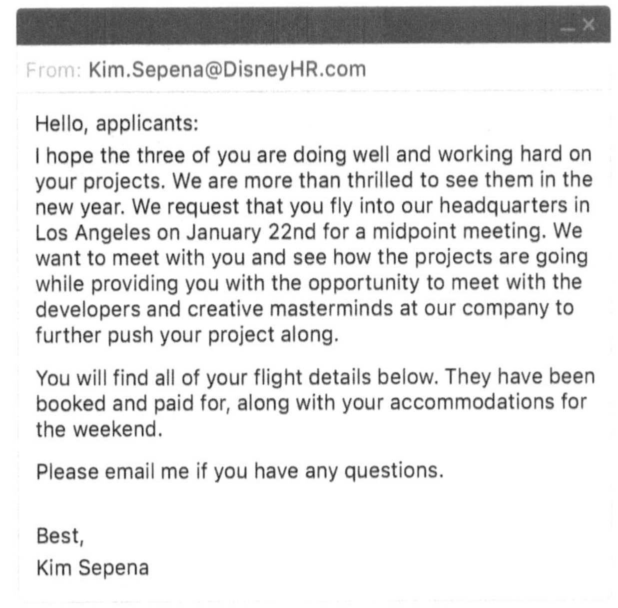

Nerves churn in my gut at her email, not because I'm not ready, but because I'm nervous about not impressing them. I need this job, not just for the money and security, but it's something I actually enjoy doing. Overall, it's the perfect position. I could work remotely which would allow me to move and live as I please.

The nerves settle into adrenaline, giving me the extra energy boost I need to work on some codes for a bit longer.

It was not until a few hours later that I noticed a text from Aurora, one I left unanswered because I was in the zone.

Aurora

Wanna FaceTime and swap
embarrassing stories??

Shit, that was three hours ago. I send off a quick text.

Me

Sorry, I just saw this. I've been
working on the game and didn't
hear my phone go off.
Everything okay?

I await her text with bated breath because it's a 50/50 chance with her. Either she's bored and wants to laugh, or she's panicking again and needs to calm her mind. I pray it's not the latter because then I'm going to be worried out of my goddamn mind.

I don't know how she does that to me, but whenever she's upset, it affects me more than I ever thought possible.

Aurora

Everything is great, Fields.
I was just bored while waiting
for practice.

Thank god.

Me

That's good, how was practice?

Aurora

Tiring as usual. Do you still
want to FaceTime?

Truthfully, I'm exhausted, too, and I want to finish another section of the game. That email reminded me that everything I've been working for these last few years hinges on this job. I need to refocus on my work, not on how Aurora makes me feel.

Me

Not tonight, sorry. I still have work to do.

Aurora

Oh okay. I won't bug you then, night.

Fuck, her response makes my gut twist. I didn't mean to upset her, but I think I did. My fingers itch to call her anyway, knowing it'd make the both of us smile. Yet I refrain, knowing this is exactly the kind of boundary I need to put in place.

We both can't afford any distractions. Our futures depend on it.

Chapter Eighteen

Aurora

I take a sip of my vanilla matcha latte and look out the window, letting out a quiet sigh. It's way too early to be up and at school, but when you're an athlete, it's expected.

I'm sitting next to the large window that panels across the wall, offering a view of the football stadium from inside the athletic cafeteria. Athletes at RLU have this separate cafeteria from the rest of the school since it opens as early as 5 a.m. to allow athletes who train in the morning an opportunity to fuel up beforehand.

Regular students are allowed to eat here, but they usually don't, except for the jersey chasers, of course.

"AV, baby!" Theo beams, getting me out of my head and setting his breakfast plate down across from mine.

"Hey, Theo, do you have an early workout, too?" I ask, knowing it's only 6 a.m., an odd time for the football team to have a workout. They usually work out in the afternoon.

Digging into his scrambled eggs, he talks through a mouthful. "Yeah, Coach's daughter has a recital tonight, so we're getting it in early today."

I nod, taking a bite of my toast slathered with peanut butter and honey. A quick glance around the cafeteria tells me Brad isn't here yet, which is a good sign.

"How have you been? I miss you being around the house," he comments, sincerity coating his tone as he fidgets with the cube he always carries with him.

"I miss you too. Let's hang out soon?" I ask, leaving out how I don't miss being at their house. I don't want him to question what happened with Brad.

He smiles at me. "We're hanging out right now, silly. Fill me in. What's new in the royal daughter of RLU's life?"

"Please don't ever utter those words again, Theo." I try to stifle a laugh, but it comes out anyway.

"It's true, you're the star of this place and you know it. Now, spill," he demands, shoving a hash brown in his mouth.

I sit back in my seat and think for a moment. So much has happened since Theo and I last spoke, but I don't think I want to share all that's happened. That I became so absorbed in training that my grades started to drop, and I needed a tutor. Or the part where I became best friends with said tutor…Yeah I don't want to share that.

"Honestly, not much. I've been studying, working, playing, or training. You know what it's like."

"I do. No new boys in your life?" he asks, with a glint in his eyes.

If there's anything Theo and I love to do, it's to gossip about our lives.

"Nope," I say, popping the p. "How about you?"

Theo smiles wickedly, leaning forward, his elbows on the table. "I may or may not be interested in someone."

I sit up straight with a gasp. "What?! Theo, who is she?"

"You know Marcela? She works at your brother's bar."

"Aw, she's really sweet, but kind of closed off. Best of luck in your efforts though,"

"Thanks, now let's get back to you, because you suck at lying—"

He's cut off as two hands rest on my shoulders, an unwelcome voice in my ear. "I bet you miss stuffing my cock in your mouth. Maybe you can fill it with a scout's cock and fuck your way to the pro's since that's the only way you'll make it."

Brad.

An unwelcome chill runs down my spine from his breath on my ear, the words he so crudely just spoke, his hands on my shoulders. I need him off of me now.

I aggressively shrug away from his touch, feeling like I need a shower. Theo eyes us speculatively, but I ignore it, trying to shift in my chair as far away as possible from Brad.

"Aurora, nice to see you. Theo, let's go." He jerks his head to the right, walking away like he's the greatest thing to exist.

"Aurora, what did he say to you?" Theo asks, eyeing me with concern.

I think about brushing him off but think better of it. "Uhm, something sexual. It was stupid since we're done, so I shrugged him off, that's all." I don't tell him exactly what happened, knowing it'll probably set him off, and that's the last thing I need.

Theo stands, glancing at his watch. "I'll talk to him. He needs to back the hell off. But I have to get going to work out. Catch up soon?"

I want to tell him not to bother, but I know it's useless, so I save my breath. "I will, I promise. Text me later, and we can set up a day?"

He lifts me out of my seat and crushes me in a hug. "Will do, AV. Fuck him, don't listen to anything he says. Love you."

Releasing me, he hustles out of the cafeteria, likely trying to catch up with Brad and ream him out.

I hate people sticking up for me. It's not his burden to bear, but I know I'd do it for him. So, I need to let him do whatever makes him feel like a good friend.

I glance down at my plate, seeing I'd only taken two bites of my toast, an entire slice left, but I push it aside, knowing I can't stomach the thought of eating after Brad's comment. It's turning my insides like a goddamn tidal wave is ravaging me.

And it hits me.

His comments were gross and rude, but most of all, they triggered me. Not that I think I'd have to fuck my way to the top, as he said, but that I might not make it. His words reach a place deep within me, an insecurity of not being good enough. The fear of not making it, disappointing my mom, my family, and myself. It's a cloud looming over my head, never moving, and he just made it darken.

It's Thursday, which is my busiest day of the week. I have an early workout, three classes, a practice, and then tutoring with Cameron. I know it's not smart to not finish my food, and it's not that I don't want to eat, but my stomach is in knots, unable to ingest anything but deep breaths as fear prickles my entire body. Add in my exhaustion from the previous night and lack of sleep.

It's going to be a long freaking day.

Hours later, I glance down at my phone, it's 4:50 p.m., and I'm dragging my ass to tutoring.

I had a protein bar between classes, it's all I could stomach. But it wasn't enough. Between the early workout, classes, and the grueling practice I just left, I feel a bit faint.

It takes me longer than usual to get to the library because of the snow. I don't want to fall, and I just don't have the energy to walk faster. I pull out my phone again to check the time—4:58 p.m.

Shit.

I hate being late and don't want to waste Cameron's time. Time he could be using to work on his game, call his sister, or do something more productive than waiting for me. Especially after he all but brushed me off last night when I asked to FaceTime.

It was very unlike him. It reminded me more of the Cam I first met. But maybe this is what we both need, space to focus on ourselves because we're becoming too intertwined with one another. Hell, we're not even *together,* and it feels like we're getting too deep.

I shake off the thoughts, pick up the pace the best I can, and eventually, the library comes into view.

I do my best to jog up the stairs, and once I reach the landing at the top, the bookshelves seem like they're spinning. I try to shake it off as I continue to make my way to our spot, but with each step, my vision grows cloudier. Everything seems to spin now as a rush of coolness washes over me. My vision suddenly grows dark as I round the corner to our spot, my knees buckling as I fall to the ground.

The last thing I hear before I fall unconscious is Cameron's pained voice yelling my name.

Chapter Nineteen

Cameron

It's 5:05 p.m., and I'm starting to worry.

Aurora's never been late and didn't text me that she would be. Unease prickles my spine. Something's off. Maybe her cramps are bad again, and she's napping? Or maybe it's something worse.

I hate not knowing. And I hate that I have no right to know. It's not like I was a very good friend last night by declining her offer to talk.

Sure, people can have boundaries and don't spread themselves thin, but I made a selfish choice. Instead of relaxing and talking to her for a bit, I decided to push forward with my work that easily could've been done in the morning.

I'm an asshole, and I know it, yet it doesn't stop me from texting her.

Me

Where are you? Are you okay?

I try to focus on the numbers on my screen, willing them to make sense as I try to develop the correct sequence for the race track I'm developing.

Pulling my glasses off, I scrub a hand over my face, my eyes landing on the take-out container in front of me. After seeing how sad she was about not getting her cake last session, I made the trek to the cafe this morning, skipping one of my classes, which I've never done before, to get her a slice. I even asked for extra peanut butter frosting, knowing that's her favorite part.

I try to look around for her, but I can't see much of the library from our spot. The only thing you can see are the mountains through the window, but other than that, we're enclosed by bookshelves.

Running a hand through my hair, I let out a frustrated sigh.

Where the hell is she, and why hasn't she texted me back?

Suddenly, footsteps float in from around a bookshelf. They're slow, staggered. Weird.

I look up at that moment, and that's when I see her. I glance at her and I'm instantly on my feet before I can comprehend what I'm doing.

Her steps are weary, and her skin pale. Before I can reach her, she collapses.

It all seems to happen in slow motion. She closes her eyes and she falls to the ground with a thud.

Fuck. No, please, no.

My stomach rises to my throat as I run over to her. "Aurora!" I yell, the strain in my voice unexpected.

I crouch down next to her limp body, and thankfully, it looks like her arms braced her fall, avoiding a concussion. I gently roll her onto her back, and a shiver goes down my spine as I take in her cold body, which seems void of life. I know that's not true, but fuck does it scare me to see her that way.

"Aurora, wake up!" I choke out, giving her arm a good shake. Still nothing. Fuck. I grip my hair, pulling it so tightly I'll have a bald spot soon. I intertwine my hand with hers, squeezing it. "C'mon, Rory, open your pretty eyes for me."

I don't have time to overthink what I said because suddenly her eyes flutter, then fully open.

"Cam?" she says groggily, trying to get a sense of her surroundings.

With my hand still holding hers, I bring my other hand up to feel her forehead. She's cold, the bags under her eyes tell me she's exhausted, and the rumble from her stomach tells me she's hungry. I need to fix it.

"I'm going to pick you up, okay?"

"Okay," she says, her tone slightly unsure.

I bring one arm under her back and the other under her knees, then stand and lift her body. The first thing that comes to my mind is how perfectly she fits in my arms. How good it feels to be holding her.

Aurora cradles her head onto my chest, her grip on my sweater tightening. I bring her back to our table, gently setting her in one of the chairs.

"Cam, I don't think I can study right now," Aurora admits shakily.

I hate hearing that in her tone. Not a fucking fan.

At that moment, I throw the imaginary boundaries out the window. The only thing I care about right now is her well-being.

I look at her over my shoulder as I shove my laptop, the container, and other things into my backpack. "We're not. I'm taking you back to my place until you feel better."

Her eyes widen at that. "N-no, you don't need to do that. I'll be fine, just give me a minute to sit. You can go, honestly."

I glare down at her, shaking my head. "Not a chance. Let's go." I walk toward her, then crouch so I'm at her level. "I'm giving you a piggyback ride. No walking for you."

Aurora scrunches her nose at me. "I didn't know your friendship was so demanding."

"I'm good at taking care of people, so let me," I plead, not in the mood for her quips when I need to know if she's okay and what the fuck happened to get her to that point.

Her eyes study mine for a beat. Then she blows out a breath. "I don't want it getting back to my dad that I was carried out of here."

I want to ask her why she doesn't want her dad to know whatever's going on, but I don't. She's not going to tell me anything right here, right now. Hopefully, after food, a blanket, and some rest, she will. So, I shrug off my plain gray hoodie and hand it to her.

"Wear this. I have a jacket I can wear instead. That way, no one will notice you."

"Are you sure?" Aurora asks, her pretty eyes so damn tired.

"I wouldn't offer it if I wasn't," I tell her softly.

She nods, then takes her sweater off, and I avert my eyes as I wait for her to put mine on. I hear the zip of her bag and the sound of her shoving her sweater into it.

"Ready," she murmurs.

I clearly didn't think this through because seeing her in my hoodie does something weird to my heart. It makes it squeeze tightly, warmth seeping out at its pressure.

The material swallows her up, and, as she puts the hood over her head, she's unrecognizable behind the material.

I step forward, reaching for her, which causes her eyebrows to shoot up. "I thought you were giving me a piggyback?"

"I am, but with my backpack on my back, I'll need to carry you in the front," I tell her. "Or I can carry you bridal style, up to you, but it'll be easier to see your face that way."

"Front it is," she mumbles shyly.

I lean down, wrap my arms around her thighs, and hoist her up to me. Her legs wrap around my waist instantly while her hands drape around my neck. I can't help but think how this feels all too natural between us.

"You okay?" I ask her while I adjust my hands to grip her thighs. Truthfully, it'd be easier to grip her ass, but I've already pushed enough boundaries.

She doesn't respond, but I can feel her smile and nod against me as she nestles her head into my chest, hiding her face.

With a deep breath, I inhale a familiar sweetness, coconut, and lime filling my senses. It's nearly intoxicating.

I walk carefully with her in my arms, making sure not to slip or falter. With every step towards my house, I'm hyper-aware of her body against mine. Every. Single. Part. Especially her pussy resting just above my cock, tempting it to wake up, but my worry for her trumps everything else.

I want to make sure she's okay, and I do my best to focus on doing exactly that.

Once we get to my house, I set her down on the couch, tuck her in with a blanket, and she dozes off a few minutes later.

Finn's not home yet, and I say a silent thankful prayer for him having a placement day where he works as a trainer with athletes. He plans on becoming a full-time trainer once he gets his degree, wanting to specialize in sports rehab.

Waiting for the water to boil, I think back to having her wrapped around me. The walk here was… interesting. It was nearly impossible to avoid stares, as she clung to me like a koala clings to bamboo.

The scowl I gave people had them turning their attention elsewhere, but I'm sure people will be talking about it. As long as they don't know it was her in my hoodie, that's all that matters. They can say whatever they want about me. I couldn't care less.

The kettle whistles, and I pour the steaming water into a mug with a peppermint tea bag. It usually soothes my anxiety, and I imagine it'll help her feel better. Mug in hand, I turn toward her and take her in from afar.

Her dark blonde hair is splayed out against a pillow, a fuzzy blanket wrapped around her body that's curled up in itself. She doesn't look like the Aurora I've gotten to know, and I fucking hate that.

I set the mug on the side table, sitting at the opposite end of the couch.

Aurora sits up instantly, looking a bit dazed. She shakes her head. "How long was I out?"

"Only ten minutes or so. I made you tea. Do you like tea? It's peppermint. It helps me feel better, so I'm hoping it makes you feel good," I ramble, suddenly nervous. I need to relax. This is just like taking care of Lexa or my mom, and I did it just the other day, despite it really messing with my head.

But this time feels different.

She smiles at me. It's short-lived, but it was there. "I love tea. Peppermint is in my top three."

"Good," I say, passing her the mug. It's too hot to drink, but it'll help warm her up if anything.

"Thank you for…all of this," she says quietly, her hands wrapping tightly around the mug.

"Stop. Thanking. Me." I chuckle, trying to lighten the mood. She doesn't laugh, but her lips tip up at the corners, so I'll take it.

Knowing she likes to have her dessert before dinner, I pull the take-out container from my backpack and put it on the coffee table.

"What's that?" she asks, perplexed.

"Since someone is a sore loser," I tease, opening the container, "I got this for you."

Aurora's eyes soften at the gesture, her pretty hazel eyes meeting mine with something I can't name. "Cam, this is…going to make me cry."

"Please don't. I don't think I could handle seeing you cry."

She swipes at a tear before it can fall, and the sight twists my insides just like I knew it would. "Sorry, I just had a rough day, and this is so sweet. No one has done something like that for me."

I hate that she's yet to be treated as she should, with so much love and kindness. It makes me want to give her that and more. To give her everything I can.

"Enjoy. There's extra frosting, too," I say, motioning toward the cake and fork that was already inside the box.

She smiles, a bit bigger this time. "Your future wife is going to be so lucky," she swoons, forking a piece between her plump lips.

My cock twitches at the motion, imagining something else between those lips.

Little does she know I've imagined her as mine more times than I'd like to admit.

Wanting to switch the conversation back to neutral ground, I pull up a food delivery app on my phone and ask, "What kind of food are you feeling? Mexican? Italian? Lebanese? Thai?"

"You don't need to feed me. I can just eat at home," she insists.

I level her with a stare that says *don't even think about it*. "I heard your stomach growl when you passed out, so I'm feeding you."

Knowing it's a losing argument, she gives in. "Thai, please."

We place our order—two pad thai's, two miso soups, and spring rolls. Reaching for the remote, I turn the TV on and load up Disney Plus.

"What do you want to watch?"

She blushes, something I haven't seen yet. I like it, the pink hue suits her. "I'm a huge Marvel fan, so anything related to that works for me."

I know it sounds silly, but when a girl has the same interests as you, it's a goddamn turn-on. Trying to keep this friendship strictly friendly will be hard if I keep finding out how perfect she is for me.

A wide smile forms on my lips as I search the Marvel category. "I'm a fan as well. The comics are the best, though."

"Aw, you really *are* nerdy, huh?" she teases, bringing the mug to her lips and taking a small sip.

"Be happy that I am. Otherwise, coding would still be kicking your ass," I give her shit right back, enjoying that we can do this now.

"Thanks for that, by the way. I'm up to a 62. Still not enough, but better."

I don't know why, but my hand reaches out and grips her knee, giving it a reassuring squeeze. "I've got you, don't worry."

Aurora nods, her appreciative gaze on mine for a beat, before she turns it to the T.V.

After swiping through a few options, we decided on *Guardians of the Galaxy*. The intro music plays, and that's as far as we get before my curiosity gets the best of me.

"Tell me, are you really okay?" My tone is gentle, coaxing her to open up to me just like she did on Saturday.

Aurora fiddles with the blanket, her eyes locked on her hands. She lifts her eyes to mine, and I can see she's anxious.

"I'm not going to judge you. We're friends. There is nothing you can say that will push me away, okay?" I tell her, sensing that she needs reassurance. I don't even know if she cares about me pushing her away or if our friendship means that much to her.

After a minute, she nods, then sucks in a breath, a small sigh leaving her lips. "So the reason I even needed tutoring to begin with was because I…I struggled to balance a healthy lifestyle. I upped my workouts, increased my training hours, got rid of proper rest, and some days I would forget to eat. My grades started to suffer because I put all my energy into practice and workouts. What little I had left wasn't enough."

Fuck, that makes me feel like even more of an ass for how I reacted at our initial meeting. She was going through some shit, and I didn't make it any easier.

"What made you do that?" I ask.

"It started in September.…I was hooking up with this guy, and when I told him I wanted to end our exclusive hook-up-ship, he told me that I wasn't good enough to make Team USA. It sent me in a downward spiral." A single tear falls down her cheek, and I itch to wipe it away, but my fists are balled up on my lap.

"H-he also told me that he would love to tell my dad what a whore I am…how that's all I'm really good at," she says with a sniffle, more tears trailing down her face now.

"So, I let his words get to me because that's my driving force, making the team. It's like I have this ball of pressure around my chest when it comes to volleyball, and he cranked the notch, making it even tighter. I don't know if it's because he's also an athlete, so I worried his opinion meant more, but looking back now, I know it was stupid. I have so much proof that I'm damn good at what I do, but it's funny how one negative comment can derail you if you let it. I started to worry he was right and that I needed to work harder, working myself to the bone every day. But then my dad pulled me into his office about my grades. I've been better about resting and whatnot, but what happened made me so anxious that I couldn't eat, and then I just forgot to as my busy day went on."

Aurora pauses, inhaling a deep breath. My hand reaches out, rubbing circles on her upper back. Her body relaxes a bit, but she stiffens again as she starts talking.

"I put on this confident act, and while most of it is real, a deep part within me still wonders every goddamn day if I'm good enough, worrying if I'll ever make my mom proud. If I will honor her." A sob breaks free from her throat as she cries, her body wracking from the sensation.

It fucking tears me up from the inside out.

I instantly pull her onto my lap, cradling her into my chest, my arms wrapped tightly around her. Using my fingers to tilt her chin up to mine, I wait until her watery eyes meet mine to talk. "You honor your mom every day by going after your dream, just like she did. You make your mom proud every day simply by being you. I may have never met her, but I'd bet my life that it's true."

More tears fall down her cheeks now, and, this time, I brush them away with my thumb. She leans into my touch.

"And who the fuck is this douchebag?" I ask, my tone clipped.

Aurora attempts to avert her gaze, but I bring it back to mine with my fingers on her jaw. "It's uh, Brad. Theo's going to talk to him about leaving me alone."

It's cute that she thinks I'll be okay with just that. I'm still fucking pissed about what happened in the hallway the other day, and now I'm about to explode. Despite the rage threatening to unleash within me, I won't use my fists as per my rule, but if I ever see him, I will give him hell.

"Who's Theo?" I ask, wanting to get off the topic of Brad before I lose it. I find myself trailing my fingers up and down her arm, for her comfort and mine.

"My friend. He's also on the team," she says, the words making me feel…oh hell. Jealous?

Fuck. My feelings for her are getting harder and harder for me to deny.

"Nice," is all I reply because I'm apparently inept with words when I'm envious.

A slow smirk forms on her face. "You're my friend too, don't worry." But it quickly falls as her next words tumble out of her mouth. "Don't you want to know why he called me a whore?"

My brows narrow, my lips flat. "No, because I know Brad is a fucking idiot. Whatever he says isn't valid."

She stares back at me. "I know, but… he may be right. As my friend, I feel like you should know that since I started here, I've only had exclusive hookups. I never dated anyone, just had committed, monogamous sex with people until we both decided to call it off."

"And as your friend, I feel like you should know that I don't think that defines you in any way. Your body, your choice."

Her bottom lip wobbles in shock, her wide eyes boring into mine. "Not many people think that way."

Tucking a piece of hair behind her ear, I say, "I'm not most people."

"I know, Cam, trust me," she nearly whispers.

Our eyes stay glued to one another, acceptance and appreciation in hers. A whiff of coconut and lime invades my senses, swirling through every part of me and filling me with something I've never felt before.

Before I can analyze it, a knock on my door interrupts our moment, causing Aurora to jump off my lap. Internally, I sigh, then go to the door to retrieve our food, setting it down on the coffee table when I return. It smells delicious.

We dig into our food, a comfortable silence settling between us as we watch the movie while we stuff our faces. I glance at her every few seconds, happy to see her eating, warm and lighter than before.

"Cam?" Aurora asks once our food is finished.

"Hmm?" I hum, turning my face to look at her.

"Earlier… when I passed out. Did you call me Rory?" she asks, her voice small.

Shit, I didn't think she'd hear me, I wasn't thinking at all, for that matter. I was too concerned about her to care.

"Uh, yeah. The nickname just came to mind at that moment. Is that okay, or what do your other friends call you?" I ask, running a hand across my jaw.

Her lips part as she sucks in sharp breath, a lone tear rolling down her cheek. I'm about to ask what's wrong, but she beats me to it. "That's…it's what my mom used to call me. She's the only person that's ever used that name. Everyone has always called me Ro, Rora, or Roro. No one has ever called me Rory since my mom passed, but you."

"I'm so sorry, Aurora, I didn't know. I'll just call y—"

"No," she cuts me off sharply, her hand resting on my knee now, squeezing it. "I like it. Call me Rory, please."

I'm too stunned for words. The emotions crawling their way up my throat prevent them from escaping. I stiffly nod as my heart screams at me, loud and clear. I like her. I really fucking like her. And not as a friend. It's more than that.

So. Much. More.

After today's events, from watching her faint and nearly losing my shit, to feeling her body in my arms and everything in between, I know I'm falling for her.

In one quick moment, I choose to say fuck my rule. I did what I needed to do in school and job-wise. She's already in my thoughts 24/7, distracting me anyway from my previously narrow path. But she's a distraction I'm starting to crave. To need.

Suddenly, the sound of the door being unlocked from the outside fills the room, and I sigh. Finn's home.

This should be fun.

Chapter Twenty

Aurora

"Aurora, nice to see you here," Finn winks, hanging his jacket on the coat hanger.

Cameron greets him while I wave. I've seen him around the bar a lot more lately, and we usually chat for a bit each time. But I think back to the comment he made a few weeks ago, about how he can't wait to watch Cameron fall in love with me.

At first, I laughed at the prospect, but now, it worries me. Because every second I spend with him, how he's treated me today, and all the small stuff in between, it's becoming difficult not to like him.

The icing on the cake is him calling me Rory. I can't help but notice how weird it is. How my mom was the only one to call me that. Now, here's Cameron, the first person using it again.

Is it a sign or something from my mom? I'm not sure I believe in that stuff, but it is…interesting.

I've always had a physical pull towards him, but now that emotional aspect is there, and we can't undo it.

I have no idea if my feelings are mutual, but part of me hopes they're not. Because then, it'll be easier to ignore whatever this is. And honestly, I love our friendship. I'd hate for us to try to be more and lose what we have. I'm not sure it's worth the risk. Sure, we've only been friends for a short time, but our connection trumps that.

Plopping down onto the loveseat across from us, he steals the remaining spring roll. "Mmm, I wuv dese," he swoons through a mouthful.

"You idiot, that wasn't for you to eat," Cameron grumbles beside me.

"Now I'm going to starve tonight, and you'll carry that guilt forever," I join in on the teasing.

"I don't think you should keep her. I take it back." Finn looks at Cameron, and if I were eating something, I would be choking.

What's that look?

I feel Cameron freeze beside me, which only makes me more…nervous? When the hell did they have that conversation? What did Cam say? When?

I have questions, clearly.

"Tough shit, we know too much about each other now. She's stuck with me." Cameron tilts his head at me with a sly smile, dimples in full effect, then winks.

Someone needs to check on my heart state because I don't think it's functioning properly after that. God, that's cheesy for me. I have never once felt that way from a simple wink, but here I am.

Finn eyes us, his gaze bouncing back and forth. His mouth tilts up at whatever he sees. Then, he shifts to face me, scratching at his thick beard. "I heard for the next project in cardiovascular systems that we get to choose our partner. Do you want to be mine?"

"Sure, a little F&A time," I gleam, feeling lighter and happier than this morning. It almost feels weird that it even happened today because everything inside me feels peaceful and calm after being cared for by Cam and opening up to him.

Cameron halts mid-sip, his water jug halfway to his lips, eyebrows scrunched together. "F&A time?"

Finn winks at Cam. "Yeah, it's our code name. We have secrets. Are you jealous?" He asks, waggling his brows.

I chuck the pillow beside me at Finn, emitting a laugh from him. "It's not a secret if you tell people."

Cameron presses his thigh against mine, unconsciously or not I'm not sure, but the slight touch sends a shiver through me.

Is he jealous?

I doubt it. That's not why he's nudging his thigh with mine.

We fall into comfortable conversation, the three of us joking and telling stories from our childhoods. It feels good. I don't have a close group of friends because being the dean's daughter makes you wonder who *really* wants to be your friend or who gets close to you for perks.

I once had a girl I met freshman year with whom I thought I had a good bond with, but then she started asking me to ask my dad for favors. Getting her into certain courses, and extending due dates. Needless to say, that friendship did not last very long.

The girls on the team are great. I get along well with all of them, but it doesn't go beyond the court for us. I don't go out of my way to hang out with them beyond practices, workouts, or games. Some may say I'm too focused, but I have goals to accomplish.

Yet, sitting here with Finn and Cameron, I feel full in such a good way. I've always enjoyed my small circle of Jasmine, Theo, Pickles, my dad, and Nate, but I think I can add room for these two.

Finn finished the movie with us, and then he retreated for the night, leaving just Cameron and I together on the couch.

Throughout the rest of the movie, Cameron's body had stayed close to mine. His muscular thigh pressed against mine, and I had to consciously remind myself not to rest my head on his shoulder. I never felt so comfortable yet so uncomfortable while sitting next to a man.

I was uncomfortable because I was aware of every inch of our bodies touching. How the sensation sent warmth to my core. I was aware of his every breath, every slight movement he made. The way it sent a wave of sandalwood and fresh linen over me, and I wanted nothing more than to wrap myself up in it like a blanket.

Try sitting next to a man you've thought about when using your vibrator and just realized you may have feelings for. It's not fun, not when you're friends and can't be anything more than that.

"What time do you have practice tomorrow?" Cameron asks as he cleans up our mess from the coffee table.

"I don't have one since it's a game day. Coach would rather we rest," I tell him as I attempt to untangle myself from the softest blanket I've ever used.

Cameron doesn't respond. He just nods as he tidies the space, but I can tell he's thinking. His tongue pokes the inside of his cheek when he's in deep thought, a tell I've learned.

We clean up in silence until Cameron's hand stills mine as I attempt to fold the blanket. "You didn't have to help me clean. I can do that."

Finn was right. Cameron truly is the kindest man I've ever met. He's always thinking of others and how he can help them. He's grown up being the caretaker, and I don't think that will ever stop. His mom raised him well. He's a good one. "I've learned that you like to take care of people, Cam, and you're great at it. But, I can also help you, too, you know?"

His lips twitch, cinnamon eyes focused on my face intently as we begin to fold the blanket together, our hands meeting in the middle to bring the long halves together. "I'm beginning to learn that."

"Good," I smile at him, taking the folded blanket, setting it on the couch, and wishing it was coming home with me instead.

Cameron must notice the longing look I'm giving his blanket because he snickers.

"Hm?" I hum, wanting to know exactly why he's laughing.

He shakes his head, "You're looking at my blanket as if it's someone you want but can't have."

If only he knew how that also applied to him.

Ignoring the pit in my stomach, I tell him, "Because I do. That is the softest blanket that I've ever been wrapped up in."

"We may be best friends, but it's not going to happen," he says, his brows set in determination, but I can see the glint of playfulness in his eyes.

"You keep telling yourself that, Fields," I chuckle, my eyes locked onto his, watching how they watch me. It's almost unnerving, the way he looks at me, but I kind of like it.

"I'm going to go, though. I have an early class, and then we meet in the locker room for tape reviews," I tell him, feeling bummed that I have to leave. I like it here, being with him and watching Marvel movies. I could do it all night. "Thanks for everything today and for being there for me. How much do I owe you for the food?"

A scowl instantly takes over his previously playful face, his tone rough. "You don't owe me anything, ever, okay?"

I roll my eyes. "I do, and I will eventually. I need to take care of you, too. That's what friends do."

Ignoring my comment, he runs a hand through his hair, then asks, "Are you okay? I know you said you were doing better at not burning yourself out, but I need to make sure."

I take a minute to think it over and realize that I should check in with my therapist, but I don't think anything's majorly wrong. I'm going to be okay. I saw what happened today when it did, and that shit is not becoming a repeat. I need a strong body and mind to make the team. Overworking myself isn't going to achieve that.

"Yeah, I am."

He stares at me for a moment, looking at me as if he can see through me. If he could, he wouldn't find anything but honesty.

Seeming to come to that conclusion on his own, he nods. "Okay, but if you ever need something or if he ever says anything to you again…" He tenses, then takes a deep breath before continuing, "You'll tell me, right?"

I reach out for his hand that's balled up into a fist, and I instantly feel his arm relax with my touch. "I will, I promise."

Releasing it, I step toward the door to grab my boots and jacket when he hits the automatic start button on his car's key fob.

"Cam, I can walk. My house is only a few minutes from here."

"No chance. Just get in the car and don't argue, please?" he pleads, his eyes bouncing back and forth between mine.

I relent because no matter how much I try to push it away, I like his overprotectiveness. It's new to me, along with the feelings it brings.

Our car ride is short, about three minutes, if that. In the driveway of my house, I look over at his handsome face, taking in each detail. The fullness of his lips, his straight nose, the sharpness of his bare jaw, his dark brown eyebrows, his cinnamon eyes, and his chocolate-like hair that curls slightly under his beanie. I never appreciated brown in all its different shades until recently.

"Next time, I'll walk, but thank you for the ride and everything today," I nearly whisper, my voice low and soft.

He pins me with a glare, his deep voice filling the space. "No, you won't, and you're welcome."

I twist my lips at him and scrunch my nose. Does he ever turn it off? Being so damn nice and caring.

His lips slip from his previous stern look, bringing a grin to his face. "No, I never stop, if that's what you were wondering. Still sure you want to be friends with me?"

I'm not sure if I only want to be friends with you.

I look at him, a warmth filling my chest. "Positive." I let myself out of his car and turned to wave at him through the windshield, only to see that he got out too, rounding the hood of his car to meet me.

"What are you doing?" I ask.

"Walking you to your door," he says nonchalantly.

I peer at him through narrowed eyes, my lips scrunched up.

"Stop being cute and just let me," he smiles, those dimples pulling in at his cheeks.

Did he just call me cute? And why does my heart feel like it just ran a mile? He called me cute. It's it's not like he said he loves me or just fucked me senseless.

I can feel the heat covering my cheeks, so I look away and walk toward my door with Cameron beside me.

We come to a stop right outside my door and face one another. Cameron instantly pulls me into a hug, his arms around my lower back, and I melt under his body. I stay under because he's that freaking large between his height and the mass of his muscles that I feel hidden when he's holding me.

I let out a soft sigh at the contact, nuzzling my face into his chest. Cameron pulls me in tighter, his chin resting on my head.

I feel safe and like I never want to leave his arms, but I also feel like it's too much for me, the feelings I have for him rushing to the front of my heart and mind. Maybe this is normal when you like a friend so much. Maybe it's not normal because Theo and I sure as hell don't hug like this.

Releasing me, he steps back, a peaceful look on his face. "Good night, Rory," he whispers, then turns and heads to his car, taking my heart with him.

No, wait, I take it back. That can't be happening. No heart taking, nothing. Volleyball and a Team USA spot are the only things my heart has room for. At least, that's what I'm trying to convince myself of anyway.

A text pings from my phone on my side table just as I crawl into bed thirty minutes later. I shuffle over to the side and retrieve it, seeing a text from Cameron.

Fields

I can't believe you think
Groot is better than Rocket.

A small laugh bubbles from my lips. We argued during the movie about whether Rocket or Groot was the better character. He claimed Groot can't talk and is annoying half the time with not knowing things, whereas Rocket, in his opinion, is far funnier and a mastermind.

Ah. There's that nickname again.

While part of it makes me sad at the reminder of who used to call me that, part of it makes me happy. It brings me joy to hear it again. It's almost like I'm reunited with my mom somehow whenever he says it.

I thought about telling him not to call me that, but my brain worked faster, somehow knowing I needed it.

Me

Night, Cam.

Chapter Twenty-One

Aurora

This morning, I woke up extra early before my only class at nine, wanting to savor the quiet and beauty of the sun rising on my back porch.

A new day full of new possibilities. It sent a thrill down my spine, at how much life could be lived today. I never took a day for granted, not after seeing how it can get cut short at any time.

With my notebook in hand, I drew until it was time for me to leave, wanting to let out all my confusing feelings from the night before.

Cameron… that man. He is the sweetest, most caring man I've ever met, and I bet I haven't even seen half of it yet. That boyish yet sharp face of his, combined with his large frame that could swallow me whole, had me using my vibrator last night before I dozed off into a blissful sleep.

I'm in the locker room, changing for the game, when the drawing I sketched this morning keeps materializing at the forefront of my mind.

It was a third-person perspective of me on Cameron's lap last night, spilling my worst fears as he held me tightly. He looked at me like I was precious to him.

I included the cozy blanket I loved using, and the Marvel movie playing on the TV. It's becoming one of my favorite drawings.

"Roooo!" Jasmine chimes, plopping down beside me as I slide on my knee pads.

"What's up?" I ask her, noting that she's ready to go.

Her uniform is on, the number 31 on her back evident as she bends over to tie her shoe. Jasmine's birthday is July 31st, mine November 25th, and ever since we met in high school, all of my passwords that require numbers have been a combination of our birthdays—2531. She's my platonic soulmate.

Swinging back up straight, her curly pigtails flipping, she answers me. "You ready to kick some ass tonight?"

I clap my hand over her knee, giving it a squeeze. "You know it"

"Do you want to go out after? I'm feeling a drink or two or five," she giggles at herself.

"Sorry, Minnie, I have a shift at the bar tonight, and I can't cancel. Nate's gone to a wedding for the weekend, so I'm in charge."

Jasmine perks up at the mention of my brother's name. "How's Nate doing?"

I swat her arm playfully, knowing she pretends to have a crush on my brother. "Still heavily into men."

"Darn," she mutters, then says, "I'll come to you then, keep you company while you work."

"I can't drink while working, Minnie." I frown at her, not wanting her to just sit and watch me work all night. She also knows I don't care to drink much anyway. When I do, it's usually a beer or two.

"Pft, as if I care. I just want to hang out with you, and since you can't drink, you can be my DD."

We agreed to ride there together after the game, and then head to the court to warm up.

Students are piling in left and right, filling the gymnasium. As Coach Tilly goes over game details and what our opponents, the Stingers from Arizona, are like, I zone out since I studied this beforehand.

I look out into the crowd, spotting my dad sitting by himself on the lowest bleacher with a freaking foam finger and popcorn on his lap. He's always been my biggest fan, and I don't see that changing anytime soon. A few students near him seem shocked from casually sitting so close to the dean. Scanning the left side of the court, I notice Finn and Ash sitting in the midd—wait.

Is that…?

I see my best friend, the one who I can't seem to keep off my mind. Cameron. He's here, watching me play for the first time. Even though we didn't know each other before, I would have recognized his face, and it's not one I've seen here until today.

Butterflies take flight in my stomach, a flight full of turbulence because they bounce around so fast that I nearly feel sick. My cheeks grow hot, and at that moment, he looks directly at me as if he sensed me staring.

Cameron's dimples pull in, his smile wide as he stares right back. My grin breaks free, and I nod at him before turning my attention back to Coach Tilly.

I feel a bit more nervous than usual. Sure, Cameron is just my friend, but I want to impress him. He only knew me as the star of the team before, and I want to show him that there's a reason for that. I want him to see my potential and believe in my ability to reach my goals more than he already does.

With that motivation, I play one of the best damn games of my life. All of my serves are bullets, half of them hitting the ground before the other team has a chance to move for it. My spikes are brutal blows that leave one girl constantly rubbing the area on her arm where my ball had hit her.

Whenever I do something that gets us a point, I can feel his eyes on me. I glance his way and see his smile, so big and proud smile, as he cheers me on.

It only makes me smile and play that much harder.

"Vallacourt, nice work today," Coach Tilly tells me during our brief after the game, in which we won all three sets.

"Thanks, Coach," I beam, feeling damn good about my performance today and my ability to make a good impression on the scouts who will be coming out after the holidays.

Jasmine and I quickly shower and then get dressed. I change into my work clothes. A black golf skirt and a long sleeve black V-neck, along with my black Converse. All black is the dress code at the bar.

I release my ponytail, blonde curls falling past my breasts, and then I apply some makeup.

"Woah," I gasp, taking in Jasmine as I tear my gaze away from the mirror where I was doing my makeup.

She's wearing a plum long-sleeved crop top that accentuates her not-too-big but not-too-small rack. It also shows off her narrow waist, highlighting the muscles in her stomach. Paired with leather tights and black booties, she looks amazing. Her midnight curls are pulled into a low pony on one side, and her face is bare.

"What?" she asks shyly.

"You look fucking hot, Minnie. If you wanted to give up that V card tonight, I'm sure people would be lining up outside the bar," I joked, taking her in again. My best friend is so beautiful. It's a shame no one has caught her interest yet.

"Alright, and we're done. Let's hit the road, Ro. Your shift starts in 25 minutes."

We drive over in Minnie's car, wanting to avoid the cold since neither of us is dressed appropriately to make the ten-minute walk it would have been.

The bar is full as we walk in. A mixture of letterman and school sweaters with numbers on the back tells me it's full of different varsity teams.

I let Craig, my brother's right-hand man, know I'm here and that he can leave. Behind the bar, I clean up the dirty glasses and wipe stuff down, needing a clean space before I get busy.

I'm fiddling with the register when Jasmine rasps her knuckles on the bar.

"What does it take to get a drink around here?" she teases.

I walk over to her and ask, "White, red, or rosé?"

"Rosé, please!" Jasmine loves wine and refuses to drink anything else, claiming why waste time drinking anything else when you find what you like.

I grab a wine glass and fill it a bit more than I would anyone else, perks of being best friends with the owner's sister. While sliding it over to her, she pulls out a book.

"Are you going to read while drinking wine at a bar?" I ask, bemused.

She looks up at me from behind her book, arching her eyebrow. "Yes, is that not okay?"

"Nope, not at all. I'll come and chat when I can," I tell her, seeing a group of men flock to the bar top.

Time flies as I constantly fill drinks, wipe down counters, and restock the bar. I glance at the clock and see that it's 10:30 p.m.

Jasmine and I have chatted here and there, but I've been slammed for the most part.

Theo's also here with his team, and he came up to talk to me. I introduced him to Jasmine, not intending to hook them up because I've seen how many glances he's shot at Marcela, my waitress tonight.

Theo and I planned to meet next week to hang out, and he promised me that he wouldn't let Brad leave the table tonight without his supervision.

I take advantage of a mini-break from serving customers and crouch below the bar to fix the glasses, lining them up perfectly.

"Ro!" Jasmine nearly squeals, causing me to jump to my feet.

"What?" I ask, searching the area for any immediate threats.

Leaning forward on the bartop, Jasmine whispers, "Look who showed up in the booth over there."

I follow her line of sight, and that's when I see them. Finn, Ash, and Cameron all sitting together in a booth.

While I'm excited to see him here, I wonder how he's handling it. With his dad and all. But, like he said, he's a grown man who can make his own choices. With him coming here tonight, I'm sure it means he's confident he can handle it.

"Why are we staring at that booth with heart eyes?" a voice snaps me away from my thoughts, and I turn to see Theo standing beside Jasmine.

"Because Aurora is totally into her tutor, and they have this soulmate crap going on, but both are too stubborn to make a move," Jasmine tells him casually, her tone cool and collected as if she didn't say the most ridiculous shit I've ever heard.

I *do* have feelings for him, but soulmates? Let's slow down.

I suddenly regretted spilling everything to her last night when I got home, but she saw us hugging on the porch, so I couldn't avoid it. The only reason I didn't want to tell her was because I was afraid she'd react like this.

"AV, baby, what the hell? When were you going to tell me this?" Theo glares at me, but it's more like a sad puppy look.

"Never, because there's nothing going on. Jesus, Jasmine, look what you did," I mutter, gesturing toward Theo, who's entirely too wrapped up in her fantasy.

"I did nothing but speak the truth. And I'll have you know, since Theo came over, Cameron's been glancing your way every ten seconds. Cameron looks kinda pissed, maybe a little jealous, I might say?" Jasmine tells us, all too pleased with herself.

Theo swivels his head, then turns back to us. "Oh yeah, he's jealous. As a guy, I know that look," he says, his gaze lingering until it lands on Marcela, watching her deliver food to a table.

I quickly glance at Cameron, and he's staring right at me. He does look a bit annoyed, with his brows furrowed and his jaw set tightly. I smile at him, and it takes a moment, but he smiles back.

The hush words between Jasmine and Theo have me averting my gaze from him. "What are you two whispering about?"

Theo looks at me with a glint in his eyes, "Don't worry, AV. Jasmine and I are just bonding, that's all."

I glance between them and shake my head. "I'm not sure I like this trio we're forming."

That makes Jasmine laugh, setting her wine glass on the bartop. "Too late. I like ganging up on you with him."

I secretly like it, too, seeing two of my closest friends finally bonding. While they had met when we had to share the workout room for a month, they rarely crossed paths over the years despite being friends with me.

A few customers approach the bar, so I leave my friends to chat while I serve more drinks. I end up getting a rush of customers, which takes me away for longer than I'd like, and now, I urgently need to use the washroom.

I let Marcela know I'm going for a quick bathroom break, and if anyone needs anything, to tell them to wait. I rush to where the bathrooms are, but another hallway leads to the staff washroom, and I take a right to beeline for it.

I quickly do my business and rush back down the hallway when I turn the corner and run into a solid chest.

I look up and see that it's Brad. His sand-colored waves nearly cover his eyes, but the smell of alcohol wafting off him tells me everything I need to know. He's drunk.

A wave of nausea hits me, and I nearly shake, but I control it, not wanting him to see it. I try to step around him, but he shifts, blocking me.

"What do you want?" I bite out, my tone harsh. I need to get back to the bar far away from him.

"You," he drawls, raising his hand to squeeze my hip.

I shove away from his touch. "I told you no before. We're done."

I attempt to squeeze around him again, but he grips my wrist this time, tugging me into his chest. His hold on me is bruising. I can feel it because it hurts like hell as his fingers dig into my skin through my shirt.

"Let go, Brad, you're hurting me." I wince, trying to free my wrist from his grip. It only makes him tighten his grip, and I nearly whimper from the pain.

"Not until you say you'll come back. I miss being inside your tight-"

He doesn't get to finish his sentence because my knee drives up and into his crotch. Brad keels over, falling to the ground as he writhes in pain. Good, serves him right for laying a hand on me.

Jumping over his body, I run down the hallway and don't stop until I'm behind the bar. I'm panting, feeling breathless and shaky. Jasmine and Theo are on me instantly, leaning over the bar top with concerned looks on their faces.

"Ro, what happened?" Jasmine asks, her face morphing into anger. I know I must look as overwhelmed as I feel right now.

"AV, baby, talk to us," Theo urges, trying to get me to speak because I've been silent, trying to catch my breath and process what the hell just happened.

I feel like my mind is spinning, and my breath feels hard to catch, so I just shake my head, unable to form words. In the background, I hear someone yelling at someone that they're not allowed behind the bar.

Worried that it's Brad, I quickly turn to see who it is. Cameron. He's stalking toward me like a man on a mission, and I can tell by the scowl on his face, the tightness of his jaw, and the heat off of his body once he's in front of me that he's pissed off.

"Rory, what happened?" he asks, his tone controlled and calm despite the signs his body is giving off.

But I can't talk. My breaths feel choppy, and I need to ground myself. Cameron must sense this and pulls me into him, wrapping me up in sandalwood and fresh linen.

In safety and warmth.

I feel hidden and safe here. It allows me to slow my mind and my breaths as my ear rests against his heart, listening to the beats that eventually mine mimic. Cameron rubs his hands up and down my back, soothing me as I tightly grip his back, feeling like he's my personal safety raft.

"Talk to me, please. It's killing me," he murmurs against my hair.

I pull back from him, but he doesn't let me get far, keeping his arms around the small of my back.

I take a deep breath, exhaling quietly. Cameron grew up with an abusive parent, and I know how much he hates any kind of violence. So, if I'm being honest, I'm a bit worried about telling him. I don't want to upset or trigger him. "Fields, it's not—"

"Don't do that, not with me," Cameron says, an edge to his voice now as he's on the verge of losing it the longer I keep him in the dark.

From the corner of my eye, I can see a customer at the bar, and I try to wiggle my way out of his arms, but he only tightens his hold on me. Not the way Brad did. This is gentle and welcomed. "They'll wait."

Bringing my hands up to his chest, I rest them there, needing to touch him and feel the heat of his body under my palms. Cameron takes a step toward me, pulling us in a bit closer, but the angle brings pain to my wrist, where Brad gripped me. I can't stop the wince I make, and Cameron notices.

He instantly steps back, removing his hands from around my waist. But, within a second, he's back in front of me. His cinnamon eyes are darker as they look at me intently. "Where are you hurt?"

I know it's a lost cause to argue at this point, so I point to my left wrist.

"Can I touch you there, or will it hurt you?" he asks softly, yet there's still that underlying rage bubbling below the surface the entire time.

"You won't hurt me," I tell him, letting him know it's okay. Cam gently places his arm under my left one, then using his other hand, he pushes my sleeve up ever so slowly to avoid causing me any pain.

My black sleeve is rolled up, stopping just past my wrist, revealing red marks that clearly resemble fingers. I knew he hurt me, but I didn't think they would be this bad. Jasmine and Theo gasp, then curse as they begin to ask me questions, but it's the primal-sounding growl that I listen to instead.

The snarl that rips out of Cameron is feral and causes me to gaze up at him instead of my arm. I've never seen someone look the way he does now. He's not just pissed off, he's fucking fuming. If smoke could be coming out of his ears, it would be.

His defined chest is moving up and down rapidly, and I could swear his body is slightly shaking.

"Who did this to you?" he demands, the chords in his throat clenched tightly.

I swallow the lodge in my throat from feeling everything. I'm overwhelmed with what happened. By Cameron and his body that's become my safety net, by Brad's actions, how his words made me cringe, how grossly he talked about my body, and how he felt the right to manhandle it.

Part of me still can't believe it. That he *hurt* me. It makes me feel slightly less emotional and more pissed off.

Feeling the anger return to my body gives me the bravado I need to tell Cam what happened. "I was coming back from the washroom when Brad cornered me. He's drunk, and when I asked him what he wanted, he said he wanted me." I shudder remembering it and the fact that he's been inside of me before. He was never like this when we were hooking up. He was fun and easygoing, but I still feel like an idiot now after he's shown his true colors.

"I told him no and tried to escape him, so he… he gripped me by the wrist and tugged me into him. I tried to break free, and he only tugged harder. It hurt. Then he started saying some gross stuff, so I kneed him in the balls. And now I'm here."

Jasmine breaks out in a fury of curses while Theo glances over to his team's table, looking for a certain someone. But Cameron…

Cameron swallows, the cords of muscle in his neck straining as his Adam's apple bobs. His eyes are darker than before, his jaw ticking and clenching as his eyes bounce between my face and my wrist. The breaths leaving him are ragged and heavy. His body is burning with rage, ready to spark at any moment.

"Rory," he breathes, resting his forehead on mine, my name soft on his otherwise harsh features. The name nearly breaks me, but also mends me at the same time. Hearing it from his lips will never get old.

"Cam, it's okay. I'll be fine," I reassure him, bringing my right hand to his cheek, trying to calm him down.

Cameron removes his head from mine, his brows narrowed. "You've been hurt. There is nothing fucking okay with that. It's not okay, Aurora. It's not fucking fine," he snaps, shaking his head at me, then looking up to the ceiling as he takes in a deep breath.

In my peripheral vision, I see a figure emerging from the washroom hallway, and I freeze.

Aware of my stillness, Cameron follows my line of sight, turning his head over his shoulder, and then he's gone.

Chapter Twenty-Two

Cameron

Turning on my heel, I rush out from behind the bar. My strides are long and quick, with a certain target in mind.

I can see him over the crowd, rushing out of the door, and I follow him just as quickly. I'm so wrapped up in my rage that I don't hear or see anything but Brad and fucking red. My bones are shaking, muscles tight, and ready to go. I've never fought before and made a vow to never turn to violence, but I'm breaking that vow.

For her.

My mind flashes to the bruises on her tiny wrist, to the hurt in her eyes. It causes a blaze of fury to run through me. Somebody put their hands on my girl. It fucking triggers me like nothing else could.

The cold hits me as I step out of the front door, but it does nothing to simmer the burning rage within me. "Brad!" I call out, my tone rough.

He swivels around, his eyebrows tilted in amusement. "It's flavor of the wee—"

Brad doesn't get to finish his sentence because my fist connects with his jaw, shutting him the fuck up. He stumbles back from the hit, and I don't give him time to recover.

I'm on him instantly, delivering blow after blow to his face, hearing the crack of his nose.

"Touch her again, and I'll break more than just your nose," I bite out between punches while dodging his own.

I'm nearly lost in the anger until I see a flash of blonde at my side. My eyes snap to Aurora, trying to wedge her way between us.

Absolutely fucking not.

I gently move her to the side and step in front of her. The millisecond I took my attention off of Brad gives him a chance to land a punch, connecting with my forehead, and I can already feel the split of skin above my eyebrow.

Aurora shrieks from behind me, her hand pulling at my shoulder.

"Get her out of here!" I shout as a blur of auburn hair arrives at my side and grabs her.

I dodge another hit from Brad and lunge forward, but we're suddenly broken up. What I'm assuming is the football team is pulling Brad back while two sets of hands are yanking me backward as well.

"Cam, it's okay," Finn's voice breaks through the anger vibrating in my body.

I take a deep breath, trying to calm myself down. The set of hands holding me back let go of me, and I turned around to see Finn and the guy at the bar with them. Theo, I think.

I look past them, my eyes frantically searching for her. I find her a few feet away with Jasmine. Her hazel eyes are locked on me, wide and scared.

Fuck, I hope I didn't freak her out or that she thinks I'm just like my dad. Because I'm not. Amid my rage, I was able to control myself when she nearly got in the middle of it.

I begin walking toward her, then hesitate. Aurora's eyes lower, and she shakes her head as she walks toward me on wobbly feet, so I meet her halfway.

"No, don't even say it. You're not him," she whispers to me, bringing her hands to my cheeks, forcing me to look at the sincerity in her eyes.

"Then why do you look scared, love?" I ask her, noticing how the name of endearment flowed off my tongue so easily. I like it, and I don't think she minded it. Despite her eyes widening at first, they also softened.

"Because I didn't want you to get hurt," her voice cracks as a tear strolls down her cheek.

Only she could ever hurt me.

I bring my hands up to her cheeks, mimicking her, swiping the stray tears that have fallen. "I'm okay. Let's get you inside, it's freezing," I murmur, gesturing with my head toward her bare legs.

When I first saw her in that skirt, I thought about how good her legs looked, how perfect her ass was. But now, I want her covered up and warm.

A cop siren in the distance pulls our attention away, our hands sliding off each other's faces. I interlock my hand with hers, needing to keep her close.

Theo walks over to us, with Finn trailing him, looking between Aurora and me. "You guys okay? What's the game plan?"

"The cops are coming, Ro. They're going to want to know what happened. You don't have to speak up, but I really think you should. If he hurt you, who's to say it won't happen to someone else when she says no?" Jasmine points out.

"I agree with her, AV," Theo chimes in, leaning his head towards her.

"Me too, Aurora. But it's up to you. We will support you no matter what," Finn tells her, Ash in front of him, a protective arm wrapped around her waist.

I give her hand a squeeze. "What do you want to do?"

Her worried eyes bounce between the five of us, then land back on mine. I see a steadiness come over her. She's sure of herself. "I want to tell them what happened."

Aurora spends the next few minutes talking to an officer, recounting what happened and showing them her wrist. They take fingerprint measurements to see if they match Brad's.

I don't leave her side the entire time, nor do I let go of her hand. Once she explains what happened, I begin to tell them that's why I did what I did. The cop nods, tilting his hat to me in a universal sign of respect.

They'll take him to the station and run the fingerprints. If they match, he will be expelled from the university immediately. Aurora isn't pressing charges, so he's getting off a lot easier than he should be.

At least he'll be gone from RLU, and no longer around her.

Jasmine, Theo, Finn, and Ash wait for us in the bar, so we head back inside once we finish with the authorities.

We tell them everything that happened with the police.

"Good, serves him right," Jasmine mutters, while the rest nod as they take in the information.

I still haven't let go of her hand, sitting next to her in a booth with her friends and mine. She attempted to let go when we walked in, but I only held on tighter, shooting her a sideways glance that made her cheeks blush.

"Looks like I'll get that quarterback position sooner than I thought." Theo pumps his fist enthusiastically, bringing some humor to the situation.

"You're still a sophomore, don't get ahead of yourself," Finn pesters him, and they both laugh at that.

"Are you okay, Aurora? Do you want anyone to call your dad before he finds out through the police?" Ash asks, fiddling with her braid.

Aurora sits up straighter at the mention of her dad. "Shit," she groans, "Yeah, I should call him."

I let her out of the booth but stop her before she moves.

"You okay? Do you need anything?"

She smiles at me, but it's fleeting. "No, I'm just going to use the office to call my dad and Nate."

"Okay," I say, feeling anything but that at the idea of her telling them by herself.

Jasmine slides out of the booth then.

"I'm coming with you, don't even argue. I want to say hi to Papa Vallacourt," she says, linking her arm with Aurora's, walking them toward the office in the back.

I spend the minutes she's gone worrying, wondering if she's okay. How her dad and brother will react, or if she needs anything. Occasionally, I join the conversation, but I mostly just listen to Theo and Finn chat. Ash joins in at times too.

My leg bounces under the table, and I find myself glancing toward the hallway Aurora and Jasmine left down every few seconds.

"Ronnie boy, talk to me. What are your intentions with AV?" Theo asks, pulling my head toward him. Ronnie boy? Jesus, his nicknames need work.

"To be a good friend to her, to take care of and support her," I answer, not wanting to tell them I like her more than a friend should.

A lazy smile forms on his face, his blue eyes bright. "Good answer."

Finn coughs, muttering "And more." Ash slaps his shoulder, while I kick him under the table.

Theo's smile grows as he looks at Finn, a knowing look on his face. I don't like it. But before they can interrogate me further, Aurora and Jasmine approach the table, her jacket clutched in her hands.

I instantly searched her face to see how she was feeling.

She seems no more upset than she was when she talked to the police, which is good, but not good enough.

I want her to rest and take the time to process everything. It's been a hell of a night, and I can tell she's wiped. Add in what happened yesterday, and I can't even imagine how she's feeling.

"How did it go?" Theo asks.

Jasmine looks at Aurora, a proud look on her face. "Ro's the strongest person I know, and her family is very supportive. She'll be okay."

"Damn right, she is!" Finn cheers, holding his fist out to Aurora, who bumps his with her own. He always does this. When shit goes down, he tries to cheer people up, whereas I go into caretaker mode.

Jasmine slides into the U-shaped booth beside Ash, but Aurora hesitates. I shuffle out of my seat, already knowing what she wants.

"Can you take me home, please?" Aurora asks me because, after the fight, they closed the bar for the night, only serving food and closing early instead. Which means she doesn't need to stay and work. Not that I'd want her to continue to work the rest of her shift anyway.

I don't know why she asked me when she lives with Jasmine, but I'm not complaining.

"Of course," I say, grabbing my jacket off the hook. Aurora bundles up in hers, the long-style coat hitting her bare knees. "Just wait here a few minutes. I'll warm the car up."

I don't miss her appreciative gaze before I turn and head for the door. It makes me smile while I freeze my ass while I walk until I'm close enough for my remote start to work. I head back inside, say goodbye to everyone, and leave with Aurora warm and safe inside my car.

Right where I know she's meant to be.

Chapter Twenty-Three

Aurora

During our car ride to my house, Cam kept glancing over at me, and I could see his hand twitching at his side. As if he wanted to reach out and touch me, but thought better of it.

He held my hand after everything that happened without hesitation. I frowned, but then, it made me freak out internally because I shouldn't be upset by that.

We're just friends, friends who comforted each other in a time of need through physical touch.

"Why did you do that tonight?" I ask as he parks his car in my driveway.

Cameron's brows snap together, and he turns in his seat to fully face me. He looks annoyed. Not with me, but with my words. "Are you honestly asking me that?"

I press my lips together, then say, "Yeah, I am. I know you never wanted—"

Cameron cuts me off, "I'm going to stop you right there. You're right, I never wanted to get violent with anyone. But when I saw bruises on your wrist, none of that shit mattered." He stops, takes a deep breath, then continues, "I'm going to protect you, always. I don't regret it, and I chose to do it. Okay?"

His words wrap themselves around me so tightly it makes my chest ache, in a good way. I never had anyone in my life who wanted to protect me, at least not this way. All I can do is nod, feeling myself overcome with how much I appreciate him.

"How are you feeling?" he asks me, his eyes roaming my features.

I shift in my seat, turning to face him. "I'm okay. I think I'm still processing what happened. It just scared me a bit. But, feeling the support from my friends and family helped."

My dad was furious, along with Nate. They both wanted me to go home to my dad's house, but I insisted I was okay and Jasmine would take care of me. And the truth is that I wanted to stay with Cameron.

He makes me feel good, and I want more of that.

Cameron listens, then takes a moment to think, his jaw twitching. "Why did you try to get in between us, Rory?"

Oh… *that*. I panicked. I didn't like seeing Cameron in a fight, the potential of him getting hurt. I needed it to stop, and I thought I could pull him away somehow.

I'll never forget the look in his eyes, the fear in them. He maneuvered me so swiftly and gently in the midst of his rage, it did things to my heartstrings. Pulled them and crossed them in every which way until my chest felt too tight.

"I…was scared. I didn't like seeing you fight and wanted to stop it."

Cameron shakes his head in disbelief, sucking in a breath. "Rory, you could've been hurt. If you got hit by him, I don't know if I could've stayed in control. I would've fucking lost it."

I could see it. Cam would've gone ballistic if I had been hurt in the process. Hell, everyone would've. Jasmine would probably try to beat his ass too.

"Bu—"

"No, there's no buts, love. You mean too much to me. Please don't ever scare me like that again, okay?" he says, his voice rough and low.

That damn nickname again makes me feel things I don't want to feel but also crave.

It makes me ask him something I probably shouldn't. "Okay. Want to come inside?"

Cameron answers by twisting his keys in the ignition, turning the car off, and opening my door for me before I could think about my suggestion twice.

He follows me up the porch steps and then up to my room, all without asking any questions. I quickly glance around my room, making sure there are no bras or underwear in sight, which there isn't.

Thank god.

Cameron's eyes fly around my room, taking it all in. My walls are a pale pink, and the one above my bed is full of Marvel posters. His eyes linger there for a moment, then move to my bed, with a white headboard and deep green duvet comforter.

He walks over to my white dresser, looking at the pictures attached to the mirror. He stills at the one of me and my mom, his eyes floating between us in the photo, taking in our similarities and differences. While I was taller, my mom was short. Her eyes were green, mine hazel. But her hair was the same dirty blonde as mine.

"She's beautiful," he murmurs.

"Yes, she was," I whisper softly, admiring the photo with him.

I'm on my mom's shoulders at the zoo. I'm smiling down at her while she looks up at me, overloaded with joy. I miss her more than words could ever accurately explain, and I could drown in the grief, but I learned over the years that I have a choice. While some days it's harder to make it, I choose not to let grief weigh me down day in and day out.

It's not what she would want, so to honor her, I live my life to the fullest.

Cameron shifts to my bookshelf, filled with more trophies and awards than actual books. "Are you good at volleyball or something?" he teases, looking at me over his shoulder with a smirk.

"You tell me since you came to my game earlier," I mention, the now familiar feeling of butterflies swarming in my stomach at the memory.

His smirk deepens, those dimples coming out. "You were amazing. I can tell you work hard from the accuracy of your spikes and the power of your serves." With a teasing glint, he adds, "I may even be your number one fan now."

I roll my eyes playfully and tug on his navy blue waffle long sleeve. "Thanks. Now go sit on the edge of my bed."

He raises a brow at me, "And you said I'm the pushy one?"

I can't help but chuckle, the sound bubbling from my lips. "Just go sit down, please, and don't move."

He does as I say, sitting on the edge of my bed while I slip into my bathroom.

I quickly wet a towel with warm water, then found the rubbing alcohol, gauze, and a Band-Aid. When I return, he's in the same spot, staring at the posters above my bed, until he hears me walking towards him.

Cinnamon eyes meet mine, and a whirling sensation runs through me. He is so beautiful, truly. I used to think he was this big, sexy guy, but it's more than that now. His heart and personality are unmatched.

I set the items on the bed beside him, and he finally asks, "Rory, what are you doing?"

"It's my turn to take care of you now, is that okay?" I ask softly, staring at him eye to eye when he's sitting like this.

His large, muscular frame takes up our space, making it hard to ignore how much I'd love to feel him hover over me. His corded arms surrounding me.

I need to stop.

He looks at me for a moment, a bit uncertain, but then he nods. "I've never had someone do that for me."

A rapid, piercing pang hits my chest. I ache for this man who's done nothing but take care of everyone around him, that he doesn't know what it's like to have someone take care of him.

"If I hurt you at all, let me know," I tell him while pouring the alcohol on a gauze pad.

He just nods, his eyes locked onto me and my every movement. I lift the pad to his forehead, right above his right eyebrow, and dab lightly at the small wound.

Cameron doesn't wince or flinch. He just keeps his gaze on me, watching intently with a softness I've only seen when we were at the lake. I dab it a couple more times, wanting to make sure there's no bacteria left.

Taking a step back, I throw out the pads in the garbage. When I return to Cameron with the warm cloth in hand, he widens his legs, letting me step between them to get even closer to him.

I don't overthink it, I just do it. But once I'm in his space, his scent invading my senses, the heat from his body cloaking mine, I realize how bad of an idea it was.

Cameron's breaths seem to rise and fall more rapidly than before, and that only makes my heart race even faster as we stare intensely into each other's eyes.

Ignoring the thoughts of sitting on his lap and tasting his lips, I continue on with my task. Bringing the cloth to his wound, I dab it lightly to clean him up, wiping away the dried blood around the cut. I run my fingers through his hair, pushing back his strands. Cam's breath hitches, and my fingers halt their movement in his hair.

"No. Keep going, please," he breathes out.

I continue running my fingers through his hair softly while I finish. I grab the Band-Aid next when he puts his hand over mine.

"I don't need that."

"Yes, you do," I pout, my bottom lip jutting out.

"Can you massage my head again? That feels really nice," he asks, ignoring my comment and looking at me with pleading eyes.

I learned in that moment that I don't think I could deny him anything because I do just as he asks, returning not only one hand but both to massage his head.

I'll give the guy credit because my boobs, although not large, are nearly spilling out of my shirt, and not once does he look. He keeps his eyes on mine, watching me with pure admiration as I run my fingers over his scalp, eliciting soft sighs from his lips.

A large, warm hand suddenly lands on my thigh, sending a bolt of energy through my body as he gently moves me to sit on his thigh. Our faces are closer now, only a few centimeters apart, so close that I can see the golden specks in his eyes.

My hands are still in his hair, my right one dropping to his cheek, stroking the smooth skin there.

Cameron's eyes shut for a brief moment, and when they open, they're darker. Hungry as they look into mine, then dip to my lips. Does he… does he want to kiss me? Because while I want to, I'm also not sure if I want to make this next step and potentially ruin our friendship. He deserves more, and I'm not sure if I can give it to him.

He leans in. I barely notice, but it's there because I'm hyper-aware of everything between us right now. His chest rises and falls quicker than normal, the heat of his body underneath me, his gaze on my lips, the bob of his throat on his next inhale.

I remain still, unsure if I'll meet him halfway when his hand cups my cheek.

But before I can decide, Jasmine walks in.

"Hey, do you want t—" she starts, then stops as Cameron and I pull apart. Her eyes widen as she takes me in on his lap. She apologizes, "I'm so sorry, I didn't realize you guys were, uhm, yeah, I'm going to go, bye."

That makes Cameron laugh, and I jump off his lap, cutting his laugh short. "Rory, you okay?"

Maybe her interruption was a sign. A sign that we're not meant to take things further than friendship? I don't know because it doesn't explain why I feel so disappointed that I didn't get to feel his lips on mine.

I must be quiet for too long because Cameron's standing up, his hand resting lightly on my shoulder as he turns me to face him. "What did I do wrong?"

"Nothing, nothing at all. I'm just tired from the day," I tell him, feeling like an ass for saying it.

Cameron studies me for a beat, a tight look covering his features. He dips his chin. "I'm sorry. I'll let you rest then."

Why does this hurt so much? Why can't I tell him I wanted him to kiss me? But I also don't know how to deal with the intense feelings he gives me.

"I'll walk you out," I whisper, the words faint and barely there.

The room's energy shifted entirely, and I hate that I can feel an awkwardness between us now.

We silently walk down the stairs with Jasmine tucked away in her room upstairs. The entire time, I think about how hurt he looked by my somewhat rejection or lack of regard for what almost happened.

Cameron was screwed over by his ex, mistrustful of those around him, and closed off to keep his focus on his priorities. And when he decided he wanted to try, I got scared because of how much I liked him.

God, I'm such an idiot.

Cameron and I say goodbye, and I stay in the doorway, watching him walk back to his car. It hits me then that I don't like seeing him walk away. Not like this.

I think of our friendship, about my mom, and how she would love Cameron to pieces. How good he is for me. How good I know he is to me, and how much I want him to be more than just my friend.

It's with a deep breath and a smile that I think, *fuck it.*

"Cam!" I yell, breathless, as I start to jog down my steps.

Cameron's head whips around just as he reaches his door, stopping to look at me with confused eyes.

It's freaking cold. I'm still in my work outfit, so my legs are bare, *and* it's snowing. I only have slippers on, but I couldn't care less. I run to him, needing to close the distance.

Cameron watches me as I run toward him, his expression confused. I jump into his arms, and he catches me with ease.

Hoisted up above him, with my hands resting at the back of his neck, I stare down into my favorite pair of eyes, feeling my breath catch in my throat.

With my heart leading, I lean in and press my lips lightly against his.

And then my world lights up.

The kiss starts gentle, but my hands cup his face, deepening the kiss. My lips move over his, learning how to meld with his full, soft ones. I pull back when I realize he's not kissing me back.

I'm breathless and suddenly feel awkward, so I attempt to slide down his body, only for him to tighten his grip on me. We stay like that for a moment, me above him, wrapped in his arms, our lips nearly touching and our breaths mingling in the space between.

The stillness surrounding us is deafening as I await his move.

Just when I think my world lit up, Cameron presses his lips to mine, exploding it in a kaleidoscope of colors.

Cameron's lips move reverently over mine, kissing me back with a longing I've never felt before. His touch is sweet, yet fierce, as his lips move over mine with determination.

In response, I tug at the hair on the back of his head, which gets Cameron's attention even more, causing him to snap. He holds me up with one arm around the back of my legs while the other comes up to the back of my head, allowing him to take further control.

He kisses me like a man starved, pressing his smooth lips against mine, getting a feel of me just like I did. It's unlike how I've ever kissed anyone before.

Cameron surprises me by changing the tempo, sucking my bottom lip into his mouth, then, with the open access, he delves his tongue inside. I instantly whimper at the invasion, welcoming him into my mouth as he explores it. He uses his tongue so well, knowing exactly how much to use and what to do with it.

Now, I'm imagining it somewhere else.

Wrapping my legs around his waist, he shifts his arm to better support me while our mouths meld into one. His hands come to rest on my ass, squeezing as he claims my mouth in every way possible.

An inkling of desire starts to spread throughout my body, every inch of my skin attuned to him. His mouth on mine, his claiming grip on me, the groans he's stifling resulting in a rumble of his chest.

The kiss is intoxicating, his lips kissing mine with expertise. I know he's not experienced much, but somehow he's a great freaking kisser.

I prod at his mouth with my tongue, and he releases a groan this time, another deep rumble from beyond his taut chest. Unable to control myself, I roll my hips against his, a shiver rolling down my spine at the feeling.

When has kissing ever felt *this* good?

Cameron pulls back, the both of us breathless and panting. "I want to taste more of you," he breathes, licking his lips. I can feel my clit throbbing in my panties. I was already wet from our makeout session, but those simple words opened the floodgates.

I squirm against him. "The feeling is mutual."

Resting his forehead against mine, he sighs. "I wanted to try and take this slow, but I don't know if I can, love. Not after I've got my first taste. I want more."

I run my fingers up and down his back, reveling in how his muscles flex at my touch. "You can have whatever you want," I tell him honestly, knowing I would give it to him.

He mumbles some curse words, then sets me down on my feet, causing me to frown up at him. "You're freezing. Go back inside, Rory."

It's then that I feel just how cold I am. I look down at my legs, seeing how red they are from the chill. Cameron's touch had heated me up on the inside, distracting me from the cold.

I wrap my hand around his, walking backward. I flirtatiously smile at him. "Come back inside with me."

Cameron halts, causing me to nearly slip at the abrupt stop. But of course, he catches me before my ass meets the snow, holding me close to him. "Rory, there's something you should know."

I scrunch my nose at him while playfully narrowing my brows. "You can't be with someone who likes Groot over Rocket?"

That earns me a laugh, and I love the sound coming off his lips. It's deep and raspy. His hand comes up to my face, tucking a stray strand of hair behind my ear. "Funny, but no. I…fuck," he sighs, running his hand through his hair.

"Cam, I'm not going to judge you. What's wrong?" I ask, feeling myself become anxious. What the hell does he need to tell me?

His gaze locks with mine, and his body visibly relaxes after seeing the sincerity in them. "I'm a virgin."

Wait…is he joking? He has to be. This beautiful, sexy, smart, amazing man is a virgin? Not that you can't be those things and be a virgin, but it still shocks me. He did say he took time to himself for his family, but I assumed he'd slept with his cheating ex.

I assumed wrong, and I'm really happy about it, to be honest.

"That's not a problem, Cam. But does it make you uncomfortable that I'm not?" I ask him, wanting to know if this changes anything for him.

I'm the opposite of a virgin, and I don't know how he feels about that. I know it makes me nervous but also excited. The idea that I'll potentially be the one exploring his body with him is thrilling. There's something primal about knowing I can have something no one else can from him.

He shakes his head at me, a sly smile forming on his lips as he stares at me intently. "No, because I'll be the last. You won't care about anyone before me, just like I don't."

The last? That sends my heart into a sprint and my mind into a tailspin. I don't know if we could be forever, only because of my goals, but I'm willing to be what we can be for now. "You talk a big game for a virgin," I tease him, pecking him quickly on the lips, but then I go back in for a deeper one because that wasn't enough.

He nips at my lip, pulling back with a grin. "I want to learn how to please you. Think you can handle me?"

"You're talking to Aurora Vallacourt, bub. I *know* I can."

Cameron scoops me up and carries me back into the house, up the stairs, and into my room, setting me gently on my bed. Anticipation unfurls in my gut, curious as to what he'll do.

He leans down, his body hovering over mine. "Not tonight, though, love. Too much shit has happened. I want to just lay with you. Is that okay?" he asks, his tone gentle yet raspy.

At that moment, I could see his need to just hold and be near me. To be intimate emotionally, despite our teasing minutes prior. While we meant what we said, it doesn't need to happen right now.

Part of me feels relieved because I don't want to rush that. Especially since he's a virgin, I want it to be perfect for him.

"I'd love that," I tell him, leaning on my elbows to take his lips with mine again. I think I have a problem because I can't seem to stop. But I think he has the same one because he kisses me back just as fiercely, taking over each time.

He pulls back, standing up straight and nodding his head toward the bathroom. "Go get ready for bed, Rory. I'll find us a movie to watch."

Minutes later, I've brushed my teeth, washed my face, and changed into my satin pajamas, a lilac set with shorts and a tank top. I always wear it to bed, loving how the silky material feels against my skin. Pants are overrated and roll up during sleep, so I avoid them at all costs.

I step out into my room, placing my dirty clothes into the hamper, when I hear a rough grumble from my bed. My head flits that way, seeing Cameron lying on it, his mouth agape as his eyes rake over my entire body.

I feel myself heat from his perusal, liking how his eyes are on me, taking me in like a meal he wants to devour.

"You have nothing else to wear to bed?" he asks with a pleading tone.

I chuckle at him as I step toward my bed, noticing the ice pack in his hand. "Nope. All I own are silk sets. It's my guilty pleasure, along with lingerie."

His eyes nearly bug out of his head, his fist coming up to his mouth. "Stop talking, please, and put this on," he says, gesturing to the ice pack in his hands.

I smile at him as I sit on the bed next to him. "Are you saying you wouldn't find me sexy in pajama pants and a loose t-shirt?"

He pins me with a look that says *seriously,* then says, "Love, I'd find you sexy in anything. But this silk thing, it does something extra for me."

"Good to know," I wink at him. He rolls his eyes, then gestures for me to fill the space between his open legs. I feel bad

I don't have anything for him to wear that'll fit him, but he seems comfortable enough in his black jeans and long sleeve top.

Crawling into the open space, I turn so that my back is to him, resting against his chest as he wraps his arms around my front, holding me. I melt into him, feeling his heart beat erratically against my back, his body heat seeping into me. His strong and defined arms are holding me tight while also being gentle. It settles me, a feeling of peace overcoming my entire body.

Cameron kisses the side of my head, and I relax into him even more, a soft sigh emitting from my lips. He gently places the ice pack under my wrist and whispers, "You okay?"

"Never been better," I tell him, truth wrapped around every word.

While browsing for a movie to watch, he pauses and asks, "What's on the inside of your foot?"

My heart swells at the mention of my tattoo, as it does every time someone asks. "It's a tattoo for my mom. Her name was Vivian, so it's a V with hyacinths wrapped around the letter because those were her favorite flowers."

Those large arms wrapped around me squeeze a bit while his lips press into my cheek. "I'm proud of you," he whispers into my ear.

"For what?" I ask, my voice choppy with emotion.

"For being you. For being so goddamn strong, confident, and an amazing person overall. It's inspiring, and I'm proud of you. Not because you kick ass at volleyball, but because you add extra light to this world just being who you are."

His words process in my head and land with a thump in my chest. Cameron sees more than the athlete trying to honor her mom, and it scares me because I don't know who he sees. I haven't met that version of me.

I don't say anything, afraid of Cameron being able to see past my exterior even more and peel me back until I'm bare. Although he's already close to that. I pull one of his arms off of me and bring his hand to my lips, where I pepper it in soft kisses.

He kisses the top of my head in response while settling on a movie.

He presses play on the second *Guardians of the Galaxy* movie, and within minutes, I'm drifting off to sleep.

While distorted with near sleep, I faintly hear him whisper, "I've got you, Rory," as he removes the ice pack and adjusts me so I'm snuggled halfway onto his body.

He has me, more than anyone else ever has.

Chapter Twenty-Four

Cameron

Gently, I reach over to the nightstand table, checking the time on my phone. It's 7:21 a.m., and I feel more awake than ever despite not falling asleep until about 1 a.m.

Aurora's snuggled halfway onto my body, her head resting on my chest, her leg draped over me, and an arm over my stomach.

I woke her up at the end of the movie and told her I should go, but with one look at her pleading eyes and her tiny, sleepy voice saying, "Stay," I remained right where I was. Not that I wanted to leave, but I didn't want her to think she didn't have the option to tell me to go.

It's the best sleep I've had in years. I have never felt so relaxed and awakened as peacefully as I do now.

Well, mostly peacefully if I could ignore the morning wood I'm sporting.

Waking up to her body against mine, it's impossible to not react this way. Her tits pressed against my chest, toned thigh over my own, causing her shorts to ride up, making my mouth water at the swell of her ass.

Aurora has an hourglass figure, a narrow waist under the swell of her breasts that aren't too small or too big, not that I'd complain either way, and the curve of her backside is fucking phenomenal.

Needing to drift my thoughts to something that won't make my raging hard-on worse, my eyes flit to her arm draped over my stomach. I can see the forming bruises on her wrist. Fury threatens to boil in my gut at the sight, but I tamp it down as soon as I look at her content face on my chest.

She's safe and happy now. That's all that matters. Never again will I let anyone hurt her.

Aurora stirs against me, a soft moan leaving her lips. The sound does nothing to help my cock straining painfully against my zipper. It *really* doesn't help when she grinds herself against it.

"Cam," she moans, her tone heady from sleep.

I've never liked my name more. Her hips grind against me again, her soft sigh fanning against my chest.

"Please," she whimpers in her sleep, her hips rocking furiously against me.

Jesus Christ, I'm going to come if she doesn't stop.

I pull her body on top of mine, my hands resting on her lower back, stirring her awake, her pretty hazel eyes finally opening. "Morning, beautiful," I whisper, a grunt nearly escaping my throat as I feel her supple body on top of mine.

Why the hell did I think this was a better choice?

A pout forms on her pretty pink lips, her chin resting on my chest. "I was having the best dream."

I run my hands up and down her back, causing her to shift against me, right against my hardened cock. She gapes in surprise, and then a devilish smirk forms on her lips.

"Let me make it real for you," I tell her.

Aurora rubs herself against me in response, and I can feel the damp silk between her thighs.

Fuck. Me.

I sit up, leaning against her headboard, causing her to adjust and straddle my lap.

I lean close to her ear, "Can I touch you?"

"Please," she whines, tugging at the hair at the back of my head. I love how physical she is. Some part of her always moves when I touch her as if she can't get enough. It makes me feel wanted, something I've never felt before.

Pulling back, I kiss her, hard. My lips devour hers, coaxing them open with my tongue. She matches my energy, clashing our tongues together. But before we get carried away, I want to make sure something important is very clear.

With a ragged breath, I pull back, staring at her intently. "Rory, I need you to know something before anything happens."

Aurora raises an eyebrow at me, "I already know you're a virgin. What else is there to know?"

My lips twitch at her words, but I control it, wanting her to know how serious I am. Clearing my throat, I tell her, "I want more than this. I want all of you, okay?"

She blinks at me, staring into my soul, a deep breath leaving her. "W-what are you saying?"

I rest my hands on her hips, drawing lazy circles there and loving how her hips rock against mine at the contact. Stifling a growl, I focus on the words I need to say. "I don't want this to just be a hookup. I want to be yours, all and only yours."

Wide hazel eyes stare back into mine, her chest pumping slowly up and down as her fingers massage the back of my head. "So… you want to date?"

I smile at her, a full one, my dimples pulling in. "Yeah, I do. I know you said you didn't want a boyfriend, but I'm hoping I can change that."

"And you said you didn't want a girlfriend either," she says, her brows pinching together.

Yeah, I need to make this clear for her so there's no miscommunication about what I want. "I also told you that I would if I found someone who was worth it and, love, you surpass that. It's me who doesn't feel worthy of you. But I'm willing to try. Let me, please?"

Her eyes dart between mine, then dip to my lips and back up, a softness grazing her features. "Cam," she whispers, her voice full of emotion. "I don't know if I know how to be anything more, but I want to try. To be enough for you, like you are for me." Her chin tilts down, and she shakes her head.

I bring my hands to her cheeks, gently cupping her face and forcing her to look at me.

"Rory, you already are. Just by being you. You could wait ten years to get physically intimate with me, and I'd happily wait because I don't need that from you. All I need is *you*."

Aurora answers by kissing me, her lips warm and soft on mine. Her hand comes up to my cheek, tilting my head so that she can deepen the kiss, and it does nothing but stoke the fire burning inside of me whenever I'm near her.

She pulls back all too soon, her lips brushing mine as she whispers the words that set us ablaze. "I'm yours, all yours."

I flip her onto her back, hovering over her body, caging her in as I take in how breathtakingly beautiful she is. "All mine?" I ask, kissing her jaw.

"Yours," she breathes, her hands going to my back, digging into the muscles there.

"And me?" I urge, peppering kisses down her neck, earning me a soft whimper.

My cock threatens to explode at the sound.

"Mine," she pants as I nip, then lick a sensitive spot on her neck right below her ear.

"Good answer," I whisper. "Now tell me, what was I doing to you in this dream?"

Part of me is asking because I want to give her exactly what made her moan and rub up against me, and the other half is asking because I am so far out of practice when it comes to intimacy. Other than my hand, who I've become far too intimately acquainted with in the last five years.

I want to ruin her for any other man. I know she finds me attractive, but I don't know how to please her and what she likes. My ex and I messed around a few times. We were both cool with hand stuff, and I would go down on her, but she never returned the favor. Not that she needed to, but not once did she give me a blowjob. And it's not that she had an aversion to it because I caught her on her knees for the captain of the boys' soccer team.

Aurora lights up, her lips turning into a devious grin, as her hands rub up and down my arms. "You were shirtless for one," she tells me, her fingers trailing to the hem of my shirt.

I sit back on my knees, and with one hand, I pull it over my head.

"Oh my god," Aurora pants, eyes wide and dazed with desire. "How the hell…you look like one of those marble god statues."

Her compliment makes me avert my gaze, a boyish grin on my face. I've never been complimented on my body. I've worked hard on it, so it feels good to have it noticed.

Aurora puts her small fingers on my chest, snapping my attention back to her. My muscles flex under her touch, especially as she drags her fingertips down, tracing over every ab and indent.

I shake my head, my hand stilling hers right above my jeans. "If you touch me there, love, this will end far sooner than I want it to."

Pulling her hand from mine, she trails a single finger down my zipper, causing me to bite my lip. She hasn't even touched my cock, and I'm already on the edge. This is not going to go over well.

"Why's that?" she antagonizes me, running her finger farther down, right over my aching cock. Desire pools in my gut, thick and heavy.

"Because it's been too long, and I'm so goddamn attracted to you. Your body is sexier than I can even comprehend, with those plump lips I want to fill and your pretty eyes I want to see rolling in the back of your head as you scream my name." I hover back over Aurora, my body caging hers in as her eyelids hood with lust, teeth pressing into her full bottom lip. I press open-mouthed kisses to her chin, jaw, and neck, stopping above the swell of her breast. "So, if you keep touching me there, I'll finish embarrassingly fast," I bite out, my teeth clamping down, nearly grinding my molars to dust as she still drags her finger up and down.

Aurora sucks in a breath as I yank her satin tank top down, exposing her perky yet full, perfect breasts. I'm tempted to pull her nipple between my lips, my mouth watering at the idea, but I need to know what she wants. "Tell me, Rory, what was I doing to you?"

Her hands come up to squeeze my biceps. "You were everywhere, your lips, your tongue," she says.

"Where exactly?" I ask, licking the top of her breast, earning me a breathy moan. God, her sounds are so fucking hot. I never knew I could be so attracted to that.

I lift my eyes to hers just in time to see a sheen of confidence over her. "You wanted to finally try the ice cream you bought me the other day."

Intrigued, I sit back on my heels and listen to her continue. "There was a trail between my breasts, down to my stomach, on the top of my pussy. You devoured every last drop, and just as you were going to eat *me* next, you woke me up."

With lightning speed, I scramble off the bed, causing Aurora to laugh, the sound echoing off the walls as I run down the stairs. Once in the kitchen, I open the freezer and find the ice cream sitting in front.

Perfect.

I shuffle to the drawer with the cutlery and grab a spoon, thanking whoever is above that Jasmine's not in the living room to see my raging hard-on that's nearly putting a hole through my jeans.

Back in her room, I close and lock the door this time—not wanting to be interrupted for the foreseeable future. Turning around, my eyes hungrily land on Aurora, who's in the same spot I left her. Blonde hair splayed against the pillow, her satin top pulled down, exposing those breasts I never got to fully taste. But what's different is that her hand is between her thighs, under the waistband of her satin shorts.

I kneel over her on the bed, placing the ice cream and spoon beside us, trying my best not to lose it at the sight of her touching herself. I can't even see anything, but just knowing her hand is there threatens to undo me completely. Just as I'm about to ask her what she's doing, she removes her hand and holds it up between us.

Her fingers are glistening, coated in her arousal. I don't think as I lean forward and suck her fingers into my mouth. Aurora gasps in shock at first, followed by a quiet moan. "Hmm, if the ice cream tastes even a fraction of how good you taste, I'll become addicted."

Aurora squirms beneath me. "Cam, take my clothes off. *Now.*"

I don't waste any more time. Aurora arches her back as I peel her tank top over her head, tossing it to the floor, then does the same with her hips as I slide her shorts down her long, slender legs.

My breath leaves my lungs in a whoosh as I take in her body below me, fucking delectable. "I have so many things I want to do with you, but we'll start here," I rasp, picking up the pint and spoon I had previously set aside.

Needy hazel eyes stare into mine as I drag the cold spoon down the valley between her breasts. Her body writhes at the coolness, but not once do her eyes stray from mine as I drag it down her stomach, over her hip bones, and teasingly over the top of her pussy.

Goosebumps erupt over her skin, and the sight makes me grin, knowing I did that to her. Not wanting to tease her too much, I dip the spoon into the ice cream and hold it above her breasts.

She watches me in anticipation as I spread the creaminess over the swell of each breast, then down her core. Aurora's body is warm, causing the ice cream to slowly melt and drip down her body, which means I need to clean it up before we have a huge mess. Not that I mind the cleanup at all.

I lower myself over her, resting on my elbows as my thighs nudge her legs apart. Hovering over her breasts, I lock eyes with her as my tongue languidly laps at her breast. Aurora's eyes close, her fingers finding my hair and tugging at the roots.

Before I get too ahead of myself, I remind her of my lack of expertise and need for guidance. "Eyes on me, love. I need to see that you're enjoying this."

Her hazel eyes fly back open, locked on mine. "I'm soaked," she pants, "Definitely enjoying this, don't stop."

A growl rips through my throat right before I dive down and ravish her. I suck her nipple into my mouth, lavishing her pink bud with my tongue. The ice cream tastes good, but she tastes fucking divine. I switch over to her other breast, sucking and licking the sticky sweetness off of her skin.

I keep going because the look of desire on her face is out of this world. Not to mention the sounds she's making, which will make me come in my fucking pants like a teenager before this is over.

I move my tongue to the spot between her breasts, lapping up the sweet cream that's melted down her core and trailing toward the top of her pussy. I lower myself down her body, sucking up the cream that settled just above her waist.

My mouth is mere inches from her pussy, the bit of ice cream that melted its way here, begging to be licked up. I bring my mouth to her mound, licking and sucking every drop off of her bare skin. Aurora's fingers find my hair, tugging as her knees squeeze into my shoulders.

I slightly lift my head, my voice laced with lust, "The ice cream was good, but it's time for the main course." Then, I settle between her legs, unable to take it slow and tease her inner thighs, and dive right into her pussy. I give her slit a languid stroke with my tongue, and she wasn't lying. She's soaked.

"Cam!" she shrieks, her grip tightening on my hair, only urging me on more.

I part her lips and suck her clit into my mouth, and it's like the first bite into your favorite meal. My eyes roll back as my tongue tingles with her taste, making my mouth water and my body crave more. I want to learn every part of her and uncover all of the different ways I can make her come.

I suddenly pull back and stand up from the bed.

"W-what are you doing?" Aurora whines, gesturing for me to come back to her.

How can she be so goddamn sexy and cute at the same time?

It's with my heart pounding that I tell her the embarrassing truth. "I'm going to come when you come on my tongue, so I'm getting the jeans out of the way."

I undo the button, lower my zipper, and shuffle out of my jeans, leaving me in nothing but my black boxers. She looks lost in a trance as she watches my movements, her eyes latching onto the protruding bulge beneath my boxers.

Before she has time to respond, I'm back between her thighs. Thank god.

I circle my tongue around her clit, not exactly touching it but driving her wild enough that she grips the sheets beside my head. I lower my mouth to her lips and suck and lap up every ounce of wetness there for me. That thought alone edges me even more because I never thought we'd get here. Only hoped and dreamed.

"You like my tongue on your needy pussy, don't you?" I ask, needing to know that she likes this beyond her physical reactions.

A half whimper, half moan fills the room. "It's needy for you," she whines.

Trailing my tongue back up to her clit, I finally give it a stroke with the tip of my tongue, barely putting pressure on it. Aurora squirms, her hips trying to seek more. I rest my forearm across her waist, pinning her to the bed.

Laying my tongue flat, I lap at her clit with different pressures, switching them up in no particular pattern to see what sets her off. Aurora's hips move wildly when I rapidly alternate from a light to a deep pressure. She likes this, a lot, evident by how she's holding my head and grinding herself against my lips.

So fucking hot.

I lift up, then lay on my back. "Get on top, love. Take me for a ride."

Aurora doesn't need to be told twice. She scrambles and adjusts herself so that her knees are right beside my head and lowers her pussy just above my lips. She's dripping down into my mouth before I've even touched her. I savor it before gripping her hips and burying my face in her. My tongue and lips devour her, eating her like she's the last meal I'll ever taste.

"Cam!" she moans with unbridled lust in her voice as she rocks herself back and forth over me.

I lift her up a bit. "You taste so fucking good."

Aurora whimpers in response, her thighs coated in her desire, and I sink her back down, lavishing up every last bit.

I bring my hand up and lift her a bit to insert two fingers inside her wet heat. Christ, fucking her is going to be insane. She feels amazing, unexplainable.

Her hips buck at that, grinding against them as her body seeks friction. "Cam…I'm going to come," she pants.

"Soak my face. I want it all over me," I rasp as I free my erection with my other hand, the pressuring swelling. I know I won't be able to rein it in when she comes on my face.

Her cry of pleasure urges me on as I pump her slowly at first, matching the stroke of my tongue against her clit. She rides me even faster now, and I pump her accordingly, flicking my tongue at her bud.

I feel her tighten around my fingers, and I know she's right there at the edge.

"Cam! Holy fu—" she starts, then breaks off into a piercing cry as my name tumbles over and over from her lips from her orgasm.

It sets off my own as a tingle of pleasure rushes down my spine to my balls, and I come all over my stomach. I hold her to me, kissing, sucking, and licking her through her orgasm, watching her climb higher and higher in bliss.

It's fucking beautiful.

She eventually stills, the sound of her breathless pants signaling that she's done. Aurora swings a leg over my head, sitting on the bed as I do the same.

Aurora eyes my stomach, eyes wide. "Did you come just from eating—"

It's with no shame that I say, "Yeah, I did. That was hot."

A devilish smile forms on her lips. "You have no idea how sexy that is, Cam. It makes me wish you had somewhere to put your cum other than on your stomach."

Holy fuck, it seems impossible, but I suddenly harden again. Rearing and ready to go.

Aurora shuffles off the bed, sinking to her knees on the floor in front of me and tugging my boxers to my ankles, but I put a hand on her shoulder to stop her from going further.

"You don't have to do that," I grit, not wanting her to feel obligated despite my cock jutting upward, loving the idea of finally filling those plump lips.

Aurora reaches out, wrapping a firm grip around my base, sending a burst of heat through my body at the contact. "Oh, but I want to. You have a perfect cock, Cameron. Long and thick. Tell me I can put it in my mouth, please," she pleads, peering up at me through her naturally long black lashes.

My eyes roll to the back of my head. Her words alone are fucking with me. "Love, I've been thinking about those lips wrapped around me for so long that I'll probably blow quickly. Add in that I've never gotten one before, and I stand no chance."

Aurora's eyebrows narrow at that, "How…you know what? I don't even want to know cause it'll piss me off. Is that a yes, then?"

The words tumble out of me before I can think twice. "Yes."

Aurora wastes no time. Leaning forward, she presses a kiss to the tip, licking the pre-cum on the slit. With her pretty eyes on mine, she wraps her lips around the head, sucking then releasing as she licks the tip.

The feel of her mouth around me sends shockwaves of pleasure throughout my body. I grit down on my jaw to avoid coming right then and there. The only thing that keeps me from doing so is that I don't want this to end. Her mouth feels like heaven, and I don't want it to leave yet.

Her plump lips wrap around me once again, and the image is one I'm going to remember forever. Aurora on her knees, naked, her fucking perfect lips wrapped around my cock.

She attempts to put me farther down her throat, but as she said, I'm a bit large, so she can't fit me all the way down, but she makes up for it by stroking the base up and down in time with the bob of her mouth.

Picking up her pace, she bobs up and down on my cock, sucking and slurping. Flicking her tongue down the underside of my cock, and massaging my balls simultaneously is a combination I never knew I needed.

"Fucking hell, love," I grunt, feeling the precipe of my orgasm building in the base of my spine.

Aurora leans back, dipping her fingers to her pussy, a soft sigh emitting from her lips at the contact. I watch her, enraptured.

She brings her fingers back up, much like earlier. "See what sucking your cock does to me, Cam? I love it."

If her words didn't already push me closer to the edge, she rubs her arousal down the length of my cock and tastes herself as her tongue licks me top to bottom.

That does me in.

The pleasure spikes in my spine, my balls tightening as I hit my orgasm, my vision darkening, and everything around me fading. The only thing I can feel is the pleasure from her lips wrapped around me as she continues to suck me through the high.

I thought she might pull out, considering I didn't warn her, but as I started to release myself inside her mouth, I felt her hum in approval, the vibration sending more waves of pleasure through my body.

Once I come back to my senses, I pull her up and onto my lap, where our lips meet in a searing kiss. Our mouths tangle at first, full of heat and desire, then slowly turn soft and sweet. Arms wrapped tightly around one another, we bask in the bliss and silence for a beat as our foreheads rest on each other's.

Running a hand down her bare back, I whisper into her hair, "You okay? Was I okay?"

Aurora tightens her grip on me, a light chuckle leaving her lips. "You were amazing, Cameron. I've never had an orgasm like that. I've never been better."

I kiss her nose, then her eyelids. "Good." I don't question if she's lying to spare my feelings because if there's anything I know about my pretty girl, it's that she's honest.

"And me? Do tell," she beams, all too proud of the job she knows damn well she did well at.

"You made me come twice within ten minutes. I think that says it all."

Her cheeks turn a shade of red I have yet to see, and suddenly, she's nestling her head in the crook of my neck. "Why are you getting shy with me now?" I ask, running a hand through her hair.

Lips brushing against my neck, she whispers, "Because nothing's ever felt like this. Imagine what it'll feel like when we actually have sex. Even if we don't for a while, it still scares me how much I feel for you."

I know the feeling. It's consuming and overpowering. Everything becomes heightened when I'm with her. Every seemingly minuscule word, touch, or smile somehow etches itself into my skin, making me feel it tenfold.

"It's intense and scary, I get it. But, you have me, Rory. I'm not going anywhere, and we'll figure it out together," I reassure her, bringing her knuckles to my mouth and planting feather-light kisses on each one.

"Even when our personal lives get busy? Me with volleyball, you with your competition for that position?"

"Even then, we'll make it work," I reassure her.

"Promise me? Promise me that no matter what happens, we won't lose sight of us, nor our dreams," her voice is small but determined as she lifts her head off my chest, staring at me with so much vulnerability it makes my heart clench. I know how much it took her to do this, to put aside her fear and try for us.

"I promise you, Rory. I don't break my promises. We're going to make ourselves proud and do it together," I say with utter confidence, knowing she's exactly where I'm meant to be.

Chapter Twenty-Five

Aurora

Holy. Fucking. Shit.

I doodled in my journal shortly after Cameron left my house this morning, using bubble letters, doodling hearts, and smiley faces around it like a middle schooler. It wasn't a beautiful sketch by any means, but that's what his tongue did to my brain.

Wrecked it. Ruined me for good.

Shortly after the first round this morning, we both got into my shower with the intent to get clean, but Cam ended up going down on me, *again.* I think he is one of those guys who not only enjoys it for my pleasure but also his own.

I went down on him again, too, loving that I'm the only one who has brought him to release with their mouth. I think we might be addicted. I don't remember ever feeling this insatiable with any of my previous partners.

Once we were clean, Cam made me breakfast, ordering me to stay put in bed since I had a game later. I told him it was unnecessary, but I think he just likes taking care of me. Because little did he know, I had the energy to fuck him for hours on end, but I know we have to take it slow.

We ate our breakfast in bed, which consisted of a veggie omelet and toast while watching an episode of a Marvel show. It was oddly peaceful, not awkward or anything like I imagined it would be like.

I never thought I'd say this, but I have a boyfriend now. It makes me nervous, but I can't let my fear determine how I live my life. Not when the fear of not having him is worse than anything else. Except for one thing, of course—not making Team USA.

I always thought I never dated because I worried it would shift my focus, which is partly true, along with not meeting anyone who caught my attention for more than just sex. But I think it's mainly because nobody is *him*.

Maybe I was waiting for him this entire time. My one and only exception.

And I'm starting to think that not dating Cameron would derail my focus more than dating him would. The constant what if is why I gave in. Cameron will make sure I keep up with my life, and knowing how important it is to me, he will make it important to him, too. And I'll do the same for him.

While I work on myself, he can work on himself. It's the perfect solution.

My phone rings through my car's Bluetooth on my way to the arena, my dad's name on the screen.

"Hey, Dad, what's up?" I ask cheerily. My mood is so high I don't think anything could ruin it.

His deep tone booms through the speakers, "Heya, Cupcake. I wanted to check in and see how you were doing."

I shrug my shoulders as if he can see. "I'm good, Dad, I promise. I have really great family and friends. It happened, and I can't change it, so no point dwelling on how messed up it was."

"I swear if I ever see that asshat, I'm going to punch him myself," he grumbles.

"And then lose your position as the dean?" I counter.

"Precisely. No one messes with a Vallacourt, especially not my Cupcake."

I love my dad. He is protective and overbearing at times, but he cares. "I know, Dad, but everything's okay. Better than okay, really." I smile, thinking of waking up to Cameron in my bed.

"Oh, is that true? Would it happen to have anything to do with the man who fought in your honor last night?" he asks, stealing the breath from my lungs. *How the hell does he know about that?* "Before you ask, I have eyes and ears everywhere."

"Dad, please don't expel him or anything. He's the sweetest guy, and he's so good to me—" My ramble is cut off short by my dad's chuckle.

"Bring him by the house sometime, Cupcake. Any man who defends my daughter is worthy of coming into our home. And he's not being expelled. Hell, if I could give him the Dean's Medal of Honor for the act, I would."

His comment means more to me than he thinks because I know how touchy my dad is about bringing people to the place where our mom lived. We don't invite just anyone over.

"Ha ha, very funny, Dad. See you at the game in a few hours?"

My dad sighs, and I know I won't like what he has to say next. "I'm sorry, hunny, but we have a faculty dinner tonight with all of the deans from the Midwest. You know I'd be there if I could. Call me after and tell me everything?"

"Deal, drive safe. I love you!" I tell him.

While a bit disappointed, I know he only misses a game when he absolutely has to. Which isn't often. Even at my away games, I always spot him in the crowd. Our away games don't start until after the holiday break. There is some weird conflict with the scheduling this year, but I'm not complaining.

"I love you more, Cupcake. Vallacourt owns the court!" he cheers, his signature chant just before disconnecting the call as I put my car into park in the athlete's lot.

It's the first time in a while I've had no one come to watch me play, not that I need anyone to, but having a familiar face in the crowd is nice. Nate's still gone for the weekend, so he won't be here, but he did ask Craig to switch my shifts, so I will be working Monday night instead of tonight, which is nice.

Theo won't be there either since they have an away game tonight. And Cam has a meeting with the network he's applying for, so I doubt he'll be able to make it.

Despite not being able to have anyone physically here with me, I know my mom always is, each and every step.

"Soooo," Jasmine purrs, sitting on the bench next to me in the locker room.

Pulling my socks on, I play it cool. "Sooooo?"

Jasmine nudges me in the ribs, "Don't be funny with me. I want details, *now.*"

"What are you talking about?" I ask, eyebrows perched as I shove my feet into my sneakers.

Looking around the room to make sure no one can hear, she lowers her voice. "I'm talking about hearing you scream Cameron's name about a hundred times this morning."

I pretended to be surprised, mouth agape and eyes wild, but truthfully, I knew I was loud and that this conversation was bound to happen. "Oh yeah, that," I muse, replaying the dirty details in my mind.

"What exactly is *that*?" she hisses. "What happened after I ambushed your near kiss?"

"It was tense because I tried to sweep it under the rug… because I was scared," I admit, knowing that Jasmine won't judge me.

She nods her head in understanding, just like I thought she would. So I continued, "I felt awful about it, and watching him walk away from me looking so withdrawn pained me. I realized then that I was more afraid of missing out on us than keeping it safe by just being friends. So, I ran down the steps and kissed him. At first, he was stunned, I think, because he didn't kiss me back, but when he did…holy hell, Minnie. I've never felt anything like it."

Jasmine squeals, drawing the attention of the other girls on the team, but they don't do anything other than glance our way. "Oh my goodness, I knew it!" she whisper-screams, throwing a fist up in victory. "That is so cute, but it doesn't explain the screaming. Keep going," she motions for me to speed up.

I love the idea of love, whereas Jasmine is partial. She just doesn't care for it, at least not until she meets the one. Then, I'll bet my spot on the Olympic team that she'll be a puddle of mush. So, it doesn't surprise me that she wants more of the hedy details than the sweet ones.

"Let's just say I woke up this morning to be greeted by his third leg," I whisper.

Jasmine rears back. "Stop it! He's huge, isn't he? Big man like that, I knew it."

I blush at the memory of it in my mouth only a few hours ago. "Yeah, he is. Biggest I've ever had. I'm kind of nervous to have sex one day…"

She blinks once, then twice. "Wait, you guys didn't even...?"

I shake my head, standing, and she follows suit. "No," I whisper, looking around to see that most of the girls have gone out for warm-ups. "He's a virgin, so all we did this morning was go down on each other. But I don't mean that lightly. It was mind-blowing, Minnie."

Jasmine's mouth drops. "Wow," she breathes, then a sly grin forms on her lips. "So when are you popping his cherry?"

I shove her forward, laughing at her comment as we approach the court. We're playing the California Bobcats, a top 4 contender in our division. It makes me a bit nervous like any game does, but I'm good at blocking it out to focus on what I need to do.

At least that's what I thought, but the first set was over, and we lost 25-17. We still have two more sets to play and potentially win the game, but it still pisses me off. I don't like to lose, especially not to a team that I know we could beat if we played better than we are now.

Volleyball is a team sport, so there's not much a singular person can do. I'm having an off-game, too, and I'm not sure why. Maybe I miss my dad's foam finger, making a ruckus in the crowd? Maybe it's the stress from last night? I have no freaking clue.

Coach Tilly gives us a pep talk after the first set that riles us up, and soon enough, we come out on top of the second set. Our game is still off though, not doing our best, which causes us to be neck and neck in the third set. It's 24-23 for us, and if I get this serve over, it's a potential game point because my serves are the hardest to return.

I'm waiting in the server's corner for the whistle while taking long, deep breaths to center myself. Just as I gather my focus, I feel a gaze burning into my side. I look over to the open archway that connects the gym to the hallway, and there he is. *My bub.*

He smiles proudly at me, his dimples pulling in, and the sight makes me smile just as big. My entire body lights up, knowing that he came, that he's here for me. No one else came, but *he* did.

The ref blows the whistle, indicating it's game time. I bounce the ball four times, then throw it up and smash it over the net. It's a bullet, hitting the ground on the Bobcat's side before anyone can react. Game over.

Coach Tilly ingrained in our brains not to overreact during regular season wins because it shows bad sportsmanship, so we all clap hands with barely contained excitement, then do the same with the Bobcats. It may not have been a playoff win, but it still feels sweet to have pulled it off since we weren't playing our best.

But when I see Cam leaning against the wall, his broad frame eating up the space he's in, I forget my coach's demands and run straight to him.

Cam pushes off the wall and scoops me up with one arm, yup, *one*, and I wrap my legs around his waist.

"You made it," I huff into his shoulder as he squeezes me tightly to him.

"It started snowing, so I took the meeting on the go to come pick you up, and luckily enough, I got to see you play."

My head rears back at that as my heart pitter-patters in my chest. He knew my stance with driving in the snow and came to pick me up so that I wouldn't be scared driving home. An unknown emotion sweeps through my body so violently that it causes me to clutch him even tighter, digging my nose into his neck and pressing a light kiss there.

"You didn't have to do that. I hope you didn't get in trouble," my voice comes out muffled since my head is still buried in his neck.

His free hand comes up to my ponytail, softly tugging the scrunchie until my hair is set free. He runs his hand through the ends. "I won't. They're very kind and would understand if I told them."

I pull back from my safe place and look into cinnamon eyes, "Told them what?"

"That I want to keep the girl I really, *really*, like safe, which meant coming to pick her up from her game," he replies swiftly, his eyes tracing my lips.

I am unable to hold back any longer, especially after that comment, so I lean in and press my lips to his. A rush of relief washes through me unexpectedly, and I feel my entire body relax in his embrace as his lips work mine so perfectly.

"Vallacourt, locker room for review, now!" Coach Tilly yells, not rudely, but she's a woman with a schedule and places to be, so she doesn't have time to watch me scale and kiss my boyfriend. Understandable.

Reluctantly, Cameron sets me down, his lower arm around the small of my back. "I'll go start the car, then wait for you in the hallway."

I smile at him, then turn and head to the locker rooms.

Our debrief is different tonight. Coach Tilly is more thorough since we just had our first loss of the season, even if it was just one set. But what she was really pissed off about was our team's attitude, claiming that we let one loss mess us up for the rest of the sets.

Playing a competitive sport at this level requires us to have the mental strength to not let that get to us and persevere to keep playing like we normally do. But we're also human, and nights like tonight happen.

Once it's over, I quickly shower and dress, not wanting to make Cameron wait too long for me.

"You look like you're in a rush to get somewhere," Jasmine points out as I quickly step into my sweatpants.

"Cameron's waiting for me," I tell her, pulling my long sleeve RLU shirt over my head.

"Yeah, I think everyone saw you claim him after the game. Are you guys official?" she asks, a sparkle in her mocha eyes.

It's with excitement and a bit of nerves that I say "Yes."

Jasmine stops, then suddenly squeezes her nearly bare body around mine. "Oh, my Ro! I am so proud of you and so excited for you both."

Patting her on the back, I laugh. "Thanks, Minnie. Now let me go so I can go see him." I grab my jacket, slide into it, and sling my bag over my shoulder when I stop and ask. "Do you need a ride home? Cam mentioned that it's snowing."

"No, I can drive my car, Ro. I'll text you when I get home, though, okay?"

I pull her for another quick hug, "Okay, drive safe. Love you."

She smiles at me, "I love you too, but not in the way that Cameron does."

I roll my eyes at that, feigning annoyance, when in reality, her words hit me like a tornado of emotions. Fear, excitement, lust, joy, and something unnamed.

But I don't give myself the time to explore it further because I have someone waiting for me, and it feels damn good.

Chapter Twenty-Six

Cameron

Aurora and I grabbed Chipotle after her game because, knowing my pretty girl like I do, she needed food after that.

Once she was fed and satisfied, I took her back home, where I've been idling in the driveway for half an hour now because we can't seem to stop talking. I would shut the car off and offer to go inside, but I don't want to bombard her. It's been a while since I've dated, and I don't want to come off as needy, but hell if I don't want to spend every second with her.

"You're my first boyfriend, you know that, right?"

I shake my head, bringing the back of her hand to my lips and pressing a small kiss there. "I'm honored."

Aurora's pretty eyes soften, then turn darker. Perfect plump lips part, her tongue darting out to lick them. I nearly harden at the sight.

"Kiss me," she whispers.

"You don't have to ask, love," I tell her just as quietly.

She smirks. "I wasn't asking."

It is impossible to deny her anything, especially when it's something I want to give her. Leaning over the console, I wrap my hand around the back of her neck while the other rests on her thigh, squeezing. Aurora inhales sharply just before my lips connect with hers, a warmth spreading throughout my body at the contact.

Kissing her feels like coming alive. Every nerve ending in my body seems to be in tune with her, lighting up. Our lips meld perfectly together, kissing slowly and sensually. It's not rushed, with no clashing teeth or nipped lips.

It's perfect.

Aurora's hands cup my face, pulling me in even more, deepening the kiss. Desire starts to flow to my cock, thrumming throughout my blood, loud and clear. I want her so badly, but I also don't want her to think we have to mess around whenever we're together. I'm so far out of the game when it comes to dating that I have no idea what to expect or what *she* expects.

A flash of headlights catches our attention, pulling our mouths away from one another as Jasmine pulls up beside us in the driveway. That's when I noticed the fogged-up window.

Aurora giggles when she sees it, a bashful smile on her face.

"I guess it's time for me to go," she sighs, looking unsure.

I want to ask why she seems that way, but I don't press. "Text me when you're cozied up in bed?"

"I will. Thanks for picking me up and everything else." She smiles, knowing it drives me nuts how much she says thank you.

Leaning over the console, she kisses me once more before getting out of the car, leaving me flustered and wanting more.

Hours later, I can't fucking sleep. Sleep has always been tricky for me because I tend to worry so much about my mom and Lexa that it makes it hard for my brain to shut off.

But, last night, it was the easiest it's ever been. I don't remember the last time I fell asleep so quickly and woke up *actually* feeling refreshed.

I've been working on the game for a few hours, knowing that I need to make some changes to my schedule.

This job is still important to me, but so is Aurora, and I'll do anything it takes to keep her and get the job. It's a balancing act, but I'm confident I can do it because when you want something bad enough, nothing will stand in your way.

My phone suddenly buzzes on my nightstand, and I wonder who it is because, last I checked, it was just past midnight.

I pick up my phone and see Rory's name.

Rory

I can't sleep.

Me

Same, how can I help?

Rory

By coming over and cuddling me. I slept so peacefully last night in your arms.

Rory

Oh gosh, is that clingy???

Rory

You know what, I'm not even sorry about it. But please don't actually come over, it's late, I'd feel bad.

I smile at her texts, seeing her get flustered is cute. It also soothes me that she feels the same way about sleeping together because I worried I was in too deep already. But it sounds like she just might be too.

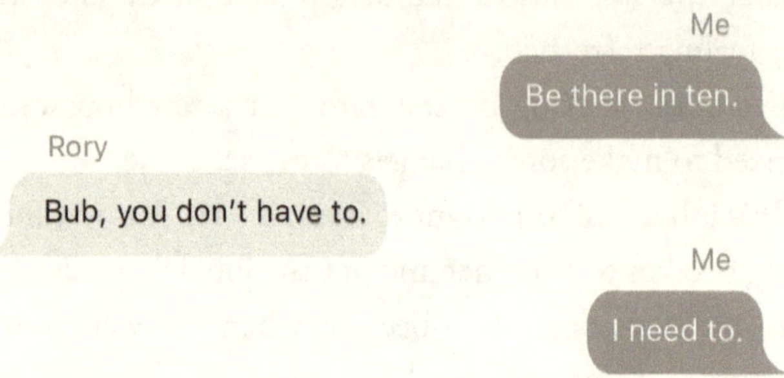

It takes me exactly ten minutes to get to her place, where I enter the code, lock up, and head straight to her room. I didn't bother changing out of my gray sweats and black T-shirt, which will be more comfortable than last night's attire.

I open the door to her room and see my girl tucked under the covers, her tired eyes on me. A lazy smile forms on her lips. "Hi," she coos.

"Hi, love. I brought you something," I say, my hands behind my back holding the blanket she loved from my house.

She sits up instantly, no longer looking tired. "What is it?"

I bring the blanket in front of me, holding it out to her as I stop at the side of the bed. "It helped you sleep that day at my house, so I figured it might help you now."

Aurora takes the fuzzy blanket in her hands, holding it against her cheek. "How are you so perfect? Is there a manual you're reading on how to be the best boyfriend?"

Sitting on the bed beside her, I smile shyly. "The best?"

"Yeah, you're crushing it. Although I think I just need you to sleep, I'm sure this will help, too."

I settle into the bed and motion for her to scoot in closer. "Come here," I whisper.

Aurora wraps the blanket around her shoulders, then adjusts her body so that her back is pressed up against my front as my arm wraps around her waist, holding her. I instantly feel more relaxed, my body suddenly heavy with the need to sleep when I've rolled around for hours earlier.

"Mmm, it smells like you," she muses.

"Keep it," I say, kissing the top of her hair.

"I'd rather keep you," she half yawns, her body snuggling closer to mine. Her body fits so perfectly with mine.

"Sleep, love. I'm here," I tell her, pressing my lips to her bare shoulder.

"I won't be able to if you keep doing that," she wiggles against me, and I harden because it's impossible not to when her body is pressed against me.

"Neither will I if you keep doing that," I groan.

"Maybe we should skip sleep," she yawns again.

"Not tonight, Rory, you're exhausted. We have all day tomorrow."

"Fine," she huffs. "Night, bub."

"Night, love."

Chapter Twenty-Seven

Aurora

The sun peeking through my blinds tells me it's already past 8 a.m., the latest I've slept in in a long time.

I'm used to being up early to work out, and even on a Sunday like today, I usually still wake up early. But not today, and I think my glorious sleep has everything to do with the beautiful man whom my body is half-sprawled on top of.

I tilt my chin up to look at him, and my breath ceases in my lungs. He's so handsome, with his sharp jaw, long eyelashes, and full lips. Asleep, he looks so content and serene that I wish I could take a picture of it because that's exactly how he makes me feel.

I'm not as good with words as he is, but I like to think I show him with my actions. Physical touch and acts of service are my kind of love language.

And right now, I really want to give him a certain service with my mouth. His morning erection is pressed against my thigh that's draped over his hips. I've seen my fair share of cocks, and let me just say that he has the most perfect cock I've ever seen. It's thick, a light dusting of hair at the base, and his length… Fuck, it'll fill me so well. I'm honestly a little scared, but it's the kind of pain I'll delight in.

A conversation from the night before plays in my mind, where we talked about our fantasies. I told him how outdoor activities were mine, while Cam said that he wanted to wake up with my mouth wrapped around him.

I can make that fantasy come true. I'm more than happy, too, to be honest.

Sliding off his body, I carefully maneuver myself so that my head is in line with his cock, trying not to wake him and ruin the surprise. I daintily slip my fingers under the waistband of his sweats when a gasp nearly makes it past my lips. He's not wearing boxers, and for some reason, that turns me on even more.

I gently pull them down the best I can. Since Cameron's lying on his back, it's not much, but it's enough that the top of his cock peeks out.

I adjust myself to lean over his body, then wrap my hand around the base and give him a quick, hard pump.

Cameron stirs but doesn't awaken, which causes a smile to cross my lips. Knowing I'll be fulfilling his fantasy and putting his cock in my mouth soon gives me near chills, a pool of wetness forming between my thighs.

Leaning my head down, I lick the underside of his length, starting at the bottom to the top, where I swirl my tongue around the tip, lapping up the pre-cum already there. Knowing I don't have much time before he wakes up, I quickly wrap my lips around him, hollow my cheeks, and suck him as far as I can go.

Tears prick my eyes because he's too much. I love it, but I can't take him as far as I would like, which would be all of it.

A groan rumbles from Cameron's chest, adding to the sound of me slurping on his cock, and it only heightens my arousal. I've always been easily turned on by sounds during sex.

Cameron suddenly jolts, causing his cock to hit the back of my throat so roughly that I gag but keep going.

"Rory?" Cam croaks, his voice like gravel.

I lift my head, my lips hovering over his tip. "Mmm, morning, bub," I purr, a smile on my lips. I hold his gaze just as I take him in my mouth again.

His eyes roll into the back of his head as his jaw tightens. I hollow my cheeks, sucking as I bring my mouth up his length.

Cameron's hands reach out and push my hair back, one hand wrapping around the strands so that he can watch me instead of my hair being in the way. "That's my girl," he praises, the words causing me to hum against his length, the vibration adding to his pleasure is evident in the way pre-cum drips from his tip now.

"You should see how you look right now," he groans, "I've never seen anything more beautiful than how you look with my cock in your mouth. So. Fucking. Perfect."

I up my efforts at his words, noting how they increased my arousal as my clit throbs in response. With my eyes locked on his, I release him for a second, watching his eyes darken at the loss of my mouth, then quickly take him in deep until I gag.

This time, he tugs on my hair, releasing me from him. I'm panting, and there's a sheen of sweat covering my body because I'm so turned on I think I could come just from sucking him off.

"Get up here and let me eat that pretty pussy," he coaxes, gentle yet demanding. I don't hesitate, knowing that if he's telling me he wants to, he does. I quickly remove my satin red shorts, then shift my body so he can have his way with me.

Except I've never done this before, and I didn't realize how hard it would be for me to continue sucking him off when his talented tongue starts to lap at the wetness between my thighs. How am I supposed to focus on anything but how his tongue drives me wild? I've never met a man so good at using his tongue and enjoying using it. It's so sexy.

I relent on sucking him when his tongue points, entering in and out of me rapidly.

"Cameron, I, ahhh," I mumble, lust taking over my voice so that I barely recognize the sounds I just made.

"Fucking love it when you moan my name," he groans, returning his tongue to my pussy hungrily, lapping at my clit with unexpected speeds and pressures, leaving me incapacitated as my orgasm hits me unexpectedly.

A rush of pleasure makes my vision go hazy. All of my senses seem to turn off except for the feel of his tongue against me, still working me through my high.

I somehow come back to my senses, remembering that he needs his release too. If the darkening tip didn't tell me that already, the rough pants from him would. I bring my hand to his balls, massaging them in my palm as I deep throat him, farther than I ever have due to the angle.

It pushes him over the edge, his muscles tightening under my body at first, then jolting upward as he releases himself into my mouth. The salty mix isn't usually my favorite, but with Cam, I like it. I lap him up until he's done releasing every last drop and I stop once he does just that.

Rolling off his body, I smile with my eyes closed, feeling sated and so damn happy.

A large, warm body is suddenly hovering over mine, and I open one eye to see Cameron looking at me with the same goofy smile. "You're so beautiful. It really messes with my head at times."

"I can say the same about you." I smile, wrapping my hands around his neck and pulling him to me for a kiss. It lights me up, his soft lips against mine.

"Go shower. We're going on a date today," he says, switching gears and throwing me off balance as he lifts off of me and stands up.

"A date?" I ask, sitting cross-legged on my bed. "You do know that the last date I went on was the movie date fiasco I told you about, right?"

"Precisely. Time to change your history with dates, and I want to take you somewhere."

I knew this was part of being with Cam, but it still makes me nervous. Because what if I'm bad at it?

"I just want to apologize in advance if I don't do well on this date," I sigh, feeling unsure of myself, which isn't something I feel often.

Cameron's lips tilt up to the right in a crooked grin. "You're acting like this date is a game. It's not a performance, love. Just be yourself, the one I like very much, and it'll be great. Trust me?"

It's with a deep breath that I know, down to the tips of my toes, that I trust this man. "I do."

He walks back over to the bed, lifting me into his arms, my legs wrapping around his waist. "Good. Now, I'm going to bury my tongue between your thighs one more time. Then, we'll shower and stop by my place to grab clean clothes. That sounds good?"

Wrapping my legs tighter around his waist as he walks us to my bathroom, I whisper playfully in his ear, "You know I can feed you if you're actually hungry?"

Cameron's hands squeeze my ass, my hips rolling into him. "I prefer you."

I have an idea of where we're going, having gone there as a kid, and I'm so excited.

We spent about forty minutes driving down a back road lined with evergreen pine trees on either side, topped with snow. Christmas is in two weeks, and the passing scene puts me in the Christmas mood.

That will only increase once we get to Snow Pine Resort. It's a ski lodge village, and it remains Christmaslike year-round. There are tons of outdoor activities like tubing, skiing, and snowboarding. Along with a ride that takes you down the hills, whipping around snow bushes for those who don't ski or snowboard but want to go down the slopes.

The village has multiple shops, restaurants, and pubs, all with the same exterior made up of wood and bricks to give it a cottage feel. In the center of the village, there's a large open seating area filled with propane fires and heaters, as well as a DJ booth where music is played throughout the day.

Many students from local universities flock here during the break, spending the day on the slopes, then partying it up in the center in-between hills, and continuing in the pubs at night. I only know this because of my co-worker Craig, who's an avid snowboarder. I've always preferred tubing, not wanting to risk breaking a leg and ruining my volleyball career.

Cameron shifts the car into park, and I reach out, gripping his forearm to stop him before he gets out.

His eyebrows narrow a fraction, a hint of concern on his face. "What's wrong? Is this not a good place for a date?"

My sweet bub, always so caring about how others feel. "This place is perfect. I'm really excited. I just wanted to give you something before we go."

His eyebrow raises, shifting to confusion. "You didn't have to get me anything."

I playfully roll my eyes at him, reaching into my tote bag for the Oreos I stashed in here before we left.

"Since you never got that Oreo," I tease, putting the package in his lap.

His lips tug up to the right, trying to fight a smile and failing. "I don't know if I should be annoyed that you remembered my embarrassing story, or happy that you did. This is perfect, thank you." He leans over the console, kissing me but pulling back before we get carried away.

We walk hand in hand toward the village when I ask, "What's the plan?" I'm a bit nervous because I don't want to engage in any activities that could put me at risk for an injury.

Cameron squeezes my hand in his, a reassurance that he has me without having to say it. "I was thinking we could go tubing, get some food, and maybe a walk through the lights later. I wouldn't put you at risk of harm, love."

I know he wouldn't. To the very depth of my core, I know Cameron will never hurt me, at least not physically. I smile wide, a blush creeping over my cheeks, and we walk up to the vendor selling tubing tickets. Soon enough, we're heading toward the slopes.

I've been tubing before, and I will say these slopes are the best. They have simple ones, a nice straight path that's not too steep, but they also have wilder ones, where they curve with steeper paths, meaning you go faster as you twist down the slope. Not only is it fun, it's safe, as long as you don't fall off.

I bend, reaching to grab the handle of the navy tube and carry it over to the clip and ride, where a belt runs up to the top of the hill, much like a ski lift, except you hook your tube up to it, and sit while it carries you to the top.

Cameron follows suit, sitting in his tube and mouthing how he's going to beat me.

In his dreams.

The first time, we went down the racing hill meant for two people to race one another. It's a simple slope, straight, not too steep, but not too flat either, giving the tubers some speed as they go down.

Much to my avail, I lost—the first, the second, *and* the third race.

I didn't want to do a fourth one because my competitive side could not handle another loss. With a huff of disappointment, I drag my tube back to the clip and ride, my lip jutting out in a pout.

I really don't like to lose.

Hands wrap around my waist from behind me, a raspy voice in my ear. "Where's that smile that lights me up?"

My body melts against his despite the frigid temperature. "Gone until I beat you at least once."

He chuckles next to my ear, the sound smooth and light. "As much as I love to see you smile, I may like teasing you more. When you get annoyed, your nose scrunches up, and it's really cute."

"I thought you liked seeing your cock in my mouth the most?" I whisper, winking at him as I sit in my tube, where it slowly pulls me up the hill.

Cameron mutters something about Jesus and a few curse words as he quickly adjusts his pants, then sits in his tube, pulling up right behind me.

Once we're at the top of the hill, we walk toward the more adventurous slope, the one that's faster and full of twisty turns.

While we wait for our turn, the girl who sends us down the hill is eye-fucking Cameron like nobody's business. Since we got in line, she hasn't taken her eyes off him unless it's to do her actual job.

She averts her gaze, sending a kid down the slope with a push, while my imagination runs wild with images of her tripping and sliding down the hill herself.

The worker turns around, looking at Cameron, then at me. "Single tuber?" she asks, but her innuendo is clear.

Irritation runs through my body, making me want to stake my claim loud and clear. It sounds irrational, having never felt this way before, but I guess that's the ugly side of jealousy.

I grab Cameron's gloved hand with my own, and to my surprise, he one-ups me, pulling me in front of his body and wrapping his arms around my middle. My smile is anything but authentic as I tell her, "We're together."

Her eyes widen, a tint of red covering her cheeks.

"Of course," she rattles off quickly, "Put your tubes down and sit in them. I'll set you up to go down together."

We oblige, sitting in our tubes as she ties them together.

"Rory," Cameron cocks an eyebrow.

"Hmm?" I hum.

"You okay?"

I tuck my lips in together, trying my best to play innocent. "Yup," I say, popping the p.

"What's up with the cavewoman-ness?" he asks, raising a single brow, a glint of humor in his tone.

I huff, sending a piece of my hair out of my face. "Because she was eyeing you like she wanted to eat you for dessert. I don't like to share. You're mine, bub."

"Damn right, I am." He smiles back at me, a cocky grin on his face. The sight makes me smile, along with the fact that he's mine. Cameron truly makes me feel more like myself. I feel safe, happy, and at ease with him.

Without warning, the worker sends us spinning down the hill, laughter breaking free from both of us.

We zip around the slope, the twisty turns making my stomach drop and my face beam from the joy of it all. I quickly glance at Cameron and see him staring at me, his smile goofy and free, those dimples appearing.

I smile back just as wide and turn my gaze back to the slope, where we slip and slide around the snow.

At the end of each slope, there's a mat followed by a half-pipe ramp meant to slow you down. But, as we pass it, we don't seem to slow down, and I think it's from our weight, making our tubes glide faster.

We slide up the ramp rapidly, with me on the tube at the top. It sends me over the ramp, causing me to fly off it.

I yelp as my body thumps into the snow, a rush of panic overcoming my body.

I really hope I didn't just injure myself.

Not moving because the fall winded me, I lie with my back on the snow and scan my body for anything that feels off. I wiggle my fingers and toes, check. Shake my legs and arms with no pain, check. And I have no headache, so I'm ruling out a concussion. Overall, I'm good.

Thank fucking god.

"Rory!" Cameron yells, the sound of his boots stomping through the snow getting closer and closer.

I remain lying in the snow, trying to catch my breath.

The snow crunches right beside me, and seconds later, Cameron's kneeling beside me, his body hovering over mine as his hands cup my cheeks. "Love, you okay?" he asks, his voice strained with worry, his eyes roaming my body to check for any damage.

"Yeah, I'm okay. Just a bit winded from the fall," I breathe.

Cameron nods, the concern still etched into his features. "C'mon, let's get you home to rest."

Oh no, we're not leaving just yet. I don't want this date to end already. Cameron sits up on his knees, and I take the chance to gather some snow in my hand and throw it at his chest.

Cameron blinks once, twice, then three times. "Did you just throw snow at me?"

I sit up now, a mischievous grin on my lips. "I did. What are you going to do about it?"

His eyes darken, going from cinnamon to chocolate in seconds as he instantly understands the sudden change in mood. "Make you beg to get on your knees for me."

My thighs clench at his words, my lips forming an O. "What makes you think *I'll* be the one begging to get on my knees?"

Cameron's head darts around, ensuring no one is around, which there isn't. The other side of the ramp consists of snow and a stack of unused tubes, hiding us from everyone.

He crawls over me, his large body covering mine, sending a chill down my spine. He wastes no time, unzipping my jacket and dipping his hands underneath my tights, his knuckles brushing against my wet thong. I inhale a sharp breath.

"Because you're already soaked at the idea of putting my cock in your mouth."

"I want you to put it somewhere else, too," I sigh lustfully as his knuckles brush over my slit.

Cameron's jaw ticks, his fingers pulling my panties to the side.

"Cameron, wait," I breathe, the sound choppy.

He stills instantly, eyes locked on me. "What's wrong?"

"I want you so badly, but I'm worried we'll get caught." While it's a fantasy of mine to do stuff in public, this feels like taking it to a whole other level.

Suddenly his lips are on mine, coaxing them open with his tongue that he expertly explores my mouth with. I relax under his lips, losing myself in the kiss, my worry forgotten but my desire heightened.

Cameron pulls back. "We're safe. Let me give you what you need, okay?"

"Please," I whine, feeling needy for his touch, and his touch only.

My words set him off, his fingers plunging inside me with no warning. I gasp at the intrusion, a spark of pleasure unfurling in my body as he curls his fingers, hitting that spot deep within me.

He fucks me with his fingers, his pace controlled as he pulls nearly all the way out, only to slam them back in, making my eyes shut from the intensity of what he's making me feel.

"Open your eyes," Cam orders, using that gentle yet dominant tone that makes me want to rip his clothes off. It's demanding while being respectful, mixed with the roughness of his voice, and it adds to my already heightened arousal.

I flick my eyes open and nearly orgasm from the look on his face. His eyes are hooded with lust, his lips slightly parted as he finger fucks me more rapidly, thrusting his fingers in and out in a way that makes me wish it was his cock pounding into me.

"Look between us. See how good your pussy takes my fingers as I fuck you with them," he says, his voice rough.

I do as I'm told, looking between us and watching his fingers disappear inside me. I've never done this before, but there's something wanton about it. It pushes me closer to the edge, my orgasm looming as his fingers coated in my arousal move in and out of me, loud enough for us to hear.

Cameron's lips descend, sucking and kissing my neck. A moan escapes me before I can stop it, causing Cam's hand to cover my mouth.

"Should I fill your mouth to keep you quiet, hm?"

"P-please," I mumble behind his hand, desperate to have my fill of him. I'm begging just like he knew I would because I'm beginning to think he knows what I need before I even do.

"Goddamnit," he grunts, desire clear in his hungry gaze.

I don't think he'll give me what I want, but then he removes his fingers and kneels beside me, quickly undoing his zipper, reaching inside his pants and pulling his cock out. *Holy hell, we're really doing this? In public?*

I go to lean up and wrap my lips around him when he pulls back slightly. "I don't think you've earned it just yet, love."

I whimper in protest, and he only grins in response. His hand returns between my thighs, but this time he goes straight for my clit, his thumb lightly brushing against it.

"Cam," I moan. I want to come so badly that it's becoming frustrating.

"That's my girl," he praises, leaning forward, the motion causing the tip of his cock to press against my lips. I open them willingly, swirling my tongue around his crown. But before I can do much else, he pulls back.

"Fields!" I whine, my body writhing in need of a release.

He pins with me a dark glare, one I haven't seen before. "Don't call me that when we're doing this. You called me that when we weren't friends. I would say we're more than friendly now."

"Then stuff my mouth with your cock, and make me come, please," I plead, giving him the begging he wants. I'd give him just about anything right now if he'd let me come.

He smirks, liking my response. "Good answer."

Suddenly, his cock is being shoved into my mouth, water pricking at my eyes from the fullness of him. I let him fuck my mouth while his thumb presses firmly against my clit, the beginning of my orgasm sparking low in my gut.

It bursts when he pushes himself into my mouth to the hilt, causing me to gag just as he rubs hard, rapid circles on my clit. I moan around him, my legs shaking as I come wildly, stars clouding my vision as the orgasm takes me to another level.

"So fucking pretty when you come with my cock in your mouth," he grunts, then stills, releasing himself down my throat.

I swallow every last drop, letting him push out every last bit of his release in me. When he's done, he pulls back, shoving himself in his pants, while I adjust my thong and pull my tights back up.

He then collapses beside me on the snow, our breathing erratic as we come down from our highs.

"Was that okay?" he asks.

I love that moments after he talks so bluntly to me, he can turn it around and be so sweet.

"That was…hot," I answer, my cheeks heating at the memory of what we just did. It *was* hot, being in public, knowing we could get caught. And the way he talked to me set my body ablaze in need for him.

He chuckles in agreement, stands, and pulls me up with him. "Does anything hurt?" he asks softly, his eyes roaming my body from head to toe.

"No, I'm good. I promise," I say, leaning on my toes to press a kiss on his lips. It's soft and sweet, just like my bub.

"Good, because we still have dinner and a market to explore," he smiles, taking my hand and leading us on the rest of our date.

We get sushi for dinner, and our meal is filled with laughter and teasing. It's the most fun I've ever had at a dinner. We roam the markets afterward, and Cameron holds my hand the entire time.

When I take a bathroom break, I come back to see him leaving a vendor with a bag in his hand. I tried to ask him what was in it, but he told me Christmas was coming and that I needed to wait.

But he did have something else he could show me, and I nearly buckled at the knees when he did. Inside a blue, velvet box was a silver chain, a dainty number 25 hanging off of it.

My number is 25. It's simple but stunning.

I thought he was giving it to me, but the moment he shook his head and put it around his neck, claiming me for everyone to see, I fell in love with him. I think I've loved him for a while now, since that day at the lake, but this moment right here solidified it for me. And that terrifies me because I can't afford to lose another person I love.

This means we're either staying together forever, which is a scary notion on its own, or I do lose him eventually, which shakes me to my core, leaving me numb at the idea.

Chapter Twenty-Eight

Cameron

"Stop looking at me like that," I mutter, trying to give Aurora a stern gaze and failing.

She's been trying to flirt with me since our session started, and I keep shutting it down because we should be studying since her exam is tomorrow.

I'm supposed to be her tutor, helping her understand the interactions between coding languages, not the interactions between us. It's what the school is paying me to do, and despite her dad not having direct control over this, I still feel a sense of duty to remain professional in this setting. To avoid getting expelled from the school only months away from graduation. My girlfriend is tempting me though, making that worry seem inconsequential.

"Like what?" she bats her lashes at me, her pouty bottom lip trapped beneath her teeth.

I rest my elbows on the table and lean forward. "Like you want me to spread you out on this table and devour you," I whisper.

Pink tints her cheeks, a bashful smile on her lips. "I always want that. Your tongue is amazing."

I cock a brow at her, "Only my tongue?"

Using her fingers, she lists off, "Your fingers, your mouth, your brain, your heart, your coc—"

"Okay, we're getting off task. Back to the flashcards," I cut her off because my cock was beginning to awaken, and we can't do that. Not in the library, and not during our goddamn tutoring session.

We make it about ten minutes before Aurora stops mid-answer, reaching for her backpack and diving inside of it frantically.

"Rory, what are you doing?" I ask, removing my computer glasses and rubbing my eyes.

Removing her hand from her bag, she pulls out a card, puts it on the table and slides it closer to me. I pick up the card, an invitation to the athletic department's annual Christmas charity gala.

The cardstock is written in black, with designs of red and green, which is noted as the event's theme, along with information on the date, Christmas Eve, and location, the ballroom of an upscale hotel in the downtown area.

"Would you like to come with me to the gala? I already paid for your ticket, but it's fine if you can't go. I thought it could be fun, and it's for a good cause, the children's hospital," Aurora says, sounding nervous, which I'm beginning to realize is normal for her when it comes to relationship-like things.

I think it's fucking adorable.

"I'd do anything with you if you asked," I tell her earnestly. "But yes, I'd love to go with you. How much were the tickets?"

She shakes her head at me, crossing her arms under her breasts, drawing my attention to them for a moment before she speaks, "Not a chance, bub. I'm paying for your ticket. You do so much for me, so let me do this, okay?"

I grunt, not liking the idea of her paying at all. "Fine, but I'm donating in our names once we're there."

"Deal," she smiles, then adds, "Also, my dad wants to meet you over the holiday break."

My stomach plummets, my heart rate picking up at the mention of her dad. I don't have a great relationship with mine, and I'm worried I won't be able to establish a bond with her dad. He's all she has parent-wise and I know how much he means to her. Which means it's important that we get along well.

"Do you…not want to take that step?" her voice cracks, sounding so unsure of herself, and I hate that my silence planted a seed of doubt in her mind.

"I do, love. I'm just nervous about meeting your dad. He scares me just from being our dean, let alone the father of the girl I'm dating."

"Don't be, he's a sweetheart. Honestly, he's really corny and caring. You'll get along just fine," she promises.

"Set up a day, and I'll be there. Also, my mom and Lexa are coming down this weekend, and I want you to meet them as well over the break."

Aurora's pretty eyes light up at the mention of my sister, "The legendary Lexa herself? Oh my god, yes, I want to meet her! And your mother, too, of course."

"Yeah, she'll lose her mind when she meets you. She's been on my ass lately about opening my heart and shit. She has our days all planned out for the entire four days they are here, but don't be surprised if she plans a whole day just for you two to hang out."

Aurora sits up straighter, her eyes alight with an idea. "My dad wanted you to come over for Christmas dinner. Do you want to bring your mom and Lexa? We can all meet at once and get to know each other. We keep it small for Christmas dinner. It's just me, my dad and Nate since the rest of our family is in California."

"I'm sure they would enjoy that. I'll talk to them about it and let you know. Do you ever visit your family, or do they come down?" I ask, wanting to know more about her family.

She had told me before that her parents met and lived in California, but they moved here so her mom could work with the best gymnastics trainer in the country.

"Just for the major holidays, we go see them. It's easier for the three of us to fly there than for all of them to fly here. But this year, we're staying here because Nate's swamped at the bar, and I have to train over the break," she admits, shrugging her shoulders.

I get the sense that she wishes she could see them, and I wish I could fix that for her, but I can't. So, I'll try to make this holiday season as special as possible for her.

Before I can say anything, she switches the subject. "Alright, let's study so I can kick this exam's ass tomorrow."

And we do just that, studying for the next hour without getting off track. Once we're done, I close my laptop while Aurora packs up her textbook and notes, and I'm confident that she will not only pass but crush her exam tomorrow.

Aurora stands, her curves prominent in her skin-tight, navy blue turtleneck dress. Her body is fucking beautiful, every dip and curve perfectly balanced to her leanness. My eyes roam her body, wishing I could peel back her dress and sheer tights to see her bare.

My cock twitches in my jeans at the image, and once my eyes reach hers, I realize she's been staring at me while I've been perusing her.

"See something you like, Fields?" she teases, her tongue dipping to wet her lips.

I see something I love, I think to myself, and the thought doesn't scare me. I've known it for some time now but have yet to say it out loud for fear of scaring her.

I nod, swallowing hard as she turns, bending over as she puts her textbook in her bag, putting her perfect ass on display. I stifle a groan that threatens to erupt from my chest, my eyes ablaze with desire as they watch her purposely rub her hands over her body.

"Aurora, don't," I warn, not wanting her to tease the fuck out of me only to have me walk out of here with the world's largest fucking erection.

She twirls a piece of her hair, tilting her head in mock ignorance. "Don't what?"

"You know what."

Aurora suddenly drops the pen in her hand, "Oops, let me get that."

Lowering to her knees, she crawls under the table, and just when I think she isn't going to do anything else, I feel her hand on my aching cock over my jeans.

"Jesus," I mutter, my thighs clenching from her touch.

"Aurora," she corrects me, pulling the zipper on my jeans down.

"Love, what are you doing?" I whisper the words strained as I internally battle with myself on what I think will happen and if I should let it.

"Putting your cock in my mouth, is that okay?" she asks as her fingers hook into my boxers, attempting to tug them down. If my hips lifting off the chair to help her isn't a sign that I'm letting this happen, then I don't know what is.

"No, but fuck if I care right now," I rasp. "I won't let anyone see you like this. If I tap the table, it means someone is coming, and no, I don't mean me," I clarify, knowing her dirty mind was going there.

Then, she gives me a fucking mindblowing blowjob underneath our table in the corner of the library, by the window overlooking the mountains. Right where our story began.

It's the best full-circle moment I've ever experienced.

Chapter Twenty-Nine

Cameron

Winter break started two days ago, and I'd be lying if I said I didn't miss Aurora like hell.

After she crushed her exam on Tuesday, the one we've been working on during our sessions, we studied for our last exams the next day.

After exams finished that Wednesday, we spent the rest of the day together in my bed, watching Marvel movies until she had to get ready for work.

And yes, I'm still a virgin.

I've wanted to bury myself so deeply inside her that she doesn't remember anything before it, but I'm also content with how we've been learning each other's bodies and building toward that moment.

Aurora hasn't pressured me, but she makes comments here and there about how much she wants me, and fuck, sometimes my restraint wants to snap like a rubber band, but I somehow hold off. Knowing it's not the time yet.

Since I've waited this long, I've always said that I want to lose my virginity to someone I care about and love. My fingers play with the metal 25 around my neck, and yeah, I think I've found that someone.

I've known about it for a while, but it wasn't until recently that I decided I was ready. Despite how vulnerable it makes me feel, I want to do everything with Aurora. I want her to have a piece of me that no one else has, just like she has my heart like no other has.

I understand what Finn meant when he teased me about being a cinnamon roll or whatever the fuck he said because that's how I feel whenever I'm around or think of her—sweet, soft, and warm.

Her laugh is an aphrodisiac, her smile the fuel that pumps my blood. She's so goddamn gorgeous that I often can't believe she's with *me*. She's funny, hardworking, caring, and confident.

I feel safe with her like all of my past worries and troubles don't matter. It's the most peace I've felt in years. All of those things pull me to her, and that pull hasn't let up since we got together, and I know it'll only increase once we have sex. Which fucking terrifies me to think about because I can't imagine having more intense feelings for her than I already do.

I hadn't seen her since that night in the library, only to end up at the bar later because I worried about her. Call it overprotective, but I don't give a fuck. Not where her safety is concerned, and it's not even the drama that happened weeks ago. It's the sleaze balls I know are eyeing her up like a piece of meat.

Aurora smiled brightly as soon as she caught sight of me walking in. I sat at the bar, my laptop in tow, and attempted to work, but I couldn't focus, not when her long legs were displayed in her mini skirt.

We chatted through the night, and I only sent three guys death stares that had them scurrying away from the bar once they received their drink.

My mom and sister arrived the next day, and Aurora went back to her dad's house for the break, so I haven't seen her since then. Knowing I won't see her for another two days is eating at me every minute that I'm not with her.

"Cameron James Fields!" Lexa announces, startling me back into the present as we sit around the tree, wrapping presents for Mom, who is attending a spa retreat today, an early gift from me.

"Yes, Lexaroo?" I ask, attaching a silver bow to a candy-cane-wrapped box.

"Is there something you want to tell me?" she looks at me with her baby blues, giving me the chance to come clean before she calls me out.

I already told my mom and Lexa about Aurora the night they got here, wanting to get it off my chest.

I haven't seen my mom or Lexa smile that animatedly in a long time as they wrapped me up in a hug, saying how happy they were for me. My mom said she never thought I'd open myself up and that she was glad her relationship with my father didn't steer me away from opening my heart up to love.

"Not that I can think of, but I'm sure you'll tell me what exactly it is." I look at her pointedly, willing her to try and argue with me.

She doesn't. "That I will. So, why didn't you tell me you were in love?"

I pause mid-cut of the wrapping paper and do my best to fight the smile that wants to spread on my lips. I don't deny it. "How did you figure it out?"

Lexa laughs and rolls her eyes, handing me a piece of tape for the gift we're wrapping. "Every time your phone lights up, so does your face. And I may have taken a peek at what you got her for Christmas," she rushes out the last bit at the admission of her invasion of privacy into my things.

"Lexa," I sigh, wanting to be annoyed that she snooped through my stuff, but I can never get mad at her.

"I'm sorry, Cam, but I was so curious. I mean, c'mon, there was a blue velvet box on your desk. I thought you were proposing, so excuse me for being intrigued."

Her mention of a ring fills me with excitement for the future because it's definitely something I've envisioned for us. But I keep my face neutral, my tone even. "Don't go through my stuff again, got it?"

"Yeah, yeah. It's really cute, though. She's going to love it, just like you love her," she answers sincerely.

I throw a bow at her. "You're slacking."

"You're deflecting," she throws it back at me, sticking her tongue out at me.

We both laugh, returning to finish our gift wrapping.

Minutes later, we're on the couch watching *Home Alone* while Lexa fills me in our schedule for when Mom gets back. We're going to the Christmas market at Snow Pine Resort, followed by heading to S'more Chocolate, a dessert shop specializing in various ways to make s'mores.

Lexa had to alter her schedule since I was going to the Christmas Eve gala, but she understood and decided a quiet night with Mom was just as good.

We're going shopping tomorrow for a tux since I've never had to get one, and to say Lexa was excited is an understatement. She's also insisting on buying a new outfit to meet Aurora's family, claiming her last name sounds fancy, somehow meaning that she needs to dress fancy.

I don't get it, but that's Lexa for you, doing things her way.

My phone vibrates during the movie, and just as Lexa said, I light up when I see Aurora on my screen.

Rory

I miss you Bub.

Me

What do you miss?

Rory

I miss sleeping next to you.
I miss being in your arms where
I feel safe. I miss your kisses,
my body needs you.

Rory

Among other things.

Me

My sister is on the couch with
me. Please do not say anything
that will give me a boner.

Me

Nvm, too late for that.

Rory

... Sorry.

Me

Don't be, love, cause I miss
all those things too.

Rory

Well now I'm all hot and
bothered too, thanks.

Me

Figured I may as well even
the playing field.

Rory

Okay. I need to go take care of
that problem before training, bye.

The urge to tell her that I love her is strong, but I ignore it because I won't text it to her before telling her in person.

Despite my weak attempt at keeping her at a distance, I love the hell out of Aurora Vallacourt.

Chapter Thirty

Aurora

The annual athlete's Christmas Eve gala is an event I look forward to every year, and despite it being Christmas Eve, it's become a part of the holiday traditions amongst RLU students.

The ballroom feels like the North Pole, with fake snow, sparkles, snowflakes, presents, mistletoes, and candy canes strung about the room.

But this year might be my favorite, and I know it's because Cam will be by my side all night. He looks stunning in his all-black tuxedo, his muscles clearly defined every time he stretches his arms. I want to rip the suit off of him.

We haven't talked about the whole sex thing explicitly because I don't want to pressure him, and I know he'll tell me when he's ready. But I really, *really*, hope it's soon.

"Aurora," Isaiah, a hockey team member and Theo's best friend, says my name a little too sweetly.

Our table consists of him, Jasmine, Theo, his other friend Ryker, Cam, and I. We all swivel our heads in Isaiah's direction.

"What, dipshit?" Theo glares at his friend, willing him not to say something stupid.

Cameron's hand on my thigh tightens, giving me a possessive squeeze that shoots up my leg, right to my clit.

"I just wanted to say your dress looks really nice. Jesus," he says, holding his hands up in defense.

I look down at my velvet, dark green dress. The long sleeves and turtleneck cover me up, minus the fact that it clings to my body, showing all of my curves and hitting my shins with a slit running up my right thigh. It's sexy, and I feel good in it.

"Thanks," I say with a small smile, wanting to be polite, but also not *too* polite.

Cameron leans in, his lips brushing my ear, and says, "You have no idea how badly I want to stick my head between your thighs and taste what's mine."

A rush of anticipation runs up my spine and back down to my toes. I have no idea where the night will take us, but I don't care as long as I'm with him. We could end up cuddling and I'd still be just as happy.

I flush and sip my water because I don't like to drink during the season or at all. I also want to support Cameron's choice to be sober, which means he won't be kissing me if I'm ever drunk—a scenario I don't like very much.

"Hey, who's that guy over there?" Theo asks Ryker, nodding his head in the direction of a tall, broad man in a maroon suit.

"Don't know," he mutters, looking like he'd rather be anywhere than here. He's been a grump all night, only speaking when spoken to and responding in short syllables. All I know is he plays on the baseball team and is a junior just like Jasmine.

"Oh, dude, I know him. He's the new assistant coach on the team. He used to play in the NHL," Isaiah pipes up, sipping some water surprisingly.

"Used to? What happened, Zee?" Theo asks.

"Get this," Isaiah says, leaning in towards the group, "He got picked up by the Denver Wolves in his junior year here at RLU, played six amazing years in the NHL, winning one championship, only to tear his ACL the year after. He's out for good now."

"What's his name?" Theo questions.

"That would be Elio. My dad coached him as a kid until he came here for school. They're good friends," Jasmine pipes up, swirling her glass of wine.

I can tell she knows more, but she won't share it with the table. I'm wondering why he's here as most coaches aren't in attendance tonight when someone coughs nearby, causing all of our heads to snap to the source.

We look up to see Elio standing right behind Jasmine's chair. He's tall, towering over her, with a dark brown beard covering his angular jaw. His hair was the same hue and styled to the side, with a single hair falling out of place near his forehead.

"I figured since you guys were talking about me, I may as well come and introduce myself. I'm Elio Mazzo, the new assistant coach for the hockey team," his tone was full of confidence, much like the rest of his posture. "I'll also be enrolling as a student next September to finish my business degree."

"How is that even allowed? You need a degree to be a coach," Jasmine points out, taking a sip of her wine.

Elio smirks, seeming entertained by her. "Let's just say, money talks," he drawls as he inches just a tad bit closer to her.

Jasmine stiffens, her back going straight at his nearness. "Oh hell, you're more entitled and annoying than I remembered."

Elio's dark green eyes sparkle as he drinks her in, his lips twitching to fight a smile. "And you're just as sweet as I remembered," he says sarcastically. He then nods at the rest of us before she can reply and leaves our table.

My mouth opens, then closes, then opens again. But it's Theo who steals the words from my lips. "That was intense. I can't believe you just talked to one of the greatest hockey players of all time like that."

Jasmine doesn't give anyone time to interject, turning it around on Theo as she asks, "Where's Marcela tonight?"

"Working," Theo responds, looking disappointed as he stares into his near-empty glass.

"Or she just didn't want to come with you?" Isaiah counters, knowing the bar is closed today, earning him a smack on the back of his neck from Theo.

"Shut up," he grumbles, downing the rest of his drink. I've seen Theo at the bar countless times, always trying to talk to Marcela, and it seems like they're friendly, but I know Theo wants more, and she's not biting for whatever reason.

"Camille!" Jasmine squeals, standing up and rushing over to the tall blonde who looks like she just came off the runway in her mermaid-style, sparkling red gown. "Everyone, this is Camille. We're in the same business program."

All of us say hello, to which she smiles back and waves. That's everyone except Ryker, who has yet to say anything since she's arrived.

"What are you doing here?" Jasmine asks her.

Cam nudges my shoulder with his, and I follow his line of sight to see Ryker zoned in on Camille, interest in his eyes for the first time tonight.

"I'm here for the school's newspaper, taking notes," she says, quickly glancing at Ryker with a small smile.

"That's no fun. Find me later for a dance." Jasmine smiles at her as they exchange goodbyes.

The rest of the night goes smoothly. Our table, minus Ryker, swap stories and laughter. Jasmine and I eventually make our way to the dance floor, dancing the night away while the guys sit and chat.

Every time I glance at the table, Cameron's eyes are on me, a faint smile on his lips as he watches me in amusement. While twirling in a circle, I spot Elio in a corner of the room by himself, a drink in hand.

His eyes never once leave Jasmine. *Interesting.*

The music changes from an upbeat pop remix to a smooth, slow one that has everyone scurrying off the dance floor to find their partner. This is when I leave every year, but, before I can move, Cameron's arms wrap around my waist, twisting me to face him.

"Dance with me?"

"Yes," I replied, wrapping my hands behind his neck, my fingers toying with the tuft of hair there as he wrapped his around my lower back, tugging our bodies tightly together.

Sandalwood and linen invade me, that familiar sense of safety washing over me. We sway softly to the music, and we remain quiet, my head resting on his chest, his chin on the top of my head.

I always imagined slow dancing to be awkward, but with Cam, our silence is comfortable, coveted even.

I never imagined I'd be here, in the arms of my tutor. But he turned out to be the man I'm dating and the one I'm hopelessly in love with. It's everything I've tried to avoid, but it's turned out to be just what I needed.

Once I get recruited for Team USA after the break, everything will be perfect.

I lift my head from his chest, feeling my love for him course through my veins, demanding to be let loose. "I love you," the words come out quiet but confident.

His cinnamon eyes widen, and I feel the breath of relief his body lets loose against mine. He tugs me even closer to him, absolutely no room between us now, his hands on my waist tightening as he kisses me reverently, like I'm precious to him.

"Can we go back to your house? I have something I want to give you since we won't see each other until dinner tomorrow," he asks, running his hand up my neck and stopping once his hand cups my cheek.

I'm not upset he didn't say it back, because that's not why you tell someone you love them. Besides, I know he deeply cares for me with his actions alone.

I nod, swirls of excitement and nerves mixing in my gut for whatever he got me. We say good night to our friends, then grab our coats. Cameron makes me wait inside while he grabs the car, and within minutes, we're driving back to my house.

The drive over is nearly suffocating, the car filled with anticipation and something else. I don't know how to explain it, except that it feels like we're about to snap, erasing the last bit of distance there can be between two people.

My theory is confirmed when we walk through my front door, and Cameron pins me to the door with his hips, his hard length felt even through my jacket. His lips come down on mine. There's nothing soft or sweet about it. He's kissing me like if he stopped, he'd die.

He takes everything he wants as his mouth moves over mine wildly, yet not sloppily. It's perfect.

"Jacket. Off," he mumbles between kisses, a ragged breath leaving his lips.

I comply, unzipping my down jacket as he does the same, and then our shoes are gone.

Cameron scoops me into his arms, carrying me up the stairs to my room, and I wrap my arms around his neck, kissing him there. His groan sounds strained, making me giggle because I love knowing the power I have over this man.

"I thought it was present time," I banter, pressing my lips under his jaw.

Kicking my door closed, he adjusts me so I'm wrapped around his waist. That's when I see the primal need in his eyes, the hunger that's there for me. "Consider this a part of it," he says while grinding his erection against me.

My core thrums in excitement, but I want to be sure this is what he wants. "Are you sure, bub? We don't have to, I know earlier I said—"

He cuts me off, pressing a finger to my lips. "I *need* to be inside of you, love. Can I?" He asks, the question making me love him even more because, despite his needs, mine always trump his.

"Yes," I breathe, and then gone is sweet Cameron. His hands squeeze my ass as his lips meet mine, devouring and relentless.

I whimper into his mouth, wanting and needing more of his touch.

Cameron sets me down and spins me so my back is to him. I shiver when I feel his warm hand at the nape of my neck, and the sound of my zipper being pulled down my back fills the room alongside our heavy breaths.

"So beautiful," he whispers in my ear, his hands coming around to squeeze my breasts through my red-laced bra.

"Cameron," I groan, wanting to feel him on my bare body— nothing between us.

He chuckles, the sound vibrating in his chest against my back. "As pretty as you are in this, it's going to have to come off," he says, his fingers moving to the clasp and snapping it undone. He slowly trails the straps off my arms, then lets it fall to the floor along with my dress.

"Need to taste you," he grunts, sliding my wet, red lace panties off next. Cameron loves going down on me, not seeing it as a means to an end like most guys do, and it's fucking hot.

In contrast to him, with his button-up and slacks still on, I'm completely bare now..

Cameron then turns my body so that I'm facing him, but before I can process what's happening, he's lifting me off the ground and onto his shoulders.

Oh. My. God.

My mountain man rests my back against the wall, my thighs around his head, my legs dangling against his back, and my pussy right in his face.

I stare at him in amazement for a moment and watch as his tongue darts out to give me one full, languid stroke. I buck off of the wall, pushing my pussy into his face because it knows exactly who it wants more of.

Cameron wastes no time, giving me what I need. His tongue laps at my pussy, then lower as he runs it along the inside of my center.

"Cameron!" I cry. The pleasure is too much and not enough at the same time.

He wraps his lips around my clit, sucking it into his mouth hard as he eats me out against the fucking wall while I'm on his shoulders.

The position already heightened my desire, but his magical tongue surpassed it. Cameron devours me as I soak his face, coming undone on his tongue when he brings his hand up to play with my nipple.

Wrapping both hands around my waist, he holds me to him while I ride out my pleasure, moaning his name, the action extending my orgasm while my back bucks off the wall, unable to control what he's doing to my body.

With me still on his shoulders, he walks us over to the bed, where he gently sets me. He makes quick work of his clothes, stripping completely, and I openly gawk at the sight. He's beautiful in so many ways. His body is just the cherry on top.

"One out of three," he says, hovering over me with a carnal desire in his eyes, his silver chain hanging off his tan skin.

"What?" I ask, sounding dazed. I have no idea what he's talking about.

"You're going to come for me two more times, *at least*," he states confidently, his nose running along the side of my neck.

I dig my fingers into his hair, loving that he has enough I can pull on. "And you only come once? Doesn't seem fair."

His lips leave my neck. "Once for this round, but we have a few more rounds to go, love."

My core heats at his words, desire flooding my entire body.

I've never had that kind of passion with a man before, where I wanted to fuck them all night long, but I get it now. Because that's exactly what I want to do with Cam.

It's why I offer him what I've never offered anyone else. "I'm negative, on birth control, and I've never slept with anyone without a condom if you wanted to do that. Go in me raw, I mean."

Cameron's gaze heats, setting my body ablaze. "You sure?" he asks, grinding his erection against my wet core.

"I love you," I tell him instead, letting him know that I trust him and want this connection between us.

"Rory," he whispers, my name full of love, longing, and need. Cinnamon eyes are locked on mine intently, our breaths mingling in the limited space between our lips as his forehead rests against mine.

Lifting his body slightly, Cameron fists his cock, and rubs it up and down my slit, causing my breath to hitch because I just remembered how large he is. This might hurt, but I don't even care.

"If I hurt you at all, I need to know, okay?" he says, his tone laced with worry.

I bring my hand to his cleanly-shaved jaw, stroking my finger up and down the bone. "You won't. Just go slow, bub."

He nods, kissing me on my forehead before sitting back on his knees. Cameron brings his tip to my entrance, and then, with his eyes on mine, he pushes the tip in.

"Holy fuck," he groans, looking pained as we both gasp in pleasure.

"More," I whimper, needing more of him.

At my plea, he gathers his control and pushes in a bit more, his eyes not leaving mine as he gauges my expression for any indication of pain. So far, it feels good, full, but good.

"See, it's not so bad," I coo, running my hand down his corded arms.

He smirks, "I have more to give you."

My mouth gapes just as he presses in a bit more, causing my walls to tighten at the large intrusion, and holy fuck. *How much more is there?*

He feels me tighten around him instantly, "Relax, love. You're safe with me."

His words reach a place I didn't know I needed them, instantly causing my body to shift from tense to calm. How he knew I needed to hear that, I don't know. My body eases him in a bit more, a grunt emitting from his lips while I stifle a whimper.

Cameron pushes in all the way in, his balls hitting my ass. He hovers over me, brushing a strand of hair out of my face. "You okay?"

I take a moment to adjust to him because I've never been so full in my life. It's a rush, feeling him inside me, raw and thick.

It's like nothing else I've felt before, and I think our emotional connection makes up a good part of that.

"Yes, move, please," I demand, my hips rocking on their own accord.

"Give me a minute," he grunts, leaning up to wrap one of my legs around his waist. I still my hips, remembering that this is his first time. I'll give him whatever he needs to make this the best for him.

The first roll of his hips causes a sharp cry of pleasure to leave my lips because I feel it everywhere. His hand wraps around my thigh, using it to keep me steady as he begins to move inside of me, not too slowly, but not too fast.

I let him adjust to the feel and pace while he garners his control because I can see it in his eyes that he's trying to keep it together.

"Rory, you feel fucking amazing," he moans, swivelling his hips and hitting a spot that fills my vision with stars.

I whimper my response, fisting the sheets beside me. "You were made to be inside me, Cam. It's so good."

His eyes darken at that before his lips come crashing down onto me, taking, devouring, and owning me with every brush of our lips and tongues as he rocks in and out of me.

"I need more. Put me on my knees and fuck me from behind," I instruct him, remembering that this is new for him and he needs some guidance.

He pulls out of me swiftly, and I whine at the loss, but before I can complain, he's flipping me so that I'm on all fours as if I weigh nothing. It's hot as fuck.

"Such a pretty pussy, dripping and ready for me," he drawls, tapping his cock on my ass before lining it up with my entrance and pushing into me more easily this time.

"Cam," I moan, looking over my shoulder. "Grip my hips and pound me as hard as you can."

Cameron's eyes are glued to us, watching himself rock in and out of me, and the sight nearly does me in because he looks entranced.

"It's not going to hurt you, right?" he asks on a strangled breath.

"No. I want all of you. Lose yourself in me, I can take it," I tell him, pushing my ass back, causing him to growl.

I grip the sheets as he begins to pound into me without pause. His thick cock hits me in all the right places, blurring my senses and making me feel everything more than I ever have.

My moaning of his name spurs him on as he fucks me even harder, and his hands tighten on my waist as he snaps his hips against my ass rapidly.

"That's my girl," he praises as I let him fuck me into oblivion, sure that I'll feel him between my thighs tomorrow. "Taking every inch of me just like your pussy was meant to."

His words throw me off an invisible cliff, my orgasm hitting me out of nowhere as I tighten around his cock, screaming his name into my sheets.

Cameron pulls out of me suddenly, flipping me back on my back, but this time, he scrambles his body down until his head is between my thighs. "Fuck, I need to taste you again."

He devours me again, his tongue everywhere as he laps up my cum, the high of my previous orgasm making me more sensitive. He doesn't stop, though, his lips wrapping around my clit tightly, sucking and moaning against me. Another orgasm pummels me because seeing how much he loves going down on me is something else. The man had to pull out of me during sex because he needed to taste me. God, I love him.

Before I come down from the high of my third orgasm, he pushes into me, his face buried in my neck as he sucks on it. I wrap my arms around his back, holding him tightly as my fingers dig into the skin there.

I can feel every brutally long inch of him inside of me and the way his cock is twitching with its near release.

His hips rock and roll into me, hitting my clit every time our bodies meet. Mix that in with his large frame dominating mine, and the pleasure is overwhelming. Sex has never felt this good.

"Cam, I can't—" I don't know what it is that I can't do because my mind is jumbled, and my body is on fire with desire for this man.

"Show me how much you love my cock pounding into your tight little pussy by giving me one more," he says into my neck, the words raspy with the need for release, and they set me off into mine.

Cameron fucks me wildly, my body shifting on the bed so much that I grab the headboard to hold myself steady. His body stills with his head burrowed in my neck, a growl erupting from his chest as he cums inside me, the feeling so erotic.

I've never been filled by a man like this before, and I'm glad it's by him, claiming me.

He lifts up rather than resting his weight on me, pulling out of me slowly before coming to lay beside me. We're both breathless, coming down from the highest high I've ever felt. I don't know how it was for him as it was his first time, but it felt like my first time, too because I've never had sex that has felt like *that*.

Cameron scoops me into his lap, sitting up with me as he leans against the headboard. Part of me wants to go clean myself up because I can feel him leaking out of me against his thigh, but I ignore it because my body is too spent to move anyway.

"You okay? Was I too rough?" he murmurs, stroking my hair gently.

I nuzzle my nose into his chest, my arms draped around his neck, inhaling my favorite scent in the world. "You were perfect… I'm not convinced you were a virgin because, wow."

He chuckles against my hair, "Your moans were a good indicator of what I should do more of, and you helped me out."

"Yeah, I'm pretty sure you've ruined me."

"Good," he hums. "You're okay, though?"

"I might be a little sore, but it was worth every second," I beam, smiling up at him so he knows not to worry, but knowing Cameron, my little caretaker, he will.

"I hate the idea of hurting you or you being in pain. It makes me sick. But," he pauses, "I'd be lying if I said I didn't love the idea that you'll be thinking of me between your legs for a bit."

"I think of you all the time anyways," I admit, unintentionally turning the conversation softer.

"That right?" he smiles, his dimples pulling in. "You've been living rent-free in my head since the day we met."

I gape at him, sounding puzzled, and ask, "Wait, what? You were such an ass to me that first day."

"I know, and I'm so goddamn sorry for that. I knew the instant I saw you that I could fall for you, and I tried to protect myself the best way I knew how. By pushing you away."

"And now?" I prompt, trailing my fingers across his defined abs, all six of them.

"Hold on a sec," he says, lifting me off his lap and throwing a pair of sweats on that he keeps here before he heads downstairs.

I take the time to throw his button-up on, leaving it undone, but it's large enough that it covers my ass, and I can pull it across my waist to cover my bits.

I sit back on my bed, noting that I will need to change the sheets before bed, but not now because I have a feeling we will go another round. My toes curl in excitement just as Cameron comes back through the door, a small gift in his hand.

"Present time!" I clap my hands together because I love gifts, no shame.

Cameron smiles, shaking his head at me as he sits on the bed with me, scooping me back into his arms.

"If you weren't so excited for your gift, I would be fucking you again, because seeing you in my shirt is doing something to me," he says, his cock hardening beneath my ass.

God, I want him inside me again.

"Then give it to me so that you can *really* give it to me," I waggle my brows at him, being corny and not caring.

He laughs, the sound filling my body with warmth. "Here, this should answer your question about how I feel about you." He hands me the small box wrapped in silver wrapping paper with candy canes and a red bow on top.

I rip the paper off, then stare at the blue velvet box. I know Cam's not proposing because he knows it would freak me out.

I open the box, and my hand flies to my mouth at the white gold necklace, a circular pendant hanging off of it. There's an intricate design of a marigold flower, which I know is his birth month flower—October 18th.

"Bub, this is beautiful. I love it," I tell him earnestly, loving how dainty and personal it is. I'll be carrying around a piece of him with me now. I give it to him, letting him place it around my neck and secure it there.

"Turn it around," he tells me once he's done.

I turn the pendant over, and the first tear falls. On the back, in what looks like his writing, etched into the metal, are the words "I love you 3000, Rory."

The tears cascade down my face because of our shared love for Marvel and the ode to his and my mom's nickname for me, but most importantly, because he loves me.

This mountain of a man, who I thought was an ass, turned out to be the sweetest, most important person in my life.

I spring forward and tackle him, knocking him onto his back as I straddle him. "I love you, I love you, I love you," I say between kissing him from his temple to his nose, jaw, neck, chest, and back up to his lips.

His arms wrap around my back, holding me to him as he looks at me intently, "I love you, Rory."

Hearing those words come out of his lips fills me with a feeling I've never had before, a sense of fulfillment and desire mixed with peace. We stay like that for a bit, smiling at one another, just gazing into each other's eyes with pure bliss.

"I believe I was supposed to be receiving another gift?" I tease, breaking the silence as I roll my hips against his erection.

"You're spoiled," he grins, using his hands on both of my thighs to lift me, running a finger down my wet slit. "And your pussy is, too. You need me again, love?" He asks while rubbing the head of his cock against my arousal.

"Always," I sigh, a cry of pleasure leaving my lips as I grip his cock and sink down onto him.

All night, he continues to satisfy my need for him, showing me with his body and words how much he loves me.

It's the best Christmas Eve I've had in twelve years.

Chapter Thirty-One

Aurora

I adjust my white cream turtleneck in the mirror, my eyes trailing down my legs to ensure my red skirt isn't too short because I'm about to meet Cameron's mom and sister for the first time.

I can't lie. I'm freaking out a bit because I've never done this before, and I'm worried I won't be worthy in his family's eyes. My dad's girlfriend and son are also coming over, adding to the nerves in my stomach.

I haven't seen Jodi since that day at the vet because I've been too busy to come home, but we've talked a couple of times over the phone whenever I've called my dad recently.

I run a hand through my blonde curls. I spent the morning trying to get the perfect blowout and even did my makeup. I also added a red bow clip, pinning my hair half up and half down. I really, really want to impress them.

I'm waiting in the foyer for Cameron, his mom, and his sister to arrive, pacing back and forth.

My dad's house is perfect for my never-ending pacing, considering the open-concept style farmhouse, with one main floor and a basement. It was spacious, but not overly large, with rooms that no one would ever use. White, light green, and gray colors popped throughout the space, giving it a bright, clean feel.

Pickles paces with me, his tongue flopping around like he thinks it is a game. A text from Cameron tells me they are five minutes away, causing butterflies to erupt in my stomach.

We finally had sex last night. Saying it was everything would be an understatement. We went for another round right after the first, and hours later, in the middle of the night, I woke up with his face between my thighs. He then woke up early and made us pancakes for a Christmas breakfast. We ate them in bed before he went home to open gifts with his sister and mom.

After he left, I showered and came here, where Nate and I opened gifts with our dad. Since then, I've been a nervous wreck.

"Cupcake, you're going to wear out the floorboards, and the dog for that matter," he chuckles, leaning against the archway that led from the foyer to the living room.

I halt in place, smoothing my pleated red skirt down. "Dad, I'm nervous. Why are we doing this?" I ask, not afraid to open up to my old man.

"Because you're in love, and I want to meet the man responsible for the bright smile on your face," he replies, wearing a proud smile.

I can feel my cheeks grow red and I tilt my chin down at the floor as I voice my fear. "What if they don't like me?"

My dad pushes off of the wall, pulling me into his arms. "Where's my confident Vallacourt girl? They would be crazy not to like you. You're kind, loving, hardworking, and your dad is great, so that's a bonus."

I laugh, feeling some of the nerves leave my body. "I love you, Dad."

"I love you more, Cupcake," he says, pulling back from our embrace. "I know today is hard because of your mom, but she's here with us. She'd be so damn proud of you two."

He was right. The holidays were always hard without her, especially Christmas because it was her favorite time of year. Growing up in California, she loved experiencing a white Christmas for the first time when they moved to Denver. From there, she made it a tradition to go all out for the holiday each year. Decorating the house top to bottom, gingerbread house making, sugar cookie decorating contests, and Christmas music always played on the stereo.

Since she passed, we endured the pain and kept her traditions alive rather than avoiding them because it was our way of feeling close to her this time of year. The day after my birthday, Nate and I would decorate the house while Dad baked sugar cookies for us to decorate.

This year, we're doing our gingerbread house-making tonight with Cameron and his family, wanting to transform the tradition and make a new one.

"I miss her, Dad," I sniffle back a tear, not wanting to ruin my makeup. "I wish I could talk to her about him. She would know exactly what to say. Not that you're not great, but you know what I mean."

"I get it, Cupcake. I do."

"And by the way, she would be proud of you too, you know," I say, hoping he knows that Mom would be proud of everything he's accomplished, from raising Nate and me to all he does at the school.

"Don't make your old man cry now," he chuckles, wiping his eyes.

A knock on the door startles us both, followed by a beep from the locking of a car I know so well.

They're here.

"You got this," my dad encourages me, making himself comfortable in the living room so I can introduce myself before he barges in.

I take a deep, calming breath, like the ones I take before a game, and then walk to the door. I open it to see Cameron standing next to two beautiful women. Lexa has dark waves accentuating her baby blue eyes, with freckles on her rosy cheeks, and while his mom has the same hair as Lexa, her eyes rival Cameron's.

"Hi, Merry Christmas," I beam, my voice giving my nerves away. I thrust my hand toward his mom. "I'm Aurora Vallacourt. It's so nice to finally meet you. I've heard a lot about you."

She stares at me for a second, and I still, wondering if I've said the wrong thing. Until she cracks a wide smile, the dimples I love on her son adoring her own cheeks. She pulls me into a hug. "Honey, stop with all the formal crap and hug me," she laughs.

I wrap my arms around her, relief washing through my body, wringing out all the nerves I had left.

We pull back, and then I shift to his sister, who starts talking before I get the chance to introduce myself.

"Hi, I'm Lexa. Thank you *so* much for dating my brother. I was worried the guy would become a crazy dog man, you know, the opposite of a crazy cat lady?" she jokes, and I instantly feel at ease.

Feisty and honest, I like her.

I chuckle as I step back to let them inside the foyer. "Nice to finally meet the superior Field's sibling. I'm Aurora."

"Yeah, I heard that when you got really nervous talking to my mom. Also, Cameron's talked about you nonstop so you can relax. We both love you already. If Cameron does, that means something because the boy's never been interested in anything for himself besides school."

I light up at her words, knowing they were true if she was saying them. They make me feel important and cherished, not that Cam doesn't make me feel that way already, but hearing that I'm the first thing he's done for himself outside of school in a long time hits a little deeper.

Two large arms wrap around my middle, hugging me to a broad chest. "Alright, that's enough out of you, Lexaroo." He kisses my cheek and whispers against my ear, "Hi, love. You look really pretty."

I twist slightly in his arms to look at my handsome man, "Thank you. You look good yourself."

He's wearing a dark gray waffle quarter zip-up with black jeans—simple but so good.

"Where can I put the taco dip? It needs to go in the oven for a bit," his mom asks, just as my dad steps into the foyer.

He takes the dip from her. "I can put it in for you. I'm Paul Vallacourt. It's a pleasure to meet you and have your family here for dinner."

Cameron's mom smiles at him, "That sure is sweet of you. Thanks, Paul. I'm Lucy Fields."

Before my dad can move, Cameron approaches him, offering him a hand. "I'm Cameron. It's nice to meet you, sir. Thank you for having us for dinner, sir."

I stifle a laugh at how serious he is because my dad is definitely not someone you need to be serious with.

"Thanks for being there for my Cupcake that night. And please don't act weird around me because I run the school. I'm a cool dad, I swear." He winks, shaking Cameron's hand firmly.

"I'll always be there for her," Cameron remarks sincerely, just as Lexa speaks up.

"If you have to tell people you're cool, it usually means you're not," she quips.

"Lexa Mae!" Lucy admonishes.

"She's fine, Lucy," my dad waves her off. "Now, Lexa, care to inform me how I can up my cool factor while we get this in the oven?"

Lexa agrees, pushing her walker to follow my dad and her mom into the kitchen, leaving Cam and me alone.

I let out a sigh of relief, emitting a laugh from Cameron.

"Rory, relax, love. My mom and sister adore you. There's nothing to worry about," he says, wrapping his arms around my lower back.

"Oh, I'm the one who's not relaxed, huh? Says the guy who just called my dad 'sir' twice," I bite down on my lip, trying to hide my smile and failing as my arms rest on his shoulders.

Cameron pinches his eyes shut. "Fuck, I did. God, that was embarrassing."

"It's okay. I think it's cute when you get all nervous and ramble."

"Yeah?" his voice turns raspier, "I think it's cute that you wore this skirt and didn't expect me to want to rip it off of you."

I don't respond with words. Instead, I lean on my toes and kiss him, our lips melding together like they were made to. His hand cradles my head, deepening the kiss as his tongue prods between my lips to access my mouth.

"Uh," Nate coughs.

I jump back from Cameron, feeling like we just got caught in the act because kissing him always feels so sensual and private. Cameron gently moves me back in front of him. I don't question it and just roll with it.

I laugh awkwardly. "Nate, this is my boyfriend Cameron. Cameron, this is my brother, Nate."

"Hey, it's nice to meet you," Cameron says, leaning around me to shake my brother's hand. It's then that I feel how hard he is against my back.

My brother grimaces. "Yeah, it's nice to meet you too. Although, I'd prefer it if you didn't have a boner, but beggars can't be choosers."

Oh. My. Fuck.

"Nate," I screech, telling him with my eyes to stop being an ass.

Cameron laughs behind me. "Agreed."

Nate folds his arms over his chest, a grin on his face. "A guy who can take a joke, good. I like him already, sis."

Dinner is going smoothly. Everyone has been getting to know each other, and we've been laughing non-stop as Lucy and my dad swap parenting stories.

I'm sitting beside Cameron, with Lexa on my other side. She insisted, and let me say, she is fiery. Her banter is quick and witty, making our conversations entertaining.

The doorbell rings, causing my dad to excuse himself and answer it. I know Jodi and her son, whom I have yet to meet or get a name, are also supposed to be joining us. It's a big, blended Christmas, and surprisingly, I'm here for it.

My dad reenters the open space from the foyer, with Jodi following him. My mouth drops open at the man following behind her because I know him.

"Cameron," I whisper-hiss, my hand landing on his muscular thigh and squeezing.

Cameron's eyes shoot up to where I'm looking, raising his eyebrows in surprise. "Well, this just got interesting."

Trailing behind his mother is Ryker—the quiet, broody man we met at the athlete's gala last night. I had no idea he was Jodi's son, which means he's now essentially family in some way. I just hope he lightens up a bit because our family can be a lot for grumps like him.

"Lucy, Lexa, Cameron, Nate, Aurora," my dad addresses, "I'd like to introduce you to Jodi, and her son, Ryker. She's a veterinarian in the city, and Ryker here is a player on RLU's baseball team."

Ryker's sporting a slightly less menacing scowl despite it being the holidays. His medium-length hair is in a half-up bun, and the tattoos on his arms are visible.

We all welcome them, and they take their seats at the end of the table near my dad. The conversation flows easily, and everyone seems to be enjoying themselves.

Cameron's pinky grazes the outside of my thigh, and I nearly spit out my water due to the desire that sparks in my stomach. I glance at him to see that he's chatting with Ryker as his pinky travels higher, inching under my skirt hidden by the tablecloth.

I can't believe he would touch me at a family dinner, but part of me isn't shocked. The man is a sweetheart in public but dirtier than I imagined in the sheets.

"Cupcake, do you mind going down to the wine cellar to get two bottles here for our guests?" my dad asks, startling me from my trance.

"Of course," I say, pushing my chair back to stand abruptly.

"I'll go with you. I want to see the basement," Cam offers, standing with me.

We walk to the cellar in the basement in silence, and tension builds between us with each silent step. My breathing becomes choppy as desire shoots down my spine to my toes.

I push open the glass door to the cellar, closing it behind us. And that's when we lose it.

I jump up, and he helps me by gripping my waist as I wrap my legs around him, our mouths colliding in a frenzy. His hands slide under my skirt, grabbing my ass as his mouth claims mine, over and over again. I grind against him, feeling him harden beneath me.

"I need to be inside you *now*," he grunts.

"Please," I whine, wanting him to take me right here, right now.

"Think you can be quiet for me?" he whispers against my neck, trailing kisses there, causing me to bite my lip to stifle a moan.

"Mhm," I mumble, rolling my hips against his.

His hands roam higher on my ass, likely trying to feel my underwear, but he won't find any. He stills once he realizes I'm not wearing any. "Rory, why aren't you wearing any panties?" he groans, pained.

"Think of it as a Christmas treat," I tease, trailing kisses from his jaw down his neck.

He bucks his hips against mine, letting me know he's just as ready as I am.

"Are you soaked for me, love? Tell me, can I eat that pretty pussy first?" he asks, giving my ass a tight squeeze.

"Fill me right now, please. We don't have time for that," I rasp against his neck, wishing there weren't so many clothes between our bodies.

Cameron sets me down for a second, quickly undoing the button on his jeans and tugging them down with his boxers low enough so that his lengthy cock can spring free. He lifts me back up effortlessly, my legs wrapping around his waist again.

Cam adjusts me so that his cock is lined up with my center, his eyes closing once he feels how wet I am. "Fuck, this needs to be quick, and you need to be quiet."

I nod eagerly just as the breath whooshes out of my lungs. He slowly pulls me down on his cock, right until there's nothing else I can take. Cameron holds onto my waist, my hands wrapped around his shoulders as he uses his to lift me up and down his cock.

He's in total control of how I ride him while keeping us both upright. It's a testament to his strength, and that only turns me on even more.

Every time I slam down his length, my body shivers in pleasure, feeling it from my head to my toes, my entire being ignited at his touch. Cameron kisses my neck, nipping then licking as he fucks me like no one ever has.

I lean forward, biting down on his shoulder to avoid screaming his name as my orgasm hits me, blinding white light crossing my vision as pleasure rolls through my body. Cameron pumps inside of me, once, twice, and then he stills, filling me as he groans against my neck, cursing under his breath.

"I think I finally see the appeal of being inside," he teases, a callback to our conversation at the lake when he told me he preferred being outside.

I laugh, not caring to control that noise. We hold onto each other for a moment, and then he pulls out before setting me down, shocking me as he quickly puts his hand under my pussy, collecting our arousal as it drips out of me.

He then holds his hand up to my mouth. "Suck."

Holy. Fuck. It's probably the dirtiest thing I've been asked to do, but also the hottest. I open my mouth and revel in the way his eyes darken. I bring my lips to his fingers coated in our cum, loving the taste as I suck and lick his fingers clean.

What is this man doing to me? I would never do that with anyone else.

"I fucking love you," he groans, and I can tell he wants to go again, but we don't have time. Instead, he goes to the bar, grabbing a napkin to wipe me up, and then we're both adjusting ourselves back to our previous state.

I select two wines, a white and a red, then hand in hand, we walk back upstairs, hoping we weren't gone longer than we thought, or worse, louder than we thought.

My brother speculatively eyes us as I set the wines on the table. "Does it take that long to get wine?" he mutters as I lean over him.

I remain composed, not wanting to give myself away. "Yeah, it does, actually, when you're searching for our best wine. Plus, Cameron wanted a tour."

A tour of my pussy, maybe, because he didn't see a damn thing in the basement.

Nate smirks, knowing damn well I'm full of shit. But he knows I have dirt on him from all the times I helped him sneak boys in and out of the house. Therefore, our secret is safe.

After dinner, I announce that I need to let Pickles out for a bit when Lexa offers to come with me. While she gets ready, I quickly run to my room to change into a pair of tights, not wanting to freeze out there. The rest of the guests settle around the table, my dad getting the gingerbread houses ready to decorate.

Once outside, Lexa hits me with a question. "So, what's it like being an athletic powerhouse?"

I giggle, loving her praise but also not wanting to come off as vain. "It's a mix, honestly. I love being able to play the sport I love, but there are a lot of things I don't like. The pressure, the draining school schedule, and the media aspect. I just want to play. The rest doesn't matter to me."

"Very humble, I like it. I wish I could hit like you do. Cameron showed me a video he took on his phone at your last game, and damnnn, girl, you got it going on," she gleams, her eyes bright with admiration.

An idea pops into my head. "Want to learn how right now?"

She looks at me like I've lost my mind. "Aurora, you know I need a walker to get around," she chuckles sarcastically.

"Who said you needed to get rid of it? I can teach you with it."

Her eyes light up. "Really? Can we try it?"

"Absolutely!" I beam, quickly running into the house to grab a spare volleyball. Everyone eyes me speculatively when I run past them, but I'm too excited to stop and explain why.

I return outside with the ball in hand, and we keep walking on the concrete patio to a large blank square, where our patio set usually is when it's not below freezing.

"Alright, the key to a good spike is your hand form. It doesn't matter how high you jump, but how you hit the ball. Sure, it's nice to get on top of the ball, but if you do as I tell you, that won't even matter."

We run through the basics, where I teach her hand form and demonstrate how to do it by spiking the ball against the brick exterior of the house. With one hand on her walker and her right hand ready to attack, I threw the ball up for her.

Lexa's right arm goes back, then swings forward, the top of her fingers curving slightly to hit the ball downward as she spikes it to the ground.

"Oh my god," Lexa whispers, then shouts, "Oh my god, I did it!"

We both cheer, and it's at that moment I realized how much I loved coaching her and seeing the joy on her face when she accomplished her goal. It's the first time I've felt as passionate about something other than volleyball and Cameron.

Speaking of, I feel a gaze burning my back, so I spin to see Cam looking at me through the glass doors. His smile is wide, dimples on display as he looks at me with gratitude.

Lexa and I spend a few more minutes outside, hitting the ball over and over. Then we head inside, joining everyone at the table to begin our gingerbread house decorating contest.

We pick names out of a hat to determine the partners, and I end up with Lexa, while Cam is paired with my dad. He looked so nervous at first, but they work well together. I even hear them laugh at some points. Lucy's paired up with Jodi, while Nate and Ryker work together.

Through a poll via social media, Lexa and I take the cake as the best gingerbread house. My dad is in disbelief, while Nate and Ryker demand a recount of the votes because they're more invested in this than they would like to let on.

It's the best Christmas I've had in a long time because I feel surrounded by Mom on her favorite day and my new family, who I knew she'd love just as much as I do.

Chapter Thirty-Two

Cameron

It was New Year's Eve, and my mom and sister went home a few days ago.

They both adored Aurora and were really happy that I'd done something for myself for once. Their approval meant a lot because they are important to me.

I enjoyed every second they were here, but I can't deny that I was looking forward to going back to my routine of working out, coding, and being with Aurora whenever possible. I've also been working my ass off on the game, making sure I could work on it whenever possible.

I came over to her place, and we decided to stay in tonight to binge Marvel movies, both of us not caring for the celebrations that accompany the holiday. Jasmine went home to spend time with her parents, which meant we had the house to ourselves.

Before coming over, I picked up food from her beloved Italian place and a slice of peanut butter chocolate cake from the cafe she loves so much.

We're about half an hour away from midnight now, and Aurora turns the TV off, putting on music instead, a mix of R&B songs with the time displayed as the background.

"I never gave you your Christmas gift because it wasn't ready yet, but I have it now," she says, twirling a piece of hair around her finger. She's nervous, a side she only shows around me, and it makes me happy that she feels comfortable enough to be vulnerable with me.

I place my hand over hers, stilling her anxious movement. "Why are you nervous, love?"

She blushes and attempts to look away. I place my fingers under her chin, lightly turning her face to me again. Her pretty hazel eyes lock with mine, and fuck, I think I just fell more in love with her. I'm not sure why, but just looking at her does that to me. Knowing she exists and loves me is enough to do that.

"Remember how you wanted to know what I've been doing in my pink notebook? Well, I like to draw. It's something I started doing when my mom passed. I would draw memories that we shared. My therapist said it was a way to process my emotions. So, I kept doing it, and now I draw whenever I want to preserve a memory or a feeling," she explains, her eyes turning glassy while her lips tug up slightly to the right. She heads over to the hallway closet, where she lifts to her tiptoes to reach the top shelf. She walks back toward me, wearing a smile on her lips, a scrapbook in her hand.

"Merry Christmas, Cam," she says softly, handing over the book to me. It's dark green, the cover plain and giving nothing away as to what's inside.

I flip to the first page to see a picture of brown eyes, but not just any brown eyes. They're mine. The detail in her work is stunning, making the eyes look life-like, but she also perfectly captured the emotion in them. My eyes look trusting, honest, and warm.

"Keep going," she urges.

I flip to the next page to see another drawing. She illustrated the time we met at Emerald Lake, her hand on top of mine on the log to comfort me as we shared our pain and where we became friends. The next is a picture drawn from above of her head on my lap from when she was sick. That was the day I realized I didn't just take care of her because it's my nature, but because I *wanted* to.

The next drawing is of us sitting on my couch, watching *Guardians of the Galaxy* the day she passed out, laughter evident on the still faces in the sketch. The one after is her wrapped up in my arms behind the bar after the incident. While that memory makes my blood fucking boil, this sketch reminds me of what we gained that night. This is shown in the following sketch, where her legs are wrapped around my waist, our lips pressed together for our first kiss as snow falls around us.

I can feel my eyes glass over with emotion, but I don't care to hide it, not with her.

The last one is a sketch from our first date, the image showing us holding hands while sliding down the slopes together on our tubes, with wide smiles on our faces. I've noticed her ability to include the emotion of that memory and what it signifies in each sketch.

"Rory," my voice croaks as I look up at her like she's the most precious thing to me, because she is.

She shrugs. "I hope you like it. It's nothing crazy nice or anything."

I tug her toward me, pressing her body against mine, needing to feel her. I possessively place my hand on her hip while my other hand sifts through the ends of her silky hair to the base where I cradle her head. "I love it, and I love you so fucking much,

Rory. You're all I can think of, from when I wake up to when I go to sleep. No one and nothing has ever consumed me the way that you do."

Aurora's pretty hazel eyes hood with lust and affection at my words, her hand coming up to stroke my smooth jaw and cup my cheek. "Promise me?"

I grab her hand, placing a kiss in the middle of her palm. "That's a guarantee, love." I seal my words with a kiss, my lips moving over hers like they were made to fit together. Our lips press against one another skillfully, not too fast or slow, just enough to savor the feeling.

Aurora pulls back, looking at me intently. "I mean it, bub. But how will this work after graduation? Scouts will be at my games after the holidays, and hopefully, I'll get picked up for Team USA post-grad. I might have to move to Sacramento, where headquarters are for practices, and then, there's all the traveling for games, for *the Olympics*. Are you sure you want this? Because if it's too much, I need to know now," she says, throwing me off.

What is she talking about? Did she not hear what I just said?

I walk backward and sit on the couch, pulling her down with me into my lap, where I cradle her. Swiping a piece of blonde hair out of her face, I say, "Rory, you're not hearing me. There's nothing that could take me away from you. Where you go, I go. My job can be remote. I want to cheer you on along the way and watch with pride as they place a gold medal around your neck in two years. And with even more pride when I place something gold around your finger one day."

Her plump lips part in an O, her gaze transfixed on me, trying to see any hint of dishonesty, which she won't find. "Something gold? Maybe I'm more of a silver kind of girl."

I scowl playfully at her. "Please, my girl is a gold girl through and through. Miss, '*I have 50 first-place trophies and medals.*'"

"You know me well," she smiles, placing a chaste kiss on my lips before turning serious. "I love you, Cameron. And I want you there with me through it all."

"Good, 'cause I don't break my promises," I tell her, glancing at the TV to see that there are five minutes until midnight. I slip my fingers under the waistband of her sweats, loving that she's not wearing any panties. We had sex earlier, and I told her not to bother putting any on because I would fuck her again later.

Her breath hitches when my fingers swipe over her wet slit. A grunt escapes my throat, loving how ready she is for me. "I plan to end this year inside of you and start the new year the same way. My favorite place to be," I inform her, just as I enter her with two fingers, her tight warmth feeling so fucking good around my fingers. I pump them in and out of her rapidly, getting right into it because we have four minutes now, and I need to be inside her. But I always make sure she comes at least once before I enter her.

Aurora whimpers into my neck as I bring her closer to the edge with my fingers, fucking her with them so that the sound of her wet heat sucking my fingers in and out of her fills the room. Mix it in with her breathy moans, and it's fucking music to my ears.

Her sweatpants limit my range of motion, causing me to growl in frustration. I remove my hand to rip them off, followed by her T-shirt. She's now bare and fucking beautiful on my lap.

I lay her on the couch, kissing my way down her body until I reach just below her stomach. Then, I spread her knees apart as I drop to mine. My mouth waters at the sight of her glistening pussy, knowing it's just for me.

"I love this pussy," I hum in appreciation as I run a single digit through her slit, making her shiver.

"It needs you," she pants, eyes hungry for more.

I glance at the clock on the wall—three minutes to go.

I dive in, wasting no time as I lap at her wet slit. I part her with my fingers and suck onto her clit hard as I lower my fingers and insert them inside her again. My fingers curl, moving up and down instead of in and out, causing her hips to buck, her orgasm ripping through her as she comes on my tongue. Her hands grip my hair for dear life as my name rolls off her lips.

I stand and quickly pull down my sweats, kicking them off to the side as I fist my cock, giving it a pump.

"I want it in my mouth," she whines, her eyes filled with hunger as she eyes up my cock, which is lined up at her center.

"Later. Right now, I need that pretty pussy," I groan, feeling like I will lose it if I don't. When we're together, everything else tunes out. The only thing in the world on my mind is her, no worries, no pressure, just making my girl feel good.

I slam inside of her with one thrust, right to the hilt. She gasps, followed by a moan as she adjusts to me. Being inside her is like nothing I could have imagined because it's better. Once I feel her hips move against mine, I know she's ready, and that's when I snap.

I pump my cock into her roughly, my hips rocking so damn hard and fast that I can barely keep up. Aurora nearly slides off the couch, too overcome by the sensation to keep her body upright, so I grip her waist, holding her steady as I fuck her.

"Cam," she moans, her legs shaking. Aurora's hands move from my shoulders to my neck and jaw until she reaches her favorite place—my hair. She tugs on it, letting me know she wants my lips on hers. I oblige, leaning forward as our lips meet, our tongues tangling as we fuck each other into oblivion, her hips moving just as eagerly against mine, our bodies in unison.

I hear fireworks go off in the distance, signaling the new year. I break the kiss, "Happy New Year, Rory," breathing heavily against her neck where I pepper kisses.

"Happy New Year, Cam," she sighs, guiding my head back up to hers, where she kisses me with so much love and passion it threatens to undo me right here. But I hold off, wanting her to come again before I do.

I grab her legs, removing them from around my waist, placing her feet behind my neck, her calves resting on my shoulders as the rest of her legs remain wide open for me, deepening the angle.

"Oh my fuck," Aurora curses, her eyes fixating on my cock, ramming in and out of her.

"Touch your clit for me, love," I rasp because I can't take my hands off her body, or she'll fall off this couch.

She moves her hand to her clit, a whimper leaving her luscious lips as she rubs fast circles over it. Her pussy squeezes my cock so goddamn tight as she comes, her orgasm ripping through her body.

Aurora screams my name, her eyes locked on mine the whole time. So fucking hot.

"That's my girl, squeezing me so fucking good," I grunt, thrusting once more before I erupt, spilling myself inside of her as I come, repeating her name over and over again as we ride out our pleasure.

A happy new year indeed.

Chapter Thirty-Three

Aurora

So far, the new year has been off to a great start.

Cameron and I have been inseparable from studying together, watching Marvel movies, going out for walks, having dates, and messing around whenever we get the chance. But the moments when I sketch while Cameron either gives me a massage or works are just as coveted.

It's a way for us to spend time on our crafts while also spending time together. We've even had game nights with Jasmine, Theo, Finn and Ashlyn. So, all around, it's been really good.

What's even better is that our team has been on a winning streak, and I've been performing really well. I still train just as hard as when I was single, if not better.

My phone rings from my backpack, and I retrieve it as I walk to my early morning training session.

"Coach?" I answer with concern because it's six in the morning.

"Vallacourt, I have good news. Scouts are coming next Friday to watch you play."

My whole world stops, and my mind whirls with the information.

"Next Friday? Wow," is all I manage to say because, of course, it's *the* day. The day my mom passed away. It's also the day Cameron is flying out for his job.

"That's what I said. I need you to keep up with your training, nutrition, and rest. This is huge. There's only one spot for the team this year, and they are considering many candidates from across the country."

A nervous chill runs down my spine at the reminder, one I hadn't been paying much attention to recently because of how busy I've been outside of volleyball. But now? I can feel that pressure weighing down on my chest, snuggling right back where it belongs as if it never truly left.

I've been working towards this for the last ten years, training, working, and perfecting my skills every chance I get. I can only hope it was enough, that *I'm* enough.

I don't know what I'll do if I don't make the team. It's been my only plan. When you know you're destined for something, you don't waste energy on a plan B or C. There's just plan A, and you put your all towards it.

And it's time I do just that. No more distractions this week. I need to focus.

"On it, Coach. Thank you."

I work out harder than normal during my training session. I bike an extra mile, extend my reps, and increase my weights where I can. I'm exhausted by the time I leave, which is an extra hour later.

After my shower, I open my locker to see a bunch of texts and missed calls from Cam.

It's 9 a.m. now, which means he's been worrying for the last hour. My chest tightens because I should've texted him and told him I was training longer today.

It's just a reminder that I'm not good at juggling all of *this*—a boyfriend, school, and volleyball. The only thing I've ever been good at is volleyball, and maybe there's a reason why. Maybe I'm not meant for love. Maybe my dream is already too much to carry with room for nothing else.

Inhaling a deep breath, I do my best to clear the panic clutching my body as I call him back.

He picks up instantly. "Rory, are you okay?" his voice cracks with concern.

"Hey, yeah, I'm fine. I had to train a bit longer this morning, that's all," I tell him as I get dressed.

"Did you eat breakfast yet? I don't want you to—"

"I'm heading to the cafeteria now," I cut him off, not wanting to be reminded of that day. This isn't the same thing. My goal has a deadline, and it's next Friday. I have to put everything aside and work my ass off this next week.

His tone immediately softens, a tinge of hurt in his voice that makes me hate myself a little. "Love, what's bothering you? Did I do something wrong?"

"Not at all, bub. You're perfect." It's the truth. He's too good to be true.

"Then what is it? You're worrying me."

"Coach Tilly informed me that scouts will watch me next Friday. Everything I've been working my whole life towards hinges on one night next week. I can't lose focus. I need to work my ass off this week and stay on top of my nutrition to be at peak performance."

"Tell me what you need, and I'll do it. Anything."

I love him so damn much. What did I ever do to deserve him? It breaks my heart knowing I'm about to hurt him.

"I need you to give me some space for the week. I can't be distracted. I need to sleep at least a full nine hours, train, practice, and rest in between." My voice cracks as a tear trails down my cheek.

He's silent for a moment, which only makes my tears come faster.

"Are you breaking up with me?"

"No, *no*," I rush my words out, panic coursing through me. "I just can't do the girlfriend role this next week. I need to focus on this. It's unfair to you, so I'm just asking that we take it easy this week. You also have your meeting next Friday, so you should focus on that."

"Okay," he breathes out, sounding somewhat relieved. "Rory, just know that I love you. I'll be there whenever you need me. You just have to let me."

I choke back a sob. Why does this hurt so much? We're not breaking up, but it feels like something's shifted.

"I love you too, bub," I whisper, then hang up. The sob I've been holding back lets loose.

I give myself ten minutes to cry, then pull it together the best I can. I can deal with my emotions another time, but the Olympic scouts will only come once.

I just hope I'll be ready.

Chapter Thirty-Four

Cameron

Two hours into the whole space thing Aurora proposed, and I'm already losing my mind.

I've grown accustomed to our routine and I miss it and her already. I know I sound lame, but I don't give a fuck. She's become a part of my life, and now it feels off.

Giving her the space she needs is the respectful thing to do, and realistically, I should be grateful for the extra time to focus on my application. But in reality, I don't want to be respectful for once. I want to tell Aurora to hell with the space, that I need her more than she'll ever understand.

But I won't because it's what she wants, and I'll always give her that.

To avoid the ache in my chest, I work on the game for hours, fine-tuning details before I leave on Friday.

It's not until Finn comes into my room that I stop.

"Ronnie boy, what's wrong?" he asks, flopping on my bed.

"Not you, too," I mutter, hating the nickname Theo's given me.

"Don't ignore me. I can tell when something's up. You didn't even leave your room when I brought pizza home for dinner. You always do when you smell the 'za."

Saving my progress, I turn my monitor off and swivel in my computer chair towards him. I take my glasses off, pinching the bridge of my nose. "Aurora and I—"

"If you say you broke up, I will sob uncontrollably. Just a warning," Finn shrieks.

That ache in my chest intensifies at the idea of us breaking up. Not a fucking chance. She's become my solace, soothing me in places I didn't know needed it. I feel complete when she's around, more like myself. She makes me laugh and smile like I never have, and god, those eyes? I'm so damn blessed to be able to stare into them. Don't even get me started on her touch. It drives me wild in the best way.

"We didn't," I nearly growl at him while I run my fingers through my unruly hair. "She wants some space this week because we both have big things to do this Friday. The scouts are coming to watch her, and I'm heading to Los Angeles."

Finn nods as he thinks my words over. "I mean, it makes sense. Aurora has worked her whole life for this. I'd imagine hearing that your dream will be determined in a week would stress anyone out. This is how she's choosing to deal with it, and you have to respect that while trusting she'll come back to you."

"I know that, truly, I do. I miss her already, that's all," I murmur.

He smirks at me, a knowing glint in his eyes. "I knew watching you fall in love with her would be fun, but seeing you as a lovesick puppy? Even better."

"Fuck off," I chuckle. "Maybe you and Ash should give each other some space, and then you can talk to me."

Finn's smirk turns into a frown. "Don't even joke like that."

As much as he likes to give me crap and tease me about being in love, he's the biggest simp. If I'm a cinnamon roll, he's an ice cream sundae with all the fixings.

Eventually, he lures me out of my room, where we enjoy pizza and the hockey game on TV.

My mind wanders back to Aurora occasionally, because when doesn't it?

I also think about what Finn said, knowing what he said was true. I know how hard she's worked, everything she's sacrificed, and how much this means to her. I want her to succeed and be there for her every step of the way as her biggest supporter.

The one question at the back of my mind is whether she would sacrifice me if it meant getting what she wanted. If she needed to break up with me to chase her goals, would she?

It haunts me long after Finn goes to bed, keeping me tossing and turning all night.

I know my dream means shit without her. It's something I realized today. I don't care what I end up doing so long as she's by my side. It's the one thing I won't compromise on.

I can lose out on the job or get a different one, but I can't lose her. I refuse.

Chapter Thirty-Five

Aurora

It's been a hell of a week.

I've been training harder, pushing myself at practice, and meal-prepping like crazy while resting whenever possible.

Whenever I rest, I think of Cam and how we've barely talked this last week. We've texted a few times, mostly him checking in on me, but nothing more.

I knew it would be an adjustment as I got used to being with him every day, but I didn't anticipate how much it would hurt. I feel like a part of me is missing, like a phantom pain that won't go away.

But I put all those thoughts on hold today because it was January 22nd. The day I lost my mom.

Grief always finds its way back to me today, no matter what. It's been an oddly warm week, melting all the snow. It makes a perfect day for a little hike to Emerald Lake to feel closer to her, as I always do on this day if possible.

I decided to skip my Friday classes, and that's how I ended up sitting on a cold log, looking at a half-frozen crystal blue lake.

I take a deep breath, the cool air filling my lungs as I remember the last time I was here with her.

I was nine, and we came here to hike during the summer. I remember it was scorching hot, sweat was sticking to my skin like another set of clothes, but my mom made it look easy, graceful even. We sat on this same log, sharing water and eating apples while we rested. My mom was looking out at the lake. "You know what I've learned, Rory?" she said, her smile so grand it couldn't be described accurately.

"What's that, Mom?" I asked, waiting on her like she held the answers to the universe.

"Sometimes, the dreams we're chasing aren't all we're meant to be."

"Uh?" I asked, my nine-year-old self not quite understanding what she meant.

She smiled at me. "It means, Rory, that just because you start on one path and it leads you astray doesn't mean you need to get back to it. Maybe we can take a path that leads us to achieve more than just that one dream."

I just scrunched my nose up at her in response, and she laughed. I wrapped my arms around her, not fully understanding her words. I'm not sure I still do.

With my gaze still on the lake, the scene of my mom and I swimming there comes to mind. My mind fills with the sound of her whimsical laughter as she tosses me into the lake, and my heart constricts when I realize the melody never fades.

I'll never forget her laugh, her love, and how she brought sunshine into everything she did.

A raindrop falls on my cheek, and I peer up at the looming gray clouds above. Pulling out my phone, I check my weather app because I don't remember seeing it call for rain today.

There's nothing safe about this situation, not when I have a game in eight hours that requires me to be healthy and not broken from slipping and falling.

Why did I think this was a good idea? I knew it was tradition, and I missed my mom, but I should've put that aside instead of what was coming later. Gosh, I'm an idiot.

Worry washes over me, much like the rain drenching my coat, making my lip quiver. My brain screams one word over and over again as I try to seek a semblance of solace.

Cameron.

I unlock my phone, seeing the 2% battery staring back at me. Unease prickles my stomach because what if something happens and I can't call anyone?

Knowing his flight wasn't until tonight, I quickly dial his number, hoping I get a signal.

"Rory?" Cameron's voice crackles, the signal weak.

"Cam, I'm at Emerald Lake, and it's raining. I-I'm scared about making it down the mountain," my voice shakes.

"Fuck," he curses under his breath. "Stay there and wait for me. I'm coming for you. Don't walk and get yourself hurt."

"I—"

The signal goes out, ending the call before I could tell him I was sorry for pushing him away. That I loved him and couldn't sleep without him beside me. Hell, I could barely function without him in my life. I didn't realize how much he became my center, the thing that grounded me and made me feel at ease until I didn't have him close.

I do my best to wait it out, but I get restless and scared, my body willing me to move to safety. I'm also worried about Cam because he's risking getting hurt by hiking up here to get me. I know he's an avid hiker, but I still worry nonetheless.

I stand, throw my backpack over my shoulders, and begin to make my way back down the path I came. The rain pours harder. The dirt path becomes slick, making it harder to trek down.

I pull my phone out again, trying to shield my screen from the rain with my other hand as I look to see if I have any bars. Distracted, I trip over a tree root in the path, falling into the mud and hitting my head off a tree stump just to the left of the path.

My vision blurs then blackens as my head starts to throb from the pain, radiating and pulsing. I feel a warm liquid trickle down my ear, and I lift my shaking hand to it, smearing it off my face.

I open my eyes to see blood on my fingers. I quickly grab my phone again, and it's now down to its last percent. I open the camera application and flip it to selfie mode. I angle it toward the side of my head to see a small cut in my hair, just above my ear. It's nothing too concerning, but my head freaking hurts, and I feel nauseous.

I attempt to stand but fall back down because my head is spinning way too much to stand upright. I kick at the dirt with my foot, feeling frustrated with myself for being so helpless. I have a game I *need* to play tonight, which means I need whatever is happening with my head right now to stop. I already know what it is, but I'm afraid if I speak the words, it'll make it more real than I want it to be.

I have no choice but to sit in the mud, the rain pouring down on me as I wait for the spell to pass or for Cameron to show up. After about ten minutes of stewing, the sadness starts to kick in, with fear not too far behind it. I don't want to be alone and possibly injured right now. I want my bub, my strong mountain man, to wrap me in his arms where I feel safe and loved.

Instead, all I can do is sit here in the mud, rain pelting on me as I think about how I'll play the most important game of my life with a concussion. I know it's unsafe, but what freaking choice do I have? This is the game I've worked so hard for, all the years of training, extra workouts, and more, for what? For nothing? Fuck that.

The tears start to fall due to my frustration over the situation, just as I hear boots slapping against the mud puddles in the distance. I squint my eyes, which are no longer blurry from my fall, to see Cameron moving faster than I've ever seen him before.

"Cam!" I call out, my voice weak and laced with sadness.

Cameron stills once he sees me in the distance, but then he charges toward me even faster now. As his face comes into view, I can see a mixture of emotions there—worry, anger, and hurt.

I hate that I made him feel that way, but right now, I can only focus on being in his arms.

He kneels in front of me, his jaw tight with tension, eyes glazed over with panic as his hands gently cup my cheeks, tilting my head from side to side. Once he sees the small cut, his eyes flare with worry, his lips parted on a shaky breath.

"Rory," he croaks, sounding worried. "What happened?"

"Can I tell you on the way down? I just need to be in your arms, please," my voice cracks, a sob ripping through me.

He obliges immediately, carefully scooping me into his arms in a front piggyback. I nestle my nose into his neck, my tears soaking his jacket. The safety of his embrace soothes something deep within me. It's been too long.

With a tight hold under my ass with one arm, he uses his other hand to rub circles on my back soothingly, trying to settle my emotions. His lips press into the side of my hair as he slowly walks back down the path, clutching me to his body like I'm the most precious thing he's ever carried.

We stay silent for what feels like thirty minutes, Cam's hold on me never waning as we make our way down the trail. The only things to be heard are my sniffles as I cry and the slosh of mud under his boots.

"Fuck, this is killing me," his gravel voice penetrating the only noise of rain hitting the dirt.

"I'm s-sorry," I sniffle, trying to compose myself as I take deep breaths of his scent, letting it soothe me.

"Don't," he says, kissing my head lightly. "I'm not mad at you. I just want to know what happened. Seeing you hurt and upset is eating me alive right now."

I take one more deep breath, tilt my head to look at him, and then recount how I hit my head off the stump. His hands tighten their grip on me, his body tensing when he hears the details.

"I'm okay. It just shocked me at first, that's all," I say to ease his worries and my own.

I don't realize we're in the parking lot until he sets me on the trunk of his car, his cinnamon eyes gazing past my bullshit.

"Love, you have a cut on your forehead. Tell me, do you feel nauseous, faint, or have a headache?" he asks, knowing what I already know.

I'm an athlete, and this is a no-brainer.

"It'll pass by then," I mutter, glancing to the side because I can't look at his searing eyes right now. There's so much concern in them, and it's threatening to make me feel guilty enough not to play tonight. Because we both know what I meant when I said 'by then.' It means I know there's a good chance I have a concussion, but I'll play that game no matter what.

Cameron doesn't say anything, his brows furrowing and his jaw tensing as he burns a hole into the side of my head. He lifts me into his arms again, walking us to the passenger side, where he carefully places me and buckles me in. Once he's in the driver's seat, he says, "We'll come get your car tomorrow."

I quietly agree. "Okay."

Then we remained silent during the drive to my house, the tension nearly suffocating. We haven't seen each other or spoken much in over a week. I can tell he's upset, but he's not in the mood to talk right now, either. Which is uncommon for him, and it's unsettling.

I'm already a mess over my concussion, the scouts, and now I'm freaking the fuck out that we're about to fight. I don't want to fight with him, a tremor running through my body at the thought of losing him.

He's quiet as we park in my driveway, my throat tight with emotion because it all feels like too much. I wrap my hand around the handle, opening my door, needing to clear my mind.

"Don't move," he orders tersely, and I comply because if this is it, I want to be in his arms one last time.

He lifts me gently out of the car, carrying me to the front door, where he enters the code and walks us inside.

Jasmine's car is here, but she's likely taking a pre-game nap because she's driving home after the game to celebrate the Korean New Year with her dad's side of the family. If she wasn't napping, I know she already would've been at the door, asking what the hell is wrong.

He doesn't set me down in the entryway, simply tugging my boots and jacket off while keeping me wrapped around his body. I bask in the connection, how he refuses to set me down for even a moment.

I have a dreadful inkling about what's to come.

Cameron walks up the stairs with me in his arms, my fingers tangling in his hair as if I'm holding on for dear life.

Setting me on my bed, he kneels in front of me, my hands resting at my sides. "Aurora, are you seriously thinking of playing?" he asks, looking at me as if I've lost it.

My eyes swell with tears because I know this will upset him.

"Cam," my voice cracks, "You know I have to. It's my only chance."

"No, it's not. I'm sure your coach can tell them the situation, and they can come watch you another time."

"That's all a possibility, but I can't risk my dreams on a possibility," I tell him.

"Yet you're willing to risk your life on it?" He frowns, his words like ice.

"I won't get hurt. I'm a great reactive player. A ball hasn't hit me in years," I defend myself, knowing despite that, it's never a guarantee.

Cameron stands, his muscular chest pumping up and down as he takes deep breaths. "Rory, if you play and get hurt even more, you can kiss that dream goodbye for good. Just tell them what happened, and we will figure something out. I promise."

"Cam, don't ask me not to follow my dreams. You know better than anyone why I need to do this," I plead, a tear strolling down my cheek.

His eyes soften a bit, but everything else about him remains rigid. "Fine, how about this. Can I ask you not to do this for me, then? Don't play tonight because if you do and get hurt, I don't how I will fucking function in a world without you."

"I'm not going anywhere," I whisper, hating that his mind is going to the worst-case scenario.

Cameron takes a step back as if I slapped him in the face with my response.

He smirks, but it's not playful. It's incredulous. "You are, though, because you're still going to play, aren't you?"

"I don't know," I mumble because, truthfully, I don't know anything right now.

"Rory, don't. Please," he begs, his own eyes turning glassy.

God, I hate that I'm doing this to him.

"I have a few hours until the game. Let me think about it," I say, feeling drained from the last two hours.

He nods tersely, his jaw working back and forth. His phone vibrates in his pocket. Pulling it out, he glances at the screen and curses under his breath. "Fuck, I have to go," he says. "They changed my flight. It leaves in two hours now."

"Okay," my voice is wobbly, threatening to overflow with my emotions.

"Rory, I need you to promise me you won't play, please?"

My lungs seize, my heart thumping sporadically in my chest. "I need time to think, Cam. I'm overwhelmed and can't think straight."

Cameron runs his hands through his hair, frustration evident in his movements. "Rory, I love you. I need you to know that because you have no idea how goddamn hard it is to walk away from you right now, but I have to," he says, turning on his heel, walking out of my room.

As soon as I hear the door close, I break down.

I sob into my pillow, my knees tucked to my chest as I feel everything. My mom's death, the possibility of losing my dream, and losing Cam. The last one hurts more than I imagined, my chest aching so violently at the thought that I clutch my chest as if it will help.

"Ro?" Jasmine asks, startling me.

I peer up from my pillow to see her standing in my doorway, her concern evident in how her black eyebrows scrunch together.

I don't say anything because I can't. I simply let another sob wrack my body, my head pounding and my body shaking. Jasmine runs over to me, coming up behind me to spoon me despite her being much smaller than I am.

"Shh," she coos, her voice sweet and gentle. "Ro, it's going to be okay. I know you miss her."

That only makes me cry harder because I wish I could talk to my mom. I want to tell her all about Cameron, how he makes me feel so worthy. How I can't stop thinking about him, about how I feel at home in his arms.

Who knew that was an actual thing? I want to gush about my first love, share that joy, and now, heartache with her, and hear all she would have to say.

"It's not just that," I say once my tears subside.

"What is it then?" she asks, brushing my hair off my face.

"I fell on the hike, and I hit my head. I know I have a concussion, but I still argued with Cameron about playing tonight. Seeing how much that hurt him is killing me. He left, Minnie, and he wanted me to promise him I wouldn't play. I couldn't do it," I tell her, my breaths uneven and choppy. "I think he's going to leave me."

As soon as the words leave my lips, tears stream down my face again because the idea terrifies me. It may seem dramatic, but I've never had a boyfriend before. I don't know what to expect or think. All I know is that fighting with him scares me because I've already lost enough in this life, and I refuse to lose the best thing that's ever happened to me.

"Aurora…" her voice trails off as she processes what I told her. "You know you can't play, right? It's illegal. The school could get in a lot of trouble if anyone found out. And besides, it's stupid. Talk to Coach. I'm sure she will work something out for you. It's not worth it to end up severely injured or worse, Ro. As for Cam, that boy looks at you like you supply the oxygen he breathes. I wouldn't worry. He's probably scared, just like you are. He needs to go and follow his dreams, just like you want to. But you can't chase your dreams like this. You need to take care of yourself first."

It hits me then, like a clearing of clouds on a rainy day. Between the fear of losing everything I have, the reminder of what happened to my mom, and everything in the middle, I make a choice about tonight's game.

I nod, swiping at the tears on my cheeks as I sit up. "Can I ride with you to the game? I want to tell Coach myself."

"Of course. Then, I'm staying home to take care of you after the game," she declares, standing up.

"And miss the New Year celebration? No way, be with your family. I'll be fine."

She raises her brow at me, her mocha eyes rolling in the back of her head. "Ro, you know I won't leave you alone with a concussion. My dad, of all people, will understand, and I can just drive there in the morning instead. I won't miss a thing."

"I love you, Minnie, so much," I say, my lips twitching into a fraction of a smile.

"I love you more, Ro. Now, let's get you out of these dirty pants and in the shower."

I follow her into the bathroom, where she helps me undress and proceeds to help me shower because I feel too faint to do it myself. Once we're both ready, we hop into her car and drive over to the stadium.

I want to text Cameron, to let him know I won't play and what's happening, but I never charged my phone once we got back to the house.

The walk from Jasmine's car to the locker room takes nearly everything out of me. My head is throbbing, and I feel weak, like I'll be sick.

I was supposed to be walking this hallway with excitement and pride, but instead, here I am, filled with disappointment and fear.

We're nearly at the locker room, where Coach's office is, when a familiar feeling begins to take over my body. I'm about to pass out, fuck. A shiver runs down my spine, my entire body feeling cold, the room blurring right before it starts to spin.

My knees hit the ground first, still somewhat conscious before my body gave out.

"Ro!" I hear Jasmine scream, followed by a cry for help, as darkness fills my vision.

Chapter Thirty-Six

Aurora

As I wake up, my body feels groggy, weak, and hungry, the sound of machines beeping nearby.

After I passed out, I kept coming in and out as the EMTs transferred me to the local hospital. I didn't eat breakfast, and between the concussion and the stress of events afterward, my body couldn't handle it.

Jasmine tried to come with me, but I refused. In my half-conscious state, I told her to play for me since I couldn't. It was the one thing I knew that would get her to stay. I didn't need her to come here and wait around while they gave me an IV and let me rest.

They'll send me home in the morning, so it wasn't a big deal.

Forcing my eyes to open, a blurry image of my dad sitting beside me catches my attention first. He's resting his head on the bed near my feet, his black hair peppered with gray is a familiar and comforting sight.

"Dad," my voice cracks, groggy from being out.

His head shoots up, and he takes a moment to look at me, his blue eyes welling with emotion as he scrubs a hand over his beard. "Aurora," he sighs in relief.

"I'm okay, Dad. It was just a concussion. I'll be fine in about a week," I reassure him.

"Aurora, do you have any idea the kind of near heart attack that phone call gave me? Especially on this day? Hearing that my baby girl was rushed to the hospital because she fainted after hitting her head is not something I'll take lightly."

"I know, I'm so sorry. I obviously didn't mean for all of this to happen, and I'm upset that I hurt so many people by it," I say, twisting my fingers in my lap.

My dad places his hands over my anxious ones, stilling them. "Cupcake, don't be. It was an accident. There's nothing you could have done to prevent it. Shit happens. That's what the kids say nowadays, right?"

I chuckle because if there's anything my dad can do, it's to make me laugh.

"I'm not upset with you. I'm upset it happened to you, that's all, Aurora," he explains, making the weight on my chest slightly lighter. My dad removes his glasses, tucking them in his suit pocket. "There is something I want you to know, and I think you'll finally understand it."

My body freezes, on high alert for whatever is about to come out of his mouth. "What is it?" I ask, sitting up straighter.

"Your mother is proud of the person you are, the woman you've become. And I say this in the present tense because I know it's true. She's looking down on you every day with that larger-than-life smile because of who you are. Not what you can do on the court, on your tests, or the money in your bank account, which is not much," he teases, trying to lighten the emotional dump he just gave me. "You don't have to prove anything to her. I know you want to honor her dreams, and it's very sweet, but if it takes everything you have in you, is it worth it? Because you'll be losing all of the parts of yourself that your mom loves very much."

I don't realize tears stream down my face until they drip from my chin, falling to my chest. "I want to get there so badly, because she never got to. Not only that, I want it for myself. I want the pride of playing for my country, the thrill of playing against the best of the world, and to make all the hard work worth it. It's for me, too, you know. I love what I do just as much as she did."

"I know that, Cupcake, but are you okay with not making the team? What happens then?" he asks the million-dollar question.

I roll my lips together, looking down at my hands.

Will I be okay?

I once would have thought, no freaking way. Volleyball is my life, but over the last few months, I've learned that I have other things that call to me just as much as volleyball does and that I can spend time doing the things I love outside my main focus. Drawing, spending time with Cameron and my friends, and coaching. It's filled me with joy, knowing there's no expectation, nothing to do but enjoy what brings me happiness.

Volleyball makes me happy, but since I've placed this pressure on myself to honor my mom, it's been stressful, too. It's not easy to get rid of that need to be the best, but it's a goal to work on. Something I know I can do with the support of my loved ones.

I take a deep breath, then lift my head back up, confident in myself as I meet my dad's gaze. "I won't lie and say it won't hurt because it will. But it won't be the end of the world for me, just the end of a journey. And I've been thinking of a new one I want to explore," I admit, biting my lip to contain my excitement.

My dad's mouth parted, eyebrows raised. "Spill the tea. What is this venture you're gushing over?"

I laugh at his use of the word tea. I shake my head and continue, "I want to open and run a facility for kids with disabilities and coach them in various sports. Of course, I would have to hire other athletes, because I don't think I could shoot a three-pointer or throw a football if my life depended on it. I'm not sure about all the details yet. Maybe it could lead to house league games, Paralympics even? Who knows. And even if I do make the team, I still want to pursue it."

"Aurora, that sounds like a wonderful and rewarding thing to do. I'm so proud of you. Even if you don't do this, I'm proud of the heart you have. You have always been so damn loving, kind, and empathetic. I'm glad you'll share that to help others, and your mom would, too. She'd love this idea."

I smile, a genuine one for the first time today, while a tear strolls down my cheek. "Thanks, Dad. You've always been my biggest supporter, and I don't think I thank you enough."

"You know you could come by and do my laundry whenever you're bored. I hear that's the new way of saying thank you these days," he jokes, his eyes crinkling with happiness.

"I love you, but I think I'll stick to the traditional ways of saying thank you," I laugh, but it's cut short once I hear the commotion outside my room.

"Where is she?" a familiar deep voice shouts.

He's here.

"Sir, who are you? We can't release that information to people who aren't her family," a nurse replies irritatedly.

"I'm her boyfriend," he replies, making my heart expand. *I'm her boyfriend,* present tense. It's a good sign, but I don't want to be too hopeful.

"We can't confirm this, so you'll have to leave."

"The hell I am. The girl I love has had the roughest fucking day, and if you think I'm going to be anywhere but by her side, you're mistaken," he shouts, his voice raising as his anger does.

I've heard him this angry only once before, and that was when I was assaulted.

My dad stands up, quickly heading out of my room. A few moments later, I hear, "Hey, it's okay, Barb. He can come in."

I hear his shoes squeak on the linoleum floor, and within seconds, he's barreling into my room with my dad right behind him.

Our eyes connect instantly, stealing the breath from my lungs because even though it's only been a few hours, relief courses through me.

He's actually here.

He has so many mixed emotions on his face, but I'm too tired to decipher them.

My dad claps him on the shoulder, whispering something to him before giving Cam one of those hand slaps then hug things that guys do. It makes me smile, my chest warming at the sight, because I'm glad they're comfortable with each other and have that kind of relationship.

My dad calls over his shoulder, "I love you, Cupcake. Nate's on his way from the bar. I'll wait out here for him." He continues out the door as I tell him I love him too, and then it's the two of us.

Cameron walks over to me, sitting on the stool beside my bed, his hand instantly finding mine with the needles in it. He lightly runs his finger around them, his eyebrows tugged inward as if he's in pain.

"Are you okay?" he asks softly, looking up at me like I could shatter at any second.

"Why are you here?" I ignored his question, wanting to know the most important thing.

Cameron blows out a deep breath, running a finger around the palm of my hand. "As soon as I walked into the airport, I came right back out. There is nothing in life that will fulfill me the way you do. I couldn't leave you, not like this."

My sweet man. My heart thuds in my chest while butterflies swarm my stomach.

"But what about the job? Don't ruin your dreams for me."

Cam brings my hand to his lips, pressing gentle kisses all over it. Then, he looks up at me, his eyes filled with such tenderness it makes a tear slip from my eyes. No one's ever looked at me this way.

"I opted for honesty and told them what was going on. They appreciated it and told me not to come and to take care of things at home. We're going to do a virtual meeting this week instead," he explains. "None of my dreams make sense without you in it. You are the dream, Rory."

The tears fall from my eyes rapidly, my hand squeezing his as I let his words wash over me, filling me with love and a sense of contentedness.

"Don't cry, love. I'm here," he whispers, leaning forward to kiss my forehead. He pulls back, his eyes searching mine. "What happened? Are you okay? I got a call from Jasmine on my way back from the airport that scared the fuck out of me."

"I'm sorry. I hate that I worried you. I'm okay, just tired and sore." I exhale, closing my eyes for a moment. "I was on my way to tell Coach that I wasn't playing, but my phone was dead. I was going to tell you that I chose differently," I tell him, wanting him to know I chose him. I'd rather never play a volleyball game again than be without him.

"I'm so damn proud of you. I know how hard that was for you to do," he says, bringing my hand to his lips, pressing them tightly against my skin, easing the fear coursing through me.

Unable to wait, I ask the question running through my mind on a loop. "Are we okay?" My voice is hoarse, barely there.

His eyes shoot up to mine, confusion and hurt in them. "I know I left, and I shouldn't have, and I'm so goddamn sorry about that, Rory. My mind was in a tailspin, and I needed to figure out what the hell was going on in it. But let me be clear, I never once thought about giving up on us. Sometimes, life gets messy, and that's okay. I'll be there for you through it all, just like I know you will be for me. I told you I'm in this with you forever. If the ring comment from New Year's Eve wasn't enough of a clue, I hope this clarifies things."

I can hear the monitor on my heart rate picking up, and he notices it, too. Leaning forward, he cups my cheek ever so gently, rubbing his thumb across the soft skin. "Hey, it's okay, love. We're okay. You're going to be okay."

I cover his hand with mine, leaning into his touch as a tear strolls down my cheek. "I thought I was going to lose you, and that terrified me more than not making it on that podium in two years. I can't lose you, too," I croak.

"You can't get rid of me, ever. I love you, and there's nothing in this fucking world that could keep me from you unless you asked."

I shake my head. "No, I don't want that either. I'm sorry I made it so hard on you. I just needed a moment to breathe and think about everything that happened. I knew in my mind that I wasn't going to play. It was the smart and safe thing to do. It was a matter of my heart getting the memo because it's sensitive to this topic."

He nods, his eyes pained. "I know that, love. I was trying to get you to that point, and I know if I would have stayed, none of this probably would've happened. You wouldn't be here if I didn't leave your side." He glances away, looking at my palm with the needles once more.

This time, I place my hand on his cheek, turning his gaze back to mine. "Remember what I told you about thinking we have control over everything? We don't. Odds are I still would've passed out. The only difference is that it would've been in your arms because you wouldn't have let me walk to Coach's office."

A slight smirk plays on his lips. "No, I wouldn't have. I'm still so goddamn sorry," he sighs, running a hand through his hair.

"You have absolutely nothing to apologize for, Cam. Nothing, okay?"

He nods. "I love you, Rory."

A hint of a smile cracks on my face. "I love you too, bub. Can you do me a favor?"

He chuckles faintly. "Yeah, love. What is it?"

"Kiss me," I plead.

His eyes scour my body. "I don't want to hurt you."

"You won't, it'll make me feel better."

As soon as the words are out of my mouth, his lips are on mine, and it's everything. I moan in relief as his lips fit perfectly against mine, moving in sync as our mouths express our love with every touch.

I lose myself in the kiss, forgetting everything except for him and how his mouth owns mine. He's kissing me with so much ferocity and passion, making my heart squeeze, which is evident by the rapid beating of it on the monitor.

Cameron groans against my lips, resting his forehead lightly on mine. "We need to stop."

I pout at him, but before I can say anything, my dad knocks on the door, leaning against the doorframe. We break apart, Cameron standing now, his hand reaching for mine.

"Heya, Cupcake," he smiles and Nate appears at his side.

Cameron coughs, clearing his throat. "I'll leave you guys to talk."

"Wait," I shout, gripping his wrist. "You'll come back, right?"

He smirks, his hand squeezing mine firmly in his. "You think I was actually going to leave here without you? I'll just be in the waiting room."

"Thank you," I whisper, staring at him with so much love as he squeezes my hand once more and then leaves my side.

"Cameron, you better walk your ass back over there. My sister is vulnerable. Go hold her hand while we all chat. You're family now anyways," Nate pesters him, slapping him on the back as he enters the room.

Cam walks back over to me, holding my hand in his, that familiar warmth spreading through my body at the contact. We spend the next hour or so talking about anything but volleyball, laughing and making me forget for a bit.

It reminds me that I have a choice. I can focus on the what-ifs, the negatives, and the worries. Or I can focus on the present moment, on what I have right in front of me, and all that I'm grateful for.

And I'm grateful for so fucking much. I'm grateful for my dad and brother, who always made sure I felt loved and supported growing up without a mom. I'm grateful for Cameron for simply existing and being mine. I'm grateful for Jasmine, being the best friend I could ever ask for, the only one I'll ever need. But most of all, I'm grateful for everything in my life that has brought me to this point right here.

Because it's made me realize that my life doesn't have to operate on a straight, narrow path. It can grow, create roots, and plant all over again.

The opportunities are endless, and I'll explore all the things that bring me joy, not just volleyball. I'll open up that facility and maybe do it while being on Team USA, raising a family, or drawing for a living.

I have no idea what's next, and it's refreshing as fuck.

Chapter Thirty-Seven

Cameron

It's been two weeks since I brought Aurora home from the hospital, aka the worst day of my life.

That whole day was a dumpster fire from the start. I was already having an awful week without her from the space she invoked. I was happy when she called me that day, but it quickly faded to panic when I heard how scared she was. Then to find her in the mud looking so fucking heartbroken?

Yeah, it tore me up instantly.

Luckily, it was nothing serious, and she was fine, but it still shook me to my core. Nothing could've prepared me for getting a call to say my girlfriend had passed out and was being transferred to a hospital.

I dropped my phone in the back of the Uber, everything around me ceasing to exist except the rapid beating of my heart as my breaths became harder and harder to take. In that moment, I realized how different love could be because I was terrified like never before.

She was released the next day, and I took her back to my place and took care of her. She argued with me every time I wouldn't let her lift a finger, but eventually, she stopped because she knew it was useless.

I knew it was just a mild concussion, but that didn't matter. Seeing her hooked up to a bunch of wires intensified my concern, and the image would pop up in my mind every time I'd watch her sleep on my couch or in my bed.

As she healed physically, she did emotionally, too, accepting that her dreams may not become a reality and being open to whatever happens.

She talked to her coach once since the incident, who promised to let her know as soon as she heard back from the scouts. Aurora's taken it better than I ever expected, truly embracing her new viewpoint on her life path. I couldn't be more proud of my pretty girl.

I had my virtual meeting with Disney, where I got to showcase the progress of my game, which received a lot of praise. After that, I worked with developers to fine-tune some details, allowing me to take it to the next level.

I don't know what my competition is like, and I never will, but I'm confident that I'll win. I don't know if my girlfriend's confidence has rubbed off on me or something, but I'm feeling oddly good about it.

Aurora and I were inseparable in those two weeks, only apart for classes as her schedule cleared up since she'd been instructed to no intense physical activity for three weeks. It's going to fucking suck when things go back to normal because I'll miss waking up to her every day. The way her body is always wrapped around mine, her unique scent of limes and coconut on my sheets, the kisses she peppers me with as she awakens.

Just as she is now, pressing light kisses to my neck and nuzzling her nose in the crook of my neck as she takes a deep breath.

I drag a lazy finger from her hip, trailing it over her satin shorts to her ankle and back up again. "Morning, beautiful," I murmur into her hair before placing a kiss there.

She shifts, rubbing herself against me. "Morning, bub," Aurora rasps, half from sleep, half from desire.

My cock hardens immediately, and I roll us so she's on her back. "I'm going to miss waking up and being inside you," I tell her as I grind my erection against her pussy.

Aurora's hands tangle in my hair. "Me, too."

"Move in with me," I whisper in her ear, descending down her neck with my lips, kissing and sucking.

This time, she tugs my hair so I'm at eye level with her, her hazel eyes content. "Are you sure? We haven't even graduated yet. Maybe we should wait so we're not moving stuff again in three months?"

I pause my lips, which are devastatingly close to her breasts, her hard nipples teasing me as they stare at me through her camisole. "I'm sure, Rory. I want you with me always. But that's a fair point. After we graduate, then?"

She pushes lightly at my shoulders, her way of telling me she wants to take control, so I let her as I roll to my back. Aurora throws her leg over my waist, straddling me now, sitting on my erection that's nearing painful now. She whips her top over her head.

"Yeah," she breathes, sounding slightly distracted now. "I'll need to remind Jasmine to start looking for a roommate for next year."

I can barely think straight with her perfect breasts in my sight, but I manage to keep my eyes on hers. "Are you going to let me take care of paying for it, no arguing?"

Aurora rocks herself against me, the soaked satin driving me insane. Why the hell did I choose now to have this conversation when all I wanted to do was sink into her?

"We can table that discussion for later," she sighs, and then her face perks up with an idea. "Oh, maybe Theo could be her roommate," she waggles her brows at me suggestively.

I grab her waist, stilling her as I thrust my hips up, rendering her speechless except for a moan that slips through. "Don't say another man's name while you're grinding your pussy on me."

Aurora's eyes sparkle in amusement, loving my possessive side. "Mmm, or what?"

"Or I'm going to shove my cock so far down your throat, it'll brand your tongue, causing my name to be the only words coming off of your lips."

Her lips parted, tongue darting out to trace her top lip as her breasts lifted with each deep breath. It's the most sensual yet beautiful sight I've ever seen. Aurora rubs herself more aggressively against my erection, "I'm going to come just from your words if you don't stop," she moans, fingers going up to play with her nipples.

"Up," I say, my voice tight with unleashed need. Aurora lifts her hips, allowing me to pull my sweatpants down, my cock ready for her.

Before she sits back down, I pull on the thin material of her shorts and tug at them, ripping them right off her body.

She gapes at me, "Those were ne—"

Her words are cut short as I thrust upwards, filling her with all of me at once. "Cam!" she moans, her pleasure evident in the way she throws her head back while her pussy grips my cock.

I'll never get over how good she feels or how perfectly our bodies fit together. And I don't let her forget it either, as I spend all morning with my head or cock between her thighs.

Appreciating, devouring, and honoring the woman I love.

Chapter Thirty-Eight

Aurora

Cam and I are hosting our first game night as a couple at his house tonight.

We have multiple board games on the table, card games, and various kinds of pizzas that are neatly stacked on the dining room table. Group hangouts are a weird concept for me because I've always been a lone wolf despite being, as Theo puts it, one of the most popular people on campus.

But I'm embracing this new version of my life with open arms, going where the flow takes me.

We're all currently sitting around the coffee table in the living room. I'm on the floor between Cam's legs while he sits on the couch with Finn, while Jasmine and Theo join me on the floor. Ash couldn't be here, which means Finn looks like a lost puppy.

The card game *Pay Me* has been going for the last hour, with Finn in the lead, followed closely by Jasmine.

"Jasmine, if you call pay me right now, I swear—" Finn seethes, staring at his cards like they can change if he willed them to.

"Or what?" she challenges, raising a brow at him.

"I'll be very upset," he says, knowing damn well he isn't going to do anything but sulk if she wins.

"Well, get a tissue box. Pay me!" Jasmine chuckles, a devilish grin on her face.

"Fuck off!" Finn shouts, throwing his cards down on the table.

We all laugh as Cameron tallies our points, and to no one's surprise, Jasmine wins the entire game. Finn sulks while Cameron pays her the forty dollars she won. Add that to the payments she got from calling 'pay me' so much, she's up fifty dollars tonight.

"I can't believe this school year is almost over," Theo comments, and I couldn't agree more. My senior year has been nothing short of intense, amazing, and life-changing.

"Yeah, I'm going to miss the hell out of you when you get a spot on the team," Jasmine frowns at me, her lip in a pout.

"Don't bring that up. I don't know how I'll function without you being so close by."

I also want to say that we don't know if I'll even make it.

"I'll be coming to your games whenever you're in town, and we'll FaceTime every day," she promises me, and I know it'll happen. Jasmine is the most loyal person I know, always sticking true to her word.

"But won't you also be busy with volleyball?" Finn asks, his auburn eyebrows furrowed, unaware of the plan her parents have for her.

And this plan sucks. I've known about it since Jasmine joined me here at RLU.

"No, I'm not playing this year. That's been the plan since day one. Play for a few years to get a free education, but as soon as I'm in my senior year, I'll need to focus on my studies," she tells him, seeming at ease with how she exudes confidence, but deep down, I know it upsets her.

Sure, volleyball isn't as important to her as it is to me, but it's still something she enjoys and is good at.

"Doesn't Coach Park get perks, though? Like a discount or some shit?" Theo asks, wiping the grease off his chin from the slice of pizza he just devoured.

"He does, so I'll be getting a discount, but it's still expensive as hell," Jasmine groans, and I feel that.

RLU's tuition is insane, making me all the more grateful for the scholarship that got me through my four years here because not everyone is as fortunate. Not only is RLU a prime Division I school for athletes, but it holds just as high of a standard when it comes to academics, too.

"I'm paying my rent until the end of graduation, so we have lots of time to find you the best roommate possible," I tell her, wanting to make things easier as much as I can.

"Ugh, don't remind me. Camille has a roommate, so she's out," she groans, blowing a black curl out of her face.

"I would offer, Jasmine, but an alum pays for the football house, and I can't afford to live elsewhere," Theo says, shrugging his shoulders.

"And we're all graduating, so that means we're out," Finn remarks as he points to himself, then to Cameron and me. "What about one of the girls from the team?"

"Yeah, I could ask around," Jasmine tells him, but I know she probably won't. It'll hurt her too much to see one of them all the time, knowing she's not on the team anymore.

"Anyone want to play charades?" I pipe up, wanting to take the attention away from this topic so she's not uncomfortable anymore.

The topic of Jasmine's living situation is long forgotten as we sit around the living room, playing charades, and laughing our asses off.

It's girls against guys, and currently, Cameron is up for his team, his body rolling on the ground in an attempt to be a worm or snake. I honestly can't tell past the tears in my eyes from laughing so hard.

"A worm?" Theo guesses, but Cameron shakes his head no.

"A snake?" Finn says, snapping his fingers. Cameron shakes his head no again.

"C'mon, Ronnie boy, switch it up. We have no idea what the fuck you're supposed to be," Theo yells at him urgently, seeing the timer dwindle with each passing second.

Jasmine and I shoulder bump as we shake from our laughter from watching my mountain of a man rolling around on the floor.

"Time's up," I cheer, loving that they lost because we were tied up until now.

Cameron sits up on his knees. "I was a wave, you dumbasses."

The boys begin to argue about how awful his choice was for an imitation of a wave, but my phone vibrates in my pocket and pulls my attention away. I take it out to see Coach Tilly's name on the screen.

That's weird.

"Sorry, I really have to take this," I apologize, excusing myself to Cameron's bedroom. Cameron eyes me, but I shake my head, letting him know it's nothing he needs to worry about.

Once in his room, I slide my finger across the screen as I nervously answer the call, "Hey, Coach, how's it going?"

"I'm well. Are you sitting down?" She cuts right to it. Never once has she beaten around the bush with me.

"I am now. What's going on?" I ask as I plop onto the bed.

"I got a call today from Summer Mills a few minutes ago," she casually mentions, as if that name doesn't make my spine straighten and my shoulders tense. Mills is the head coach for the women's USA volleyball team.

"What did she want?" I ask, my voice not sounding like my own.

"You, Vallacourt. Coach Mills said she has been watching you since you were a teenager and is impressed by the player you've become."

My world stills, everything else ceasing to exist except for the rapid pounding of my heart and the joy coursing through my veins.

They want *me?* I have to be dreaming.

"H-how is this possible?" I stutter, my fingers coming up to still my trembling lips.

Coach Tilly sighs in exasperation from having to spell it out for me. "It's all of the hard work you've put in since you were eleven, that's how. She mentioned they were proud of your ability to take yourself out of the game that night and how she personally respected you for it. She wants you, Aurora. What should I tell her?"

Old me would've been screaming at her through the phone, yelling the word yes over and over again. But I find myself pausing to think about it. While the news makes me so freaking happy to hear, I also know I have some things to think about. And someone I need to think of now as well when I make decisions like this.

"Can you give me a few minutes to process it and call you back?" I ask, biting my lip as I await her response.

"Of course. Mills said we have a week to give her an answer. After that, she'll be moving on to whoever is after you on the priority list," Coach informs me, although I already knew that.

There's one position this year, and if I don't want it, they'll find someone who does.

"Got it. Thank you for calling and telling me, Coach."

"You deserve that spot, Vallacourt. You will do great things for the team," she says, making me smile at the possibility. We say our goodbyes, and then I'm left alone to process what the hell just happened.

I can't believe everything I've done, all the training, sacrifices, and overloaded schedules actually paid off. They want me, Team freaking USA. If I accept, I'll be going to the Olympics in *two* years. Holy fuck.

The idea thrills me, filling my body with pride and excitement. But a part of me aches for the facility I want to open. Will I be able to do it while working for Team USA? How will I even get the finances to do so? There are so many questions I don't have the answers to, but I need to take it one step at a time.

I stand from the bed, knowing I need the support and advice from Cameron and my friends.

Jasmine and Cameron chat in the living room while Theo and Finn are in the kitchen nursing their beers.

Jasmine spots me instantly, hopping to her feet. "What's wrong, Ro? Who was it?"

At that, Cameron's up on his feet, his concern evident as he scans me up and down. "It was Coach. She had news for me."

Cameron deflates, his shoulders slightly relaxing, while Jasmine sighs in relief.

"What is it?" she asks, a smile growing on her lips once she sees the positive emotions I'm trying to hide.

I can't control the smile that feels like it expands from cheek to cheek as I tell them, "Team USA wants me. They've been watching me since I was a teen. They need an answer by next week."

I'm met with silence at first, and then utter chaos erupts.

Jasmine rams into me with her tiny body, squeezing me tightly as she hugs me and screams into my hair. She releases me, only for Cameron to pick me up, spinning me around as I clutch his neck while he tells me how happy he is for me. Theo and Finn hype me up, yelling how proud they are and clapping as they wait their turn for a hug.

Once all of the shouting and hugs are over, Jasmine suggests that she, Theo, and Finn get drinks to celebrate in my honor, but I know she's giving Cameron and me some space to talk about things.

After they leave, Cameron and I spend a few minutes tidying up in silence. I finish putting the leftover pizza in the fridge when two large hands circle my waist, spinning me toward a hard chest.

"C'mon, let's talk," Cameron suggests, holding my hand as he leads us to his room.

He sits on the bed, pulling me along so I sit across his lap.

"What do you want to do, Rory?" he gets right to the point, rubbing circles along my outer thigh.

"I-I don't know," I answer truthfully. "I want to go so badly because it's been my dream for as long as I can remember. But I also want to open the facility, and I'm worried I'll lose sight of that while trying to balance the two."

When I told Cameron about my idea, he was in awe. He made love to me all night after, whispering how proud he was of me.

"You won't, love. You'll have me right there with you, reminding you of who you are. Of how strong and capable you are of doing everything your heart desires," he tells me, soothing the worry and filling me with hope.

"There's a lot to figure out logistically for it, but I want it just as badly as I want to compete. Are you sure you're ready for this? You're really okay with moving farther away from your family?"

Cameron doesn't shy away or take a moment to think it over. "I'm ready to start our life together, Rory. Which means you're my family, too. I'm already away from them. What's a couple more miles? Plus, if I get the position, I can fly us to them whenever we feel like it. So, what's your decision?"

I inhale deeply, looking into the cinnamon eyes that transfixed me from the start, the ones that reassure me that everything is going to work out. "We're going to Sacramento, bub."

Cameron's entire face lights up with joy as he crushes my body to his, his lips pressing a kiss to the top of my head. "I heard they have great hiking trails out that way, you know."

"So that's the real reason you're following me, huh?" I tease him, running my fingers up and down his chest.

"Well…" he trails off, and I tackle him, his laughter making my heart dance in my chest. He's quicker, though, flipping us and pinning me to the mattress with his hips, which is how we spend the rest of the night.

Wrapped up in one another, he cherishes my body with his, showing me how proud he is to be mine.

Chapter Thirty-Nine

Cameron

Aurora and I are relaxing on her bed at her father's house with Pickles as we watch *Iron Man 2* when I get a call from Kim Sepena.

"Hold on, I need to take this," I tell Aurora, pausing the movie. She nods and takes Pickles with her out of the room.

"Hey, Kim, how's it going?" I answer, nerves wracking my stomach. It's only February, and the competition isn't done until April 1st. Why would she be calling me right now?

"Hi. Cameron, I'm great. Thanks. I hope all is well with you," her bubbly voice floats through the phone, making my nerves somewhat dull. She wouldn't be this upbeat if she had bad news, right?

"Are you busy right now?" she inquires.

"No, is everything okay?" I ask, needing to get to the point of this call.

"Everything's great. With the feedback I heard from the developer that aided the three of you with your projects, he had a lot of insights to share with me," she pauses, making my nerves spring back to life. "He was very impressed with your concept

306

and the follow-through with the graphics, the coding system, and pretty much everything else. With his advice, we decided to close the competition early. Congrats, Cameron, you've won. You're the newest member of our coding and programming team at Disney."

I put myself on mute and do a little dance of victory. "Fuck yes," I shout in a whisper.

Holy shit, I can't believe I *actually* did it. I was confident, but to have your dream confirmed? That you're finally about to get everything you've been working for for years?

There isn't a word that accurately describes how fucking good it feels. It's more than elation and joy.

Unmuting myself, I clear my throat. "Wow, thank you so much, Kim. I'm very grateful for this opportunity."

"I know you are, and that's another thing we liked. You're sincere and humble, something we value here. Your first project will be to finish the game you're developing, but we can discuss details in a few weeks. Enjoy your last semester of college, okay?"

"I will. Thank you so much. Talk soon," I say, ending the call.

I smile to myself, feeling a sense of pride like never before. I fucking did it.

"Rory, come in here!" I yell out as I pull up Lexa's contact card.

"What's wrong?" she asks, entering the room with Pickles on her heels as she sits beside me on the bed.

"I got the job," I smile, feeling my dimples pull in.

Aurora's hazel eyes widen, a large smile on her face. "Cam! I'm so proud of you, bub!" she squeals, tackling me to the bed as she plants kisses all over my face.

When she finally kisses my lips, I melt under her touch, letting her dictate our mouths. She kisses me lovingly, her touch gentle yet fierce.

I pull away from her before we get carried away and sit with her on my lap as I FaceTime Lexa.

She answers on the second ring. "Marvelnerd11, what do you want?" she asks.

"I have news, where's Mom?"

Her eyes widen. "Oh my god, is Aurora pregnant? Am I going to be an aunt?"

"Pregnant?" I hear my mom's voice in the background. Oh, fuck me.

"No, no, no," I backtrack. "Aurora is not pregnant. It's about me."

"What is it?" Lexa ponders, her head tilting to the side.

I tighten my hold on Aurora, and she squeezes my thigh in response.

"I got the job with Disney," I tell them, smiling again.

My mother and sister shriek, yelling congratulations, while Aurora kisses my cheek. I feel so cherished in that moment, truly loved and valued by the ones I care about most.

It's one of the best moments of my life, and I know this is just the start.

Chapter Forty

Aurora

Green needles stick out from the pine trees, the evergreens seeming to go on forever as I take in the surrounding area. The crystal blue lake in front of me looks clearer than usual, much like my heart and mind ever since I last was here.

It's been two months since that day, and life has never been better.

I remember when I first realized Cameron was poking at my walls and how afraid I was that he wouldn't find anything beyond my athletic persona. Together, he helped me uncover who I am and my worth beyond my physical abilities.

Mainly, I learned that I can be gentle with myself. It's okay to take breaks. It's okay to want more for myself and to explore those options. Not everything is a straight shot, without amendments.

Looking back on my time here at RLU, I see how rigid I was in how I spent my time. If I wasn't in class, working, training, or playing, I was studying or staying home to rest, only ever hanging out with Jasmine or Theo.

Those things were great, but part of me wishes I bonded with the girls on the team more and had late nights out with friends, the typical college experience.

But I also realized that everything happens for a reason, bringing us closer to where we're truly meant to be. So, I don't regret how I spent my time because it led me to the greatest thing in my life.

Cameron.

The overprotective man he is gave me two wireless battery charging packs just in case anything were to happen. I also now have a first aid kit in my backpack, which truthfully should have been there in the first place because you never know.

Movement near the lake catches my eye. A deer with its neck careened dipping into the water to take a drink. The gesture reminds me of my mom's graceful and quiet movements.

With a deep breath, I do what I came here to do today.

"Uh, hi, Mom? I know this is probably weird, and no, I am not losing it. I just don't like the idea of cemeteries, and I feel more connected to you here. That's why I'm talking to you now, hoping you can hear me," I stumble over my words, feeling awkward at first. I've never done this before, talking out loud like this to her.

"I miss you so much," my voice cracks, a tear strolling down my cheek. I wipe it away with the back of my hand and continue, "Dad keeps telling me how proud you would be of me, and I'm finally starting to believe it. I owe that to my boyfriend, Cameron." A smile tugs at the corner of my lips. "You would've loved him, Mom. He's everything you wanted for me and more. But we can talk about boys another time. What I really wanted to tell you is that I made it."

Another tear rolls down my cheek, but this time I leave it. "I accepted a position on Team USA. The contract will last for the next two years with a possible extension, depending on my performance throughout the years and at the Olympics. I'm going to get you there, Mom. But if for some reason I can't, I hope you know that I tried. God, did I ever try my hardest. I've finally found other things that fuel my soul and that I want to explore beyond competing. I'm hoping you'll still be proud of me. I know I finally am."

The tears flow freely now, not from sadness but rather from relief. It feels so fucking good to be at this point in my life. I was finally cleared to play the last two weeks of the season, and they were the most fun I've had in a long time because the pressure that once laid heavy on my chest was no longer there.

Golden rays peek through the gloomy day, the sunlight drifting above me. "Hi, Mom," I whisper, my heart breaking and mending at the same time. Not everyone believes in occurrences like this, but I do. And I know my mom's looking down on me right now, spreading light even when she's gone.

I bask in the warmth it provides, feeling how it lights me up from the inside out. It's healing and soothing.

I take my pink notebook out of my backpack and immediately get to sketching the moment, how the sun's rays are poking through the cloudy sky, and how it's shimmering off the aqua blue lake. It's one of those moments I want to preserve because it's the moment I finally feel whole.

Two hours later, I'm on my way to Cameron's house with a surprise.

I stopped at the grocery store with an idea in mind, and I was a bit nervous about giving it to him. It always surprises me how I still get nervous around him at times.

I used to be the one in control, but now? Cameron threw that bitch out the window, completely owning me in every way possible. He makes our every moment together feel like it's new again, with those damn butterflies and body shocks still there each time.

I knock on the door with the surprise behind me, bouncing on the tips of my toes as I wait. It hasn't been long since I left this morning, but I miss him.

Cameron opens the door, leaning against the frame with his sleeves rolled up his forearms. He smiles at me, those dimples I love appearing. My clit throbs at the sight before me because he looks so damn sexy right now, especially with the way his gray sweatpants are hanging off of his hips.

"Rory," he hums teasingly. "You have a key. Why are you knocking?"

Because apparently, I'm an idiot.

"Right," I cringe. "I forgot, but I got you something."

Before he can protest, I shove the bouquet in his hands. Cameron looks down at it, puzzled at first, but then a broad smile takes up his beautiful face, cinnamon eyes sparkling as they flit up to mine.

"I'm never going to live down that story, am I?" he laughs, shaking his head.

The bouquet consists of Oreos on skewers, all tied and held together like a bouquet, and it looks amazing if I do say so myself.

"Nope," I pop the p. "Stick with me, and I'll give you all the Oreos you want," I smile at him. I step forward, walking him backward until we're inside.

"Hm, what else? I don't know if the Oreos will cut it," he pretends to think dutifully as I lock the door behind me and remove my jacket.

"And blowjobs? And kisses? And cuddles?" I add, my eyebrow raised as I walk into his open arms, the bouquet resting on the kitchen counter.

His large hand comes up to twirl a strand of my hair, his fingers skimming the bare skin of my arm. "Better, but those are things I want. Do you want to know what I need?"

I tilt my head back to look into my favorite pair of eyes. "What's that?"

"Your love," he kisses my forehead. "Your smile," another kiss to the tip of my nose. "Your laughter," pressing a kiss to my cheek. "Your body safely wrapped in my arms," his lips land on my other cheek. "I just need you, always," he says softly, his voice like gravel as it drags across my skin, heating me from the inside out.

"You have me. All of me, forever," I whisper, standing on my tip toes so that our lips are nearly brushing. Cameron lifts me, my legs instantly wrapping around his waist where they're all too comfortable to be.

"Promise me?" he breathes, running his nose along mine.

"I promise you, bub."

And then he's kissing me, lighting up my world just like he did that first night our lips met. And just like I know he will for the rest of our lives together.

Epilogue

Aurora

Two years later

Sweat drips down my back, my thighs aching, and my belly twisting.

This is it.

I've spent the last month here in Paris for the Olympics, our team competing against the best athletes from around the globe. It's been extremely challenging, mentally and physically, but worth it for every second of joy and pride I get competing at this level.

The excitement and nerves were expected, but what I didn't expect was to make so many friends. The Olympic Village is more laid back than it seems on TV, as people from different sports mingle and get to know one another during late-night dinners, watching events, or going to parties together.

Don't get me wrong, we're all very serious about our training and competition, but when we have time to ourselves, that's what we do since we don't compete every day we're here.

What's been even better? My fiancé gets to be here by my side, and my dad. Yeah, *fiancé.*

Cameron proposed about a year ago, not long after our anniversary of moving in together in our place in Sacramento. We were hiking on one of the various trails in our area when we came to a large boulder. He hopped up first, pulling me up after, only to get down on his knee the second I was up there, the view of tree tops stretching as far as I could see, the summer sun shining down on us.

It was simple yet meaningful because of our shared love for the hobby. A moment later, after his speech and my tears, he slid the gold band (because he was right, I am a gold girl through and through) with a circular diamond taking center stage and a ring of smaller diamonds around it.

It reminded me of *Iron Man's* Reactor and made me love it even more. I hate that it's off my finger right now, but that's besides the point.

My team is currently in the championship game for women's volleyball in the 2024 Summer Olympics, and our opponent is Switzerland. It's our final set. We lost the first one, but are winning the second, meaning whoever wins this takes home a gold medal.

The score is tied 23-23. We only need two more points to secure our spot on the top of the podium. I'm more nervous than I have been for anything in my life, knowing I'm up to serve. If I mess it up, that's a point for the other team, inching them that much closer to gold.

I quickly look into the crowd, my eyes latching onto a pair of cinnamon ones that make every day feel like the best day of my life.

He mouths to me, "You got this, Rory." I smile and nod slightly, the whistle signaling I have ten seconds to serve.

I bounce the ball four times, the way I always have, and throw it up in the air, smashing it over the net with my right arm.

The opponent bumps it to their setter, who gives a beautiful set and is slammed down to the ground by their hitter. Our team can't react fast enough, the ball hitting the floor before one of us can get it.

23-24 them. *Shit.*

They rotate, and of course, it's their power server up to serve. I get low, getting ready to receive the ball since I know she likes to come my way.

My theory is correct. Her ball comes just to my right, and it's nearly out. It's a beautiful service, but my instincts are better. I quickly adjust and bump the ball to my setter, who sets up our hitter. She goes for the cross hit, and it works, gaining us another point to tie up the score.

Now we'll have to go to 26 to win, needing two points above theirs to take the win.

Our captain moves into the setter position, hitting the ball across the net. The ball nearly hits the top, but it doesn't, going right to the floor instead. It's rare to get an ace in the Olympics, but it's possible when you have a serve like Wren.

25-24 now. We need just one point to take home gold.

Sweat trickles down my temples, nerves, and excitement trying to claw their way through my stomach.

Wren serves again, but this time, they receive it, setting up a spike that our center blocks, the ball falling to the ground on the opposing side before they can move fast enough. The room is silent for a split second, then erupts in cheers and applause.

We. Fucking. Won.

My knees threaten to give out, but I somehow hold myself up as our team piles in a group hug, tears, sweat, and joy surrounding us. Before we can truly celebrate, we pull away to shake hands with the opposing team and coaches.

And then I'm turning away, looking for my family.

Cameron and my dad make their way to me with huge smiles on their faces, but Cam slows, letting my dad come to me first. Somehow, that makes me love him so much more that he knows what I need before I even do most times.

My dad tucks his foam finger under his arm along with his ancient sign, 'Vallacourt owns the court,' as he wraps me in a hug, with nothing but pride in his voice.

"You did it, Cupcake. That was a hell of a game. Your mom was on the edge of her seat watching. I just know it."

A tear escapes the corner of my eye as I pull back to look at him. "Thanks, Dad. I hope she enjoyed being here as much as I did. I won a medal, can you believe it? I won't until they put it around my neck."

Holy shit, I'm an Olympic gold medalist. I don't know if that will ever truly sink in.

"She did trust me. And I believe it. You're a Vallacourt, and we do great things," he beams, squeezing my shoulder. "I'm going to call Jodi and figure out where she is. I know she was meeting with Nate, Ryker and his wife for lunch to stream the game at a sports bar."

I could only get two tickets, so they aren't here watching me live.

"Alright, text me, and we can all have dinner later?" I suggest, and he agrees, parting with one last hug and an I love you.

Cameron approaches me with long strides, quickly closing the distance between us as he closes in on my space. He bends slightly, wrapping one arm under my ass to lift me in the air where I stay, my body tightly wrapped in his arms.

"That's my fucking wife," he says with a glimmer in his eyes.

"I'm not your wife," I remind him, although my heart is pounding from hearing him call me his wife. I like it a little too much.

"You're mine in every way that counts, so basically, you're my wife already," he explains, that dimpled smile on his face that I want to kiss so badly it aches.

"I love you," I tell him, feeling nothing but happiness and love course through me.

"I love you more. I'm so goddamn proud of you," he says, looking up at me like I'm the one who puts the sun in the sky. He grasps the back of my neck, pulling me forward so that our foreheads are touching, sweat be damned. "I can't wait to get you back to the hotel and strip you naked, nothing but that gold medal around your neck as I spoil that needy pussy with my tongue," he whispers, the vibration of his tone sending shivers down my spine.

But before we get carried away, Coach Mills calls me over, needing all of us to gather at the podium for the medal ceremony.

There are too many of us to all stand on the podium, so Coach sends up the captains to represent our country. Wren and I go to the podium because I became co-captain just a few months ago.

My legs threatened to shake from excitement, nerves, and the overwhelming sensation of being on the podium. The one my mom desired to stand on herself, albeit for a different sport, but it's still all the same. The one I'm standing on for her, but also for myself.

It feels like falling in love, scary, but you can't help but free fall into the joy because if you're going to drown, you may as well pick the happier emotion. So, that's what I'm choosing. To focus on how good it feels to be here despite my mom being unable to.

The gold medal is placed around my neck, causing tears to cascade down my cheeks. I may look silly to the thousands of people watching from home, but I don't care. They don't know my story.

I bend down, pressing the gold medal into the tattoo on my inner ankle, whispering to myself, "We made it, Mom. We fucking made it."

THE END!

Want more of Cameron and Aurora?
Head to my website carliejean.ca to get a bonus epliogue.
If you're interested in seeing Daddy Cam, I'd head over there.
Up to you though!

What's next?
Trust Me, which follows Jasmine and Elio's story,
comes out in February 2024.

Acknowledgements

Wow, I can't believe I'm writing one of these again. It's surreal, and so damn exciting to be putting more love into the world through these characters, which were created doing what I love, *writing*.

To my lovely readers, I couldn't do any of this without you, so I thank you for your support and love. It means the world to me, and I can't wait to keep creating and sharing with you.

I have to thank my editors, Salma and Isabella. These two ladies were amazing to work with. They're professional and provide detailed feedback to improve the quality of the story while hyping me up along the way. I am beyond grateful for them and all that they have done to help me deliver this story to my readers.

Next, I want to thank my betas. Sabreena, thank you for always being so excited to read my stories and messaging me with all your reactions, it gave me the confidence I needed for this story. Erin, thank you for becoming my author bestie and reading this book in its baby stage, giving it the love and advice it needed. Jessica, thank you for your constructive feedback, along with your love, it helped shape this book into what it is today. Summer, thank you for dealing with all of my text messages, brainstorming voice notes and more while I was writing this story. This story needed you, and I couldn't thank you enough for always being my hype woman even though you only like dark romance.

To my cover designer, Cat, there never seems to be an appropriate way to express how grateful I am for you. You're not only a creative genius, but the sweetest and kindest person to work with. I am so glad we met, and to call you a friend. Thank you for this beauty of a cover, I love it so much.

To Greys Promo, thank you for all that you've done to help promote and release this book. I look forward to working with you again!

To Nada and the team at Qamber, thank you for your patience and flawless formatting skills. I love working with you, and can't wait to do it again!

About the Author

Carlie is a romance author who loves all things swoon, sunshine, and spice. She lives in Canada. She has two brothers, and a dog named Milo. She loves to watch and play a variety of sports. When she's not teaching little ones, she loves reading, writing, going for walks, and traveling.

SOCIALS

Check out my website for in-depth book information,
what I'm currently writing, and bonus materials!
www.carliejean.ca

Tiktok and Insta for all book things,
snippets of my personal life and behind the scene writing
@carliejeanwrites